ALL GODS MUST DIE

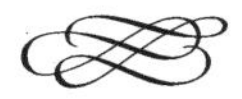

SORAYA COLE

All Gods Must Die

Edited by Polish Perfection.

Proofreading by Words of Advice.

AUTHORS NOTE

This book contains subject matter that might be difficult for some readers, including violence and torture. Readers discretion is advised.

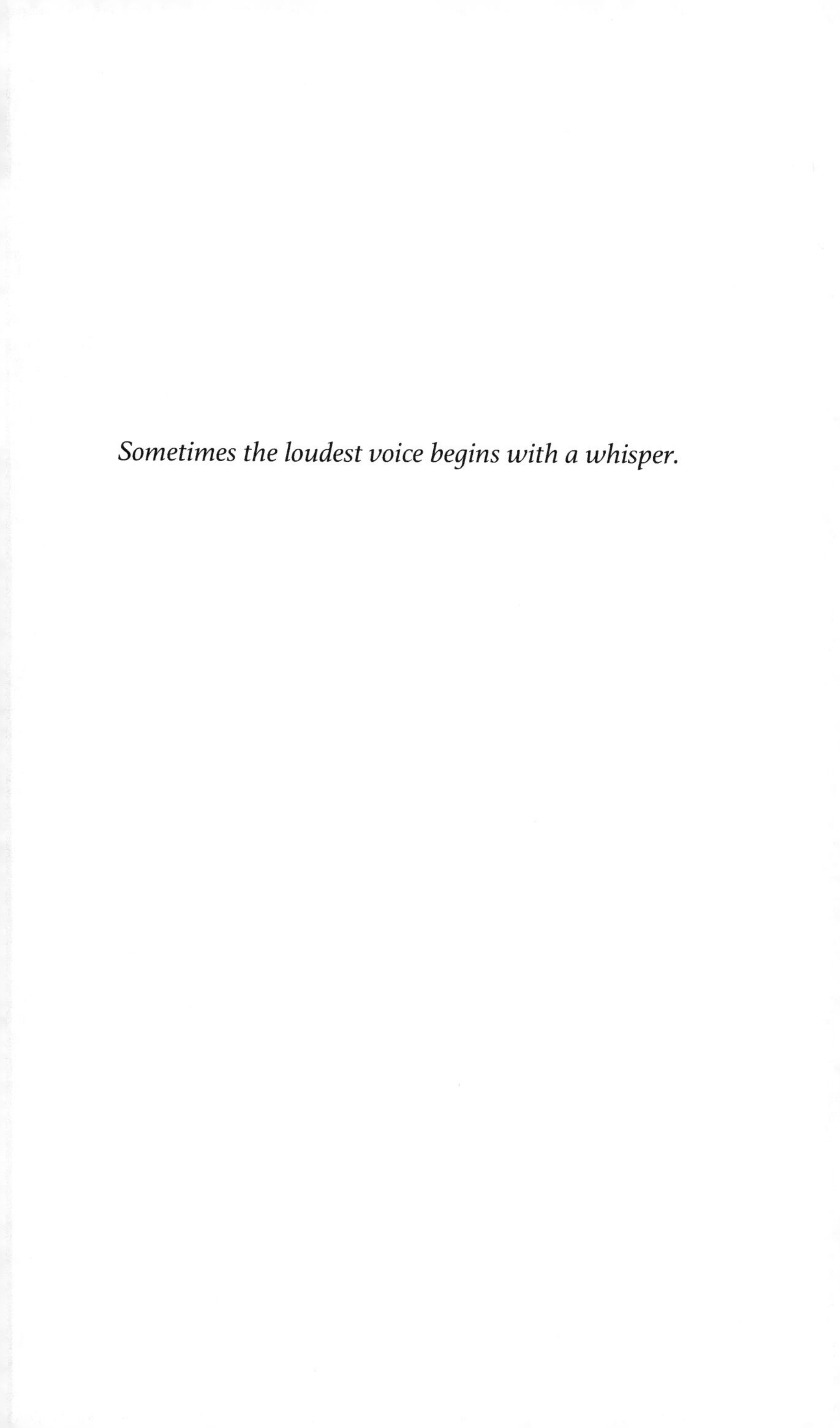

Sometimes the loudest voice begins with a whisper.

CHAPTER 1

Death draws near as darkness bleeds across the Sidus town. It crawls between the derelict buildings below me, in the small alleyways in between, and casts its shadows along the high wall that surrounds the entire kingdom of Findias.

My eyes scan the town below as the Sidus move about quickly, making their way home before the Caligo guards start their nightly patrol.

The Caligo's ability to wield shadows is what most likely gave them their position as the kingdom's guard. A position that allows them too much power over the Sidus. And even though the Sidus have their own abilities to cast light, it does not stand a chance against the Caligo guards and their abilities.

I glance over at the high wall of the kingdom and the Caligo guards who walk along it. Beyond the wall beside the Sidus town stands the dark forest, a thick expanse of wild woodland and the monstrous creatures that now reside there.

Creatures that should not exist.

The entire kingdom is a huge island that is surrounded by a sea as black as the darkest night. Nothing should be able to pass through it, not only because of the treacherous dark waters that bring about death but also because of the shield. A huge translucent barrier that was erected centuries before I was born and stands behind the high wall, keeping all those in the kingdom safe.

The last few years, it has grown to an inky, shadowed darkness at its base, tainting its very existence. But the only ones to suffer are the Sidus, whereas the Caligo sit high in the mountains near the palace.

As the shield gets higher, it curves similar to a dome and is almost translucent, matching the color of the sky with nothing but the rain and sun from the heavens above getting in or out.

There is no way to pass through it. No way out of this cage we all live in. Even the Caligo's ability to move through the void of shadows and travel to another place is blocked by it.

It keeps us caged and closed off from the rest of the world. But even with its growing tainted base, it has always protected us from the dark forest and anything beyond it.

Or at least... that is what it used to do.

The cold, hard rooftop beneath me digs into my

knees as I silently wait, watching for that wisp of shadows that is sure to materialize soon. A warm breeze flutters by me, slightly lifting my dark hooded cloak from my face, revealing a stray strand of long blonde hair. I quickly pull it back in place, concealing myself, as my eyes continue to watch the spot at the edge of the Sidus town near the wall.

Not many visit this spot anymore. Not where the now darkened forest bleeds its taint up and along the wall, with wild overgrown black forestry now seeping inward. The tall, twisted black trees lean forward, breaking it open and growing through the thick stone and outward into a huge shroud of dark thorny bushes.

The shield's tainted base grows month by month, but as no harm is befalling the Caligo, it is only seen as something harmless.

The Sidus have not been so fortunate. Not with the tainted shield and its darkness, nor the threat that is now killing them.

Nothing should be able to make it past the shield, even with its dark taint. But what is more mysterious is that the weakening shield is never in the same spot. The creatures have been showing up in different places all over the edges of the Sidus town where the wall is at its weakest. It is a mystery we have yet to solve.

The Caligo guards constantly miss the threat that is right in front of them.

But I can no longer sit around and watch as these creatures bring death upon their arrival. If my mother knew I was secretly joining their fight, she would be furious. But the small group of Sidus that tries to protect the entire town is not enough.

Two nights, both with too many lives lost. Tonight will not be their third. I will make sure of it.

I know it is only a matter of time before they show up again. I just need to wait and watch.

Around me, sound from the busy kingdom disappears. I slow my heart rate, solely focusing on the edge of the wall where the large patch of seeping dark forest sits. A couple of minutes pass before I feel a pull beside a cluster of shadowed trees.

Good. The dark trees and shrouded bushes will give me cover for what I'm about to do.

I zero in on the spot. Waiting and watching for what I know will arrive.

There.

Wisps of dark smoke start to cluster together, trying to form. Then another and another.

Closing my eyes, I call upon my own darkness and pull myself into the abyss of the void. A rush of cool ice enters my blood as I pass through it and emerge just as the tall, thick bodies of three dark creatures form.

Not giving them another second, I unhook my daggers from my side and head for the nearest one to my left. Just as its black arm forms, I slice my dagger down it, cutting it right off. It hits the ground, slowly turning to shadows before disappearing completely. The injured creature does not make a sound or act wounded. It is as if it does not feel or understand pain.

Whipping around, I slam my other dagger into the second dark creature's chest. Twisting, I spin back, narrowly avoiding a claw to the face from the third.

Though I have harmed them, the killing blow needs to be to their head. Even if I have to effectively remove it with my blade. But until the shadows fully form there, I won't be able to act.

For now, I get to toy with them, spot their weaknesses and strengths, and learn for myself instead of what has been told to me.

The creatures are silent; no sound comes from their sharp, smoky jaws as they form, which works in my favor. They will not give away my presence to the Caligo guards. And although I'm grateful for their absence of sound, their silence is dangerous. They have used it to kill under the cover of night, leaving no trace behind of what or who the culprit is.

Another thing the Caligo guards use against us.

They don't believe the Sidus, only seeing us as distrustful and liars. I doubt they would believe us even if one of these creatures stood before them.

The dark creatures' assessing eyes could easily blend in with the rest of their bodies, if not for the red tinge that bleeds around them. I feel their darkness as it reaches out to mine, searching for an answer they will not find.

Movement from the wall forces me to change my

tactic of discovering more about them and their weaknesses.

A sigh escapes my lips. I am disappointed I will have to make this quick. Delaying their inevitable fates will not help my own if I am caught.

With their heads now fully formed, I pull my darkness around me, becoming part of the shadows themselves. Appearing beside a creature, I shove a dagger into the side of its head before quickly yanking it out. Moving through the shadows, I emerge on the other side of the creature just as a claw slashes across my stomach, making me gasp from the sharp sting.

Gritting my teeth, I let go, letting years of training take over. My mother trained me for this; I just need to let my muscle memory repeat what it has been taught.

I slam my daggers into the creature's head before twisting and pulling it out. It drops to the ground, dead, before slowly disappearing in wisps of black smoke.

Two down, one to go.

I turn to the third just as it's about to grab me. I let my arm and dagger become shadows and watch its claw pass right through it before becoming whole again.

Ducking out of the path of its second claw, I grab both daggers and thrust them up through the creature's jaw, and the tips come out through the top of its head.

Yanking them out, I watch the creature drop to the ground. Its heavy thump and the sound of my breathing are the only things breaking the silence around me.

Glancing over at the guards, I turn back and watch as

the creatures take too long to disappear. Placing my daggers back at my sides, I reach out and pull the creatures into the void with me and emerge closer to the shadows at the edge of the wall and dark forest. Using the shadows to conceal us, I wait until they have completely disappeared before moving.

Glancing around once more, I make sure there is no evidence left of the fight. The quick movement sends a sharp burn across my stomach. A hiss escapes my lips as I put pressure on the wound before glancing over at the guards as they laugh at something.

There was no need for me to worry about being seen, as not once did they glance over at the tainted wall. No, to them, the only danger is the Sidus. It doesn't matter that the Caligo are more powerful, their dark shadows snuffing out even the strongest light from a Sidus.

When the new royals entered their ruling over a decade ago, people born with powers of light were cast aside and seen as the enemy. While the Caligo, people born with power from the shadows, were thrust into positions of high authority, giving them control over the Sidus.

Overnight, a kingdom once full of peace and promise became broken and divided, full of fear and distrust. While the Caligo sit in their houses of grandeur atop the mountains near the palace, with jobs that pay well beyond their needs, the Sidus scrape by below, surviving day to day in structures that could barely be called a home.

I never knew the old king before he passed, but I have heard a great many things about him. He ruled with compassion and kindness. His verdict was always fair. No sides were chosen, and all those in the kingdom were treated as equals.

Once he passed, his three sons decided to rule as one. But they are his complete opposite. They seem to rule with fear and resentment for the Sidus. And although they are neither Caligo nor Sidus but something more, as all royals are, they trust only the cruel Caligo guards to be by their sides.

The Sidus have no say and no power when it comes to the Caligo guards and the royals. The guards have twisted the position they have been given and have used it to their advantage, taking what they want at their choosing. And anyone who dares stand up to them is promised a swift death.

I glance around once more before pulling myself into the void and focus on returning home, emerging from the shadows into a familiar small jagged alley.

Keeping my head down and covered but my eyes watchful, I make my way past the neglected paths and shabby shacks that house the Sidus people. My stomach sinks at how dilapidated some of them are. Most Sidus can no longer afford the luxury a solid roof provides and have been using dirt and cloth to cover them.

Many will move on once the harder seasons arrive, to the other side of the town, where the shadows are not so harsh. Some before, if the guards are feeling bored and want something to amuse them.

I push down the quiet rage building inside me. I know it will do no good to lose my temper. The guards have no compassion, and their judgment is swift.

If I had been caught for what I just did, I would join the prisoners in the palace before an execution the next day. It would not matter that I might have saved lives. The Caligo guards would have never believed me. They only crave power, and anyone who dares defy them and who cannot be controlled should be eliminated.

They can never know what I did or what I am, as my life is worth nothing but death.

CHAPTER 2

I silently sneak in the window I left ajar for my return. My mother is somehow always able to sense my shadowing, so I need to be careful when using it around her.

Stripping off my cloak, I bundle it up and throw it under the makeshift bed made from two wooden planks, cloths, and feathers. My room is small, barely big enough to fit two people, but it is a lot more than what most have.

I grab the small box of ointment and strips of fabric and place them on the small wooden trunk sitting at the end of my bed. Opening the box, I check on my wound, pulling out a piece of fabric when a throat clears from behind me, making me wince.

"Seren, please tell me you did not just do what I think you did?"

I turn around and glimpse a look of disbelief written

across my mother's face. Her thick brown hair is pulled back, accentuating the elegant bone structure of her face and the sharp look she gives me. Her lips are taut with displeasure, ready to release whatever pent-up anger and worry she has.

My mother can be a scary person when provoked. As a former guard to the previous king, her skills and training are beyond measure, her beauty and grace hiding a ruthless warrior beneath it.

No one provokes Aloisia unless they question their mortality.

"What exactly is it you think I did?" I ask, steeling myself for the oncoming lecture while angling my injured stomach out of her view. Seeing my small injury would only further her anger and concern.

Though she knows I can take care of myself and has seen me with much worse injuries, her worry for me always trumps any sense of duty.

Her sharp brown eyes narrow on me. "Now is not the time for games. Did you or did you not just sneak out to fight one of those dark creatures?"

I open my mouth to try to end this quickly, but she steps forward, her eyes alight with fury.

"What would have happened if you were caught? If they found out what you are, what we've been hiding all these years?" She knows she has trained me well, more worried about the guards catching me using my shadow powers than the dark creatures themselves.

Though, she has a right to worry. If the guards had caught me, I would be dead, there is no doubt about it.

But I can no longer hide myself away, not when the Sidus try to push back the dark creatures night after night. Not when the creatures grow in numbers and power.

Not when the Sidus' light powers barely harm them anymore.

We need to do more. *I* need to do more.

The shield is no longer keeping the dark creatures at bay, its powers deteriorating and allowing more to pass through. We need to think ahead and plan for more than just fighting and surviving. We need a plan to live a life where we are not always fighting against some constant threat.

My hands tightly fist the piece of fabric. "I cannot stand by and watch another parent lose their son or daughter. Not when I can help. These abilities might as well come to our aid. If the Caligo choose to ignore what is right in front of them, then that is on their own consciences, but I will not spend another moment hiding when I can do something."

She says nothing, watching me closely.

"You've trained me for this." I step forward and wince, the quick movement aggravating my injury.

She growls as her eyes zero in on it. "I've trained you to protect yourself, not to become a vigilante in the cover of night."

I hide the next wince threatening to reveal me, her words closer to the truth than she knows.

Grabbing the box, she makes me sit down so she can tend to my wound. Even in her angered state, she always looks out for me. It curbs some of my own anger, making me think before I say something I might regret.

"I *need* to help."

"Seren—"

"I'm not a child anymore. I know there is more dark than light in this world. Let me at least try to find my own path in it."

"Nineteen years of age is barely on the precipice of adulthood and does not give you the right to make decisions like this."

"And what about the others? Those who cannot fight? Those who have no choice or say? Should we just ignore their pleas and sit back and watch?"

My mother stays silent, focusing on tending to my wound. I grab her hands and hold them tight, waiting for her to look at me. The anger in her face masks the true emotion seeping from her eyes.

Fear.

She fears what may become of me should I join their fight, and thinks she has to always protect me from the harsh nature of our world as she tries to be my shield. But it is about time I become someone else's.

"Let me be their voice when they cannot be heard, their blade when they cannot fight. Please don't try to make me watch on as our world grows bleak and hopeless."

Her anger withdraws, an expression of sadness taking over her face as she shakes her head. "I know you are strong; you are my daughter after all, but if you're caught—"

"I will not allow myself to be caught. I can do this. *Please* trust me."

She quickly pulls me toward her, gripping my shoulders tight before her hands envelop me. I ignore the twinge of pain in my stomach, comforted by her warm embrace.

"I *do* trust you; it's the rest that worries me." There's a tremble in her body as she holds me close. "I love you more than life itself, Seren. If anything were to happen to you, I fear the world without your light in it."

My eyes burn from the unfaltering love in her voice. I owe everything to my mother. She saved me when the very people who brought me into this world had abandoned me to the dark. I know love and kindness only through her. It is because of her love and strength that I am the person I am today. But helping is the right thing to do. She knows this because it is what *she* has taught me.

She pulls away and gazes at me before bandaging up my cut. "How many?"

Renewed energy lights up inside of me at the thought of finally having her blessing.

"Three."

She pauses, looking up at me with a frown before sighing and finishing up. I know what she's thinking. There shouldn't be so many showing up, especially not all at once. That's not normal, even for them.

"There has been a rise in the amount of them. Why?" I ask. There has to be a reason. They started showing up alone, the time spanned out between appearances. Then they doubled and now it seems that has only grown, bringing nothing but death and destruction with them.

My mother shakes her head. "Something is coming, Seren, something dark. I can feel it deep in my bones."

A cold shiver works its way down my spine as I feel the truth in her words.

She looks over my face with so much love in her eyes. As she cups my cheek, I feel the warmth seep into it. "Whatever it is, I hope we may all face it together and overcome it with victory." She moves her hand and the warmth goes with it.

There will be no *all* when it comes to facing whatever may come. The Sidus will fight and die while the Caligo guards watch on.

Not all Caligo are bad; the Caligo people mostly stay to themselves and up in their mountains beside the royals.

It is essentially the guards who force the divide with their cruelty. They think us beneath them and their powers and spread lies about our distrustful natures. Lies that are only supported by the foolishness of the rebels. A group of disorganized petulant criminals who do nothing but cause havoc and sully the name of the Sidus.

Not everyone agrees with our two kinds being divided. Many are amicable toward each other and not only out of purpose or duty. But the guards make sure to halt any growing relations between the two. They will never fight alongside the Sidus. Our mighty trio of royals and their own misguided trust ensures that.

"Our royals will do the right thing." My mother nods her head to herself, thinking her words to be true. Something I immensely disagree with. Her misguided trust could be due to meeting the king, her heart still hoping his legacy of royals will be just like him.

Apart from those close to them, no one knows what the royals look like; no one has seen them leave the safety of their palace since the death of the previous king.

At first, many believed them to be in mourning. But the years passed while the Caligo guard's power grew with no sign of them.

I imagine their looks to be like their personality and actions: sharp and cruel.

"They do nothing but sit on their thrones, declaring their commands and looking down on us as if we are nothing but small annoying creatures."

All royals have great power beyond measure. They say the Gods gave it to them to assure they could protect their people, but they do nothing to protect us. *Nothing*, when they could, and I cannot forgive that, no matter if their birthright calls them my rulers.

"*They* are our monarchs." My mother's tone leaves no room for argument. But I attained my stubborn nature from her and will always do and say what I feel is right.

"They are *nothing* to me. They help no one but themselves and their selfish needs. Our people are dying. Our kingdom has been cut off from everyone for longer than I have lived, and for what? Maybe if they gave us a chance outside to fight, we could defeat these dark creatures and whatever else is beyond them and be part of the world again."

A whole world might exist out beyond the dark forest and black sea, but we'll never find out if we stay trapped inside their cage.

"You do not know what you speak of. There are thousands, if not more, of those creatures out beyond the wall in the depths of the dark forest. If not for that shield protecting us, we would all be dead."

Would we? The guards are arrogant and cruel but also powerful. If they allowed the Sidus to all train and fight instead of coming up with some foolish guard's competition every year in an attempt to prove the Sidus' incapabilities, then we might stand a chance.

The only Sidus to ever join their ranks is Ryuu, and that was many years ago. No other Sidus has joined them since, and they have made sure to keep it that way, making each competition more brutal and vicious each year.

All Sidus should learn how to fight to protect themselves and one another in order to stand a chance against this threat. But the Caligo guard would never allow it.

They don't believe any pleas we've made about the weakening shield or previous Sidus deaths. And after the last few nights of multiple deaths, I doubt they ever will.

"What are we supposed to do? Just blindly follow their rule and live our lives in a cage?" I ask.

"It is better to live in a cage than to be dead."

"Is it?" How can anyone truly live when they've never been set free?

Her sigh is long and weary, the fight no longer in her. "Get some sleep. We'll talk in the morning."

I don't want to fight with her. I know she means well, but I can no longer live my life hiding among the shadows. I need to see the world with my own eyes and not through the filtered thoughts and opinions of others.

I glance back at my mother and the worry that crinkles her eyes and forehead before she turns to leave. "I love you, always. I hope you know that."

She pauses at my door, a quiet smile warming her eyes. "As do I, Seren, always."

Before leaving, a mischievous look graces her face. "Ryuu will want to see you early. Don't be late."

I wince hearing her quiet chuckle move farther down the small hall between our two rooms. I have no problem getting up early, but *Captain* Ryuu takes early to another level.

My mother's husband has been a thorn in my side

these last few years. Ryuu is known as the only Sidus to win the Caligo competition and is a formidable force to deal with.

Though I doubt him staying on with the Caligo guards has given him a quiet life.

When our little family joined together, Ryuu never saw me as a newly acquired daughter but more of a soldier he could command at will. The crack of dawn is late for him and his form of torture that he likes to mask as training. His acquired training techniques tend to reflect the mood he's in, and my mother keeps nothing from him bar the secret of my birth and abilities. He will surely take whatever frustrations he has on my nightly escapades out in my session.

Tomorrow is going to be a long day.

CHAPTER 3

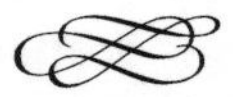

I reach up to catch the dawn as its golden rays slowly cast incandescent shades of burnt oranges and bright pinks across the sky. Everything around me is quiet, the silence a peaceful sanctuary that settles over me and keeps me warm as the cool morning slowly awakens.

The jagged cliffs conceal me from the world, a small haven that I can call my own.

I glance out upon the kingdom that is both a home and a cage, the wall's colossal size making it impossible to ignore. The shield and its shadowy foundation darken the Sidus town below, casting its tainted darkness throughout and blocking nearly every piece of light from the emerging vibrant sun.

The distant palace stands tall, even amongst the mountains themselves.

I am awed by its beauty. Its pearly whites and golds shimmer in the soaring light, casting rays of wonder among the lush greens that surround it. Extravagant waterfalls cascade down the side of it, merging into the lake below before expanding out among the homes of the Caligo. The lake carries down to the Sidus town, turning murky the closer it gets to us.

Whereas the Caligo and their homes reach the high translucent shield and, in turn, the sun, the homes of most Sidus below see only shades of blacks and grays.

A line that is deftly drawn across one kingdom divides the two furthermore.

My mother never kept the truth of what I was from me. Born both from light and dark, I eternally hover between each world while never completely fitting in either. What I am goes against the very laws of nature. An imbalance that is unholy and should be destroyed.

A smirk tilts my lips at the thought. I am an unknown, and for that, I am feared, and anything feared should be destroyed. The odds will always be against me, but I will revel in proving wrong those who question my existence.

Embracing my shadows one last time before suppressing them for the day, I pull myself into the void and straight out onto the small alley that is almost completely deprived of light this early. Its dark cover guards my secret as I walk out into the bustling dark streets.

Buildings once similar to the majestic homes of the Caligo are now nothing more than disintegrating blocks of shaded structures. The sidewalk and streets now blend as one, no longer maintained, with more important necessities prioritized, such as food and shelter.

The shield started darkening at its base years ago, but one of the side effects is that it started rotting the plant life and decaying buildings.

Since the homes and land of the Sidus are the only things to suffer under its influence, the darkening shield is otherwise thought harmless. As the Caligo are high, near the top of the shield, no harm is befalling them, while the Sidus take the brunt of its ill effect. And although the atmosphere is still thick with its murky shades, the Sidus people stand strong and proud.

Our ability to cast and control the light is not weakened; instead, the darkness makes it stronger. Though the Sidus' powers are not as strong as the Caligo's, many found a new way to use their powers and adapt to the strange new environment.

"Seren! Seren!" someone calls out, shaking me from my thoughts.

I turn, finding Meira running toward me, her little legs stumbling as she tries to catch up to me. I bend down as she reaches me and scoop her into my arms.

"Meira. Is Andro chasing you again?" I glance around for the young boy who is besotted with Meira. Though, who could fault him, with her big blue eyes, wild red hair, and never-ending ability to show kindness. Her beautiful heart makes her someone everyone adores.

"No, I lost him some time ago."

I chuckle quietly to myself. Meira is not only known for her kindness but also her cunning nature. Although only six years old, she is intelligent beyond her years.

"Seren, Mama needs your help." Meira's face grows sad, sending a bolt of worry through me. Meira's mother, Natasa, is always too proud and stubborn to ask for help from anyone. I silently beg whatever gods are up there that it isn't something sinister.

"What happened?"

"She's... stuck. Please come help her."

I frown but put Meira down to follow her.

"Show me." Ryuu will not be happy with this delay, but I cannot ignore someone in need.

We run past curious stares before coming to the edge of the town. Meira continues on out farther, until she stops beside a well. I pause beside her, giving her a questioning look. She points into the well before stepping away. It takes me a minute but finally dawns on me what she's trying to tell me. But... surely not...

I peek over the edge, seeing nothing but darkness. Frowning, I call on my light, letting it flow out and down into the deep well. Luminescent strings float downward before circling a figure completely drenched in thick mud.

"Not. A. Word." Natasa's sharp voice rings out around the dark circular walls.

I pinch my lips from the chuckle threatening to escape. It would do no good to mock her, not when she needs help.

"Just help me get me out of here." Natasa sighs. Her weary tone snaps me out of any previous amusement.

I lean forward, getting a better look. Casting my light farther around her, I push more power into it, making it grow.

"Together?" I ask her. Like the Caligo, most Sidus work together to perform larger tasks that require more power. And although I could do this in my sleep, the Sidus are unaware of my expanded abilities.

"Together," Natasa replies, calling upon her own light to join with mine.

We connect our strings of light, forming a net. It cocoons her, wrapping around her to gently lift her off the ground. I feel the slight pull as she moves upward, slowly floating toward me until she nears the top. Reaching out, I grab her nearest arm, my hand slipping slightly from the sludgy mud all over her before finding a grip. I drag her up, giving my light an extra push to help lift her over the lip of the well, before she's able to break free.

Sweat and mud cling to her like a second skin. Her face, somewhat visible through the brown sludge, is pale, making me frown. Using her powers to carry herself, even with help, has drained her.

Giving her a moment to catch her breath, I reach out to help her stand up.

After a moment, Natasa takes a deep breath, and her pallor face returns to a normal color.

"Thank you." Natasa's voice is rough with emotion.

"Anytime."

Pulling Meira into a tight hug, she dips her head before turning to leave. Just as she takes another step, she hesitates, turning back to me and clearing her throat.

"I would appreciate it if you didn't mention this… *misfortune* to anyone."

I frown, feigning confusion. "I can't say I know at all what you're referring to?" My frown turns into a knowing smile. Keeping this small secret for her is no hardship. I have my own, though one more weighty with far more severe consequences.

Her stiff posture loosens as she shares my smile. Taking hold of Meira's hand, she turns, heading in the opposite direction of the town. I doubt she wanted anyone to see her in such a vulnerable state. Vulnerable for her proud nature, of course.

"Thank you, Seren," Meira shouts out.

I wave her off before heading back through town and on to another *bonding* session with the captain.

Approaching the cusp of Ryuu's land and old home, I pause, taking in the small stretch of terrain around me. Distant memories of passing this place as a young child rise up.

Before Ryuu became involved with my mother and lived here, my innocent eyes saw a small oasis in a world full of shadows. A land once carpeted with wildflowers that flourished among the terrain is now barren. All that is left is decaying earth full of rocky ground and hard soil. An oasis no longer, but favorable for the use of training.

As I continue on past the crumbling archway, Ryuu's tall build comes into view, his rigid posture pacing leisurely back and forth. A deception in itself.

"You're late," Ryuu's gruff voice barks out. He has an air about him that demands respect and obedience. A captain through and through. He towers over my average height, while my pale skin and hair brighten against his dark and bronze tones. Though his sea green eyes are the exact shade of my own. It is the only thing we seem to have in common.

I sigh, taking up the position he expects. Eyes forward, shoulders back, legs slightly apart, and hands behind my back.

I don't need to look at his face to know what expression he wears. Ryuu is in a constant state of scorn. That is, until he is in the presence of my mother, and a different person rises up. One with warmth in his green eyes and a gentleness to his touch. My mother is not a fragile woman, but to Ryuu, you would think she was made of glass and could shatter any moment. His love for her is unequivocal, which is why I don't object to our alleged bonding sessions. That, and I'm not foolish enough to turn down an opportunity to further expand my skills.

Although my mother has trained me well, there are

always more techniques to acquire and master. Ryuu has a different viewpoint, a different approach when assessing his opponents and the ways in which he would take them down.

Where I was disciplined to be swift and silent, his attacks are brutal and unforgiving. His presence is full of raw power, and he pushes me just as hard as, if not harder than, his soldiers. And although we never see eye to eye, his unbiased nature has helped me build respect for him.

"I'm here now." There is no point making excuses with Captain Ryuu, no matter how genuine they are. Excuses to him are just that, and anything beyond death would not suffice.

"I expect you to be on time; an extra hour in the stables after our session."

Cleaning out the Caligo guard's horse stables is one of the many *punishments* he likes to dole out for disobedience. Not that it ever bothered me. Though the stables smell foul, the animals are beautiful beasts with calming natures.

"Yes, sir."

A dip of the head is the only acknowledgment given before he continues on.

"I've been made aware of your foolishness."

The hope that I would receive any form of blessing from him dashes away.

"Sir?"

"Do you think yourself some sort of champion, Seren?"

Champions are foolish beings who covet fame and fortune. I require neither, nor have I ever desired the fictitious nature of such a position.

"No, sir."

"Some sort of clandestine, then?" His taunts are only cruel words, nothing I haven't heard before.

I remind myself of my own deception—what I keep hidden from him and the guilt it holds—before letting my emotions get the best of me.

I face him, seeing the flames of anger in his eyes, his jaw clenched as his eyes pierce through mine like blades. "No... *sir*."

"Ah, maybe it is that you think yourself as one of the rebels? Maybe you would like to join them and their immoral behavior?"

The rebels are no help, causing nothing but trouble for the rest of us.

The Caligo guards believe us to be untrustworthy and incapable of any sort of alliance, and the rebels have done everything to prove them right. They cause havoc, their methods unorganized and sloppy. They speak of equality and fairness but hold no such regard for themselves. There have been many times their asserted plan went asunder, leaving the rest of us to clean up their mess. I would rather work by myself than join the group of fraudulent misfits.

"Of course not."

"Then I cannot fathom why one would sneak out and commit such a foolish act." His tone is as sharp as a whip, doing nothing to ebb my own rising ire. He turns his back to me, continuing his back-and-forth pace.

My voice is steady when I reply. "I only want to help." Seeing firsthand what our people go through should make him understand what I'm trying to do. There are not many who know how to fight anymore. No one even tries to learn, too fearful of the repercussions from the Caligo guards. Many are left unprotected and alone. We need anyone and everyone that can help.

"Your mother is under the impression that you are ready for such a responsibility. I do not agree with her on this." Of course he doesn't. He would train me to use a blade but lock me up to keep me safe. His words and actions are constantly at war with one another. He would tell me daily that I should stay out of the guard's business and any trouble, yet that very same day, he would show me a maneuver to incapacitate an attacker in two strikes.

"I can take care of myself. I handled the threat without any complications." Minus the small injury I acquired, but I am clearly not about to bring that up.

"Fool's luck is what it was."

I lock my jaw, keeping my temper at bay. It was no luck that helped me last night but years of training and hard work. He has to know I am capable enough to take care of myself.

"It's ridiculous that you think you are ready for such

a thing and incredibly irresponsible to willingly put yourself in danger."

I know I am not immortal, and although powerful, I realize I can also easily be killed. I also know it will be a risk going up against these creatures and what will happen if I am caught, but doing nothing will not help anyone.

"I have my mother's blessing on this, and although I wish I also had yours, I must continue to do what I feel is right. I *will* fight."

"You will do *no such thing*," he hisses.

My eyes widen as his anger pulses out around him, his Sidus power coming to the surface. Where two green eyes were a minute ago are now white orbs that mirror bolts of lightning.

He closes his eyes, taking a deep breath, calming himself.

Ryuu is known for his control, especially when it comes to emotions. It's one of the many reasons he became captain in an army full of Caligo. He sees daily the desolate and castaways and, among them, many a lost soul that does not have an ounce of hope left. And yet he is still able to continue with the job at hand. He puts up with the guards who constantly taunt him and make sure he knows that they see him as something beneath them.

So, for him to lose control so easily, it stuns me silent.

I swallow against the lump forming in my throat. I know deep down he has always cared in his own way. He helped raise me these last few years. But every child must grow up and leave the safety of their parents. They must forge their own path and make their own mistakes along the way.

This is something I need to do. Deep inside me, I know the gods must have created me for more than just sitting on the sidelines and watching.

"I *can* do this. Please trust what you and my mother have trained me to do."

Ryuu sighs, shaking his head, suddenly looking older than his age. "You are barely an adult, Seren, and messing with things that you have no business messing with. What if the guards were to have seen you?"

I clamp my jaw shut, facing forward once more. He doesn't know the extent of my abilities, nor the fact that I can shadow myself in the blink of an eye. A feat not many Caligo can achieve. Pushing him on this would not help my cause and only further anger him, so I try to stay quiet. It might make this lecture pass more swiftly.

"Hmm, nothing to add?"

His arrogant tone grates on me, but I push down my heightened emotions once more, feeling it unwise to behave childishly. If I want to be treated like an adult, I have to act like one. Screaming and shouting will get me nowhere.

I hold in my next sigh before speaking, but barely. "I was not seen by anyone. The guards were too busy fooling around to notice the incoming threat. They would not know what a threat was if it were to stand right in front of them." I may be above screaming and shouting, but I will always get my point across. That, and I have acquired my mother's eloquent quip. People can choose to listen and take my opinion or not. As is their right.

Ryuu stands still before shifting into my view. "Do you not think the guards capable?" His voice is but a whisper, his tone though, like quiet thunder.

Even though they mock him daily, disrespect him behind his back, he still vouches for the guards who are supposed to be under his command. I hold no quarrels with speaking the truth.

"I'm sure they are extremely capable." Being trained by Ryuu would make them so. "Though I question their intentions and complete disregard for the safety of our people. They continually overlook the glaring truth and what that means."

Ryuu harrumphs. "And you, naturally, know what this *truth* is?"

I look him straight in the eye so he can sense the absolute certainty in my words.

"Death."

Ryuu's eyes widen slightly before he composes himself, but I will not let this go so easily.

"We both know it, what is here and what is coming. It will not be long before they start getting through in droves. If we don't band together and do something now, we'll never be able to stop them." It is only a matter of time. Time we don't have.

We need to form a plan, and soon.

"This is not for you to worry about. The guards wi—"

"The Caligo guards deny the very existence of the dark creatures showing up here or the Sidus deaths. How are they going to help us when they think us liars?"

When he says nothing, I continue on. "There is something coming; we all feel it. It is in the air around us, cloaking what little hope we have and twisting it into something sinister. It won't be long until we have no choice but to fight. We need to plan ahead; we need to band together—"

"You cannot protect everyone, Seren."

"No, but I can *try*. And that should be enough."

Ryuu's shoulders deflate, a frown scarring his otherwise unblemished face. "There are things in this world... I wish... I wish that I could keep you far away from, but I know that it would be futile." A slight quirk of his lips shows a brief display of humor in his otherwise somber demeanor. "You have your mother's stubborn nature, after all."

"An annoyance she has come to regret, I assure you. But not to worry, I still remind her of it daily."

A smile that mirrors my own spreads across his face. "As is your duty."

His expression turns serious once again. "Whatever may come to pass, I expect you to keep yourself safe. Demand it, in fact. Don't make rash or impulsive decisions. Be smart about your actions and the trust you give to people around you."

"I will, you have my word." A sliver of elation rushes through me at his quiet acceptance.

Ryuu nods his head once more before taking a step back. Any previous emotion shown on his face retreats behind the distant captain's facade.

"Let us begin."

CHAPTER 4

I pass through the thick, sludgy brown fields, my only good pair of black boots now drenched in mud, and head toward the stables.

The fairly large-sized wooden structure is held up partially by its extra supported wooden beams, added by Ryuu himself, but mostly by sheer luck and hope. Hope that it will not fall apart at its seams due to rot and old age.

Once inside, I look around to find all seven stables are occupied. The horses all belong to the Caligo guards who are stationed near this side of the kingdom and wall.

My smile stretches across my face when I spot an old friend.

Blaze.

Walking up to the colossal dark horse, I take slow, measured steps. Though we are both old friends, her tricky temperament assures unwelcome visitors a swift punishment. Her glossy black fur shines even in the darkest of rooms, making the other horses pale in comparison.

"Hello, old friend," I whisper.

Blaze hesitantly steps forward, her nostrils flared. "It's just me, girl." Stepping closer to her, I slow my movements further and reach a hand out. She shakes her long dark mane before stepping closer, sniffing my hand and nudging it, looking for any treats.

I chuckle, pleased that she remembers our little secret, and rub a hand over her silky mane as I move closer to her.

"Not today, girl. I didn't realize you'd be here."

Blaze had become a prominent addition to the guard's arsenal once they realized her potential. Her raw power and strength surpassed the other horses, making her stand out. But it was her lack of fear when near the walls closest to the dark forest that made the guards choose her over the rest.

What once was a sickly young filly, ignored and thought of as nothing but a waste, is now the leader of her herd and paramount to the guard's duties.

Our training together ensured her place among the guards, and in return, I found a long-lasting friendship, now bound through years of merciless practice and preparation. Our determination and unyielding spirits gave way for a better path for her future while also giving me hope for mine.

"Tomorrow, I promise."

I lean my forehead against hers, closing my eyes, and soak up the serenity and calm of being around these beautiful beasts.

I'm so absorbed in the tranquility that I almost miss the thud of boots across the dirt floors as someone enters the stables. My body grows stiff as I wait to see who it is.

"Ah, there she is, my favorite mulch partner."

My tense body relaxes hearing Jarek's jovial voice.

Jarek has a soft roguish look that many fall for. His soldier's build and light blue eyes are the cause of many brawls. "How is the beautiful Ren today? Break any hearts yet?"

I roll my eyes at his bestowed childhood nickname.

"Physically, you mean?" With there being more important things to think about, I'm not interested in fooling around. "Not yet, but the day is still young."

Jarek's deep chuckle echoes off the stable walls. "I, for one, cannot wait to see the day you finally meet your match."

I doubt that day will ever come.

"I prefer the company of these beasts over foolish boys."

He dips his head, agreeing. "Of course you would. But how about we get you a nice guy to have some fun with? Might help you loosen up a bit."

I narrow my eyes at his idiotic idea. Most guys my age are either settling down or full of stupidity. I need neither the companionship nor the melodrama that comes along with such an arrangement.

Jarek sighs loudly, glancing over at me. "It is a pity."

"What is?" I frown, hesitant to hear where he is going with this, knowing from experience it could be anything.

"That we could never be matched." He exaggerates a sigh, shaking his head. "You and I, we could have been amazing."

I grin at his jesting. "Is that so?"

He nods his head, a serious expression on his face. "If only I were swayed by your beauty alone." A smile full of mischievousness lights up his face. "Alas, I require a certain... *instrument* the female variety do not possess."

Jarek's perpetual wit and whimsy is one of the things I love most about him. He sees the world around him in shades of color instead of the drab monochrome it usually is.

"Apart from me not being able to fulfill your physical needs, you aren't my type anyway. Too high maintenance for me to even attempt to keep up with," I tease with a smirk.

He grabs his chest in a mock blow. "Downright merciless, that's what you are."

My replying chuckle and grin are wicked. "You wouldn't have me any other way."

A genuine smile crosses his face, one he only shares with close family and friends. "Not even a little."

Tilting his head, he casts a brief eye around the stables. "What did you do to irritate the captain today?"

"Apart from existing, you mean?" The captain likes to think of me as one of his soldiers until he is dissatisfied with something I do, and then I am nothing more than an inconvenience. "I was late."

Jarek chuckles, shaking his head. "He should know by now what you're like. When are you ever on time?"

"When I'm required to be." At least I'd like to think so, but life seems to have a way of placing obstacles along the way. "Also, when the situation is dire, and training is neither."

"I'd have to agree with you on that. The amount of training you do should be outlawed."

His statement causes me to frown. "Everyone should know how to wield a blade and protect themselves."

"I agree, but not to the extent of your proficiency, nor the amount of time you spend at it." Jarek chuckles, jostling my shoulder. "Some of us like to do more than just exist in this world. We want to *live* in it too. Remember that, Ren. There is more to life than fighting."

Unless fighting is the only way to live.

I look back at him, seeing a light in his eyes that is usually dimmed by the weight of his responsibilities. "What has you in such a cheerful mood?"

His eyes are wide when he gives me a strange smile. "I didn't realize I had to have a reason to be happy."

"You don't, but you just seem... lighter. I want to know the cause." Moments of happiness should never be taken for granted, especially when of late, they're hard to come by.

Jarek shrugs as if his behavior is an everyday occurrence. Which I know for a fact, it's not. His life has been far from easy. From losing his mother at such a young age to then having to grow up quickly and provide for himself and his father. A father that is now a lost shell of a man who retreated from the world once his wife was gone.

"Today is a good day. We are all alive. There were no dark creature attacks last night, and things are looking up. I, for one, would not disregard the small gift of reprieve and hope it means something good for us all."

I face Blaze, hoping Jarek can't see the guilt on my face. The attacks have not stopped, instead getting worse with more creatures getting past the shield and wall. A reprieve will not be coming anytime soon, with the ominous stench of something malevolent on the way.

I push down the guilt and send him a small smile. There was no point in destroying his frail moment of peace, not when he looks so happy. I will just have to work hard to figure a way to make sure he and this kingdom are kept safe and, in turn, try to preserve his slight reprieve and hope.

He clears his throat, giving me a shy look. "That, and I met someone."

He mumbles it so softly I barely catch the words. They send a bolt of relief throughout me, moving away from the subject of dark creatures and my omission of the truth.

"Of course you did. What is his name and when am I meeting him?"

Jarek scoffs, waving a hand in front of me. "So you can frighten him off with your insane warrior skills or turn him to your favor with your striking beauty? I think not."

Although playful, his tone and the slight shift in his normally rested demeanor make me wonder what has him anxious.

"Is everything okay?"

"Of course. You know me, I'm always fine." His grin is brittle, and his far-off look causes me to doubt his words, which makes me want to push him on this. But I know it will get me nowhere until he's ready to tell me.

He must see the worry mirrored on my face, as his smile turns warm. "Don't worry, you'll meet him soon enough."

"I better," I warn him, but I tack on a smile so he knows I'm not being completely serious. Only just *mostly*.

Jarek chuckles, giving me a knowing look. "I overheard the guard's competition this year is being held in the palace grounds."

I quirk a brow at his quick change of subject. "And you're telling me this for what reason?"

A playful glint enters his eyes. "Not only do you get to see the palace up close but you also get to meet those secretive royals too."

I have no intention of ever joining the Caligo guards

and their army, nor do I care for meeting any of the royals that continue to have such bias toward the Sidus.

Jarek narrows his eyes. "I imagine them to be hideous to have hidden away for so long. I can't fathom why else they would not show themselves."

Blaze nudges me, seeking attention. I chuckle, rubbing my hand along her soft face.

"Maybe they see us beneath them and nothing more. Maybe they prefer to stay with their Caligo up in the mountains, where everything is clean and gold and bright."

"Maybe..." That far-off look returns to his eyes once more, making me frown.

"Why does any of this matter? You have never cared for any of the other competitions." They are held each year, each one the same as the last. And the Caligo use every single one of them to make sure the Sidus know just how powerful and brutal they are, should we ever try to defy them. Them choosing to close it off and have it in the palace grounds is a small mercy we will be granted.

Being forced to watch it every year is not something I ever look forward to.

A sliver of light returns to his eyes as he focuses his attention solely on me.

"Well... none of them have ever been in the palace, nor has there been a little... *incentive* involved."

"An incentive?" I ask.

"Think about it, Ren. With your skill and abilities, you would win it without breaking a sweat."

"You're forgetting the part where I don't care for meeting the royals, nor do I ever want to join the Caligo guards."

"Yes, but—"

"Jarek. Is there something wrong?" I frown, wondering if there is something more to this. "Have your rationings gone?" If he was without food, I would make sure to find him some.

"No. No, nothing like that. I just thought it would be nice for you to show those Caligo guards how useless they really are, and should you end up with some winnings—*that you would love to share with your favorite friend*—why not give it a chance?"

I shake my head at him, the worry quickly slipping from me. "We don't need to prove just how useless they are; they do that all by themselves."

Jarek sighs but nods his head, dropping it, knowing I will not give into this with my stubborn nature.

"Come on, I'll give you a hand." He turns around, heading toward the small rack of shovels.

"And here I thought it was *I* who was giving *you* a hand." One of the many jobs Jarek has is helping the stable hand when there are more than a couple of horses present. Being that there are over half a dozen, his presence is definitely required.

Jarek scoffs. "Let's not concern ourselves with the

technical details. I'm here to save the day, *as usual.* You can just say *thank you,* and we can move along swiftly."

Giving Blaze one last rub and promising her I'll be back tomorrow with her treat, I follow after Jarek, chuckling.

"I'm still waiting on that thanks," he calls out, leaning against the tool rack, his arms crossed in mock protest.

"You might be waiting a while," I tell him, passing him a shovel and pushing him toward the pile of horse manure.

His roaring laughter rings out around us, filling me with warmth and easing the heaviness from my chest.

* * *

I play the part of a hawk, observing the people below me from the rooftop of one of the highest buildings in the Sidus town. The dark, deserted chapel still stands tall and towers over most buildings, granting me the concealment I need to keep watch.

Along with the dark cover of night, my black armor and cloak help me blend into my surroundings, becoming part of the chapel itself. Though the only way I would truly stand out is if I were to wear colorful or bright clothing. The Sidus have access to neither and end up wearing dark, muted tones that ensure we blend in.

From this height, I can see most of the town and its people, helping me ensure their safety.

It's not only the dark creatures the Sidus have to worry about. Some Caligo guards take advantage of their position and power and often need a reminder that the Sidus are not the only ones who are being watched.

This past year, I have taken on the role of sentry over the guards. No longer able to wait for permission from my mother to help join them in their fight against the dark creatures, I needed to do something. Seeing first-hand some of the disciplines the guards handed out for the simplest misdemeanor made my choice for me. I could no longer sit by and watch a Sidus child struck for asking a simple question or hear the aftermath of a Caligo guard taking liberties with Sidus women and men.

So far, no word has been carried back about a hooded vigilante helping the people of Findias. After all, the guards would have to admit their vile behavior or tell their superior how they ended up in such a position in the first place, conceding that they were weaker than their attacker. A confession no Caligo guard would be willing to reveal.

For now, my secret remains just that.

It wasn't until recently, when I came across a young girl grieving the loss of both her parents from a dark creature, that I was impelled to pursue them as well.

My nightly duties, though, are still a priority as I continue watching the guards spread out across this side of the kingdom. Some walk about, taking their jobs seriously, leaving the Sidus be, while others gossip like old crones, getting drunk on expensive wines. They mull about the town, finding unsuspecting victims for the night, thinking no one will bother them if they have some fun.

So, I listen and watch and wait. Ready to take action if needed but always hoping that it will not be the case. I know fighting amongst ourselves will not solve the bigger threat coming, nor will it justify killing.

Those who only ever see a battle overlook the war upon the horizon.

A shout comes from below, shaking me from my wayward thoughts. I use my shadowing and jump from taller to lower rooftops to reach the source of noise. Coming closer, I see three Caligo guards blocking the entrance to the small alley. A man is injured on the ground while another guard shouts above him.

"Please, don't hurt me. I don't have it. Please, just leave me be. I beg of you."

I glance around, finding a small alcove that will suit my needs.

Most Caligo are limited in what they can do with their shadow abilities, and although not as limited as a Sidus, the guards favor sticking together to combine their powers. To pass through the void to move to places farther away takes at least a half a dozen Caligo joining together.

I have no such restrictions, with my powers sometimes feeling unending. My unique differences would draw attention, even for a lowly vigilante. I need to be clever when choosing my battles and only reveal what is necessary.

"Hand it over now. We know it is in your possession." The guard's tone is full of violence as he raises his hand, forming a baton made from his own shadows, ready to strike.

I jump down, entering the void before making sure my hood is in place, and pull the dark cloth up over most of my face before emerging in the shadows beneath the alcove.

Stepping out of the darkness, I glance down at the man about to collide with the guard's weapon.

The guard pauses his attack, seeing me. "What the—"

I move swiftly, pushing my shadows toward him. They bellow out of me in puffs of black smoke, blasting the guard back against the wall. He slides down to the ground, collapsing from the force of the impact.

Feeling movement from behind, I duck, avoiding the shadowed blade directed at the back of my head, and twist around, catching sight of the three guards advancing, their powers at hand.

I unsheathe my daggers, stepping in front of the injured man. Using shadowed blades doesn't last long, and although they are efficient and useful when needed, I prefer the feel of hard steel in my hand and the control it gives me.

"Get him," one of the guards grits out.

I block a guard coming at my left, using the blunt end

of my dagger to the side of his head. He crumples to the ground just as black smoke circles me, trying to cage me in. It draws closer, surrounding me like the rising waves of a dark ocean.

Before it closes over me, I see the two guards as they join hands, both wearing smug looks as they combine their powers for an attack, hoping to snare and suffocate.

Instead of fearing the darkness, I embrace the familiar power and step through the guards' tenebrous trap. A rush of power slides through me, brushing against my heightened senses and alighting every nerve in my body.

Coming clear of the shadows, I'm greeted by mirrored looks of shock.

"How did you—"

"What are—"

I don't give the guards a chance to finish their inquiry, and use their own trick against them. I watch as my own power swirls and coils around them before encasing them whole. Connecting to my power, I feel their life force like small embers in a flame as they slowly ebb away. Just before they dim completely, I pull back, revealing their slumped forms.

In a way, it is easier fighting the dark creatures. I don't have to hold back for fear of killing them. I can let go, embracing the dark side of myself that I know we all carry deep within us. We are not wholly good nor evil but flawed as all mortal creatures are. But I am also not a god and will not kill without cause. Their judgment will come when it is their time to enter the Otherworld.

Turning around, I drop to the man's side, noticing the river of blood around him, quickly realizing we don't have long before death calls to him.

"Thank you." The man's voice is but a whisper.

I find the source of his wound, a thick gash at his side. Tearing some cloth from my cloak, I use a hand to staunch the bleeding, trying to halt any further blood loss before I can get him help.

He reaches a hand out toward me, and I grab it with my free hand, thinking he needs some comfort and reassurance, but the look in his eyes tells me different.

"We must find you a healer," I tell him—and quickly, by the looks of it. The black cloth is already drenched with blood. I'm about to call on my shadows and bring him to safety, damn the consequences, when his plea makes me hesitate.

"My pocket." His pallor is gray and each breath he takes is labored.

"I need to get you to a healer; you won't last much longer—"

"I do not fear death. I know it is my time."

I shake my head at him, pleading with him to trust me. "I can get you to someone. Just hold on."

"*Please.*" His voice is insistent yet weak. "My pocket." His eyes beg me, moving me forward.

I reach into his pocket and pull out a pulsing white

orb the size of a fist. Its power draws me in, calling out to me.

"Forgive me, but they must never have it. It will destroy everything." The remorse in his voice shakes me out of the strange spell the orb has over me. I open my mouth to ask him to explain what he means, when the pulsing orb's light expands out around us.

"You must never allow them to get hold of it," he whispers.

I try to drop the orb, but it clings to me like a second skin before continuing to expand its light. The light intensifies until it's all I can see, the bright flare engulfing everything, causing me momentary blindness before it starts to recede.

I glance down, no longer seeing an orb but a glimmer of brightness. Almost like a piece of a star, its luminous shine so delicate yet alluring.

The illuminated sphere sends out one last small pulse of light before it flickers, shrinking inward and melding with my hand. I try to shake it away, but it does no good. It continues its process until no outward light can be seen.

A flicker pulses under my skin. Once. Twice. Before it disappears completely.

"Protect it." A weak, soft voice draws me back to the man just as the light leaves his eyes.

"No," I call out, hoping it is not his end even though I see the truth right in front of me.

"Damn it." Releasing a harsh sigh, I reach over and

brush my fingers down his eyes, closing them for the last time.

My hair falls free as I bow my head and pray to the Gods that they grant this man a safe passage to the Otherworld.

"Farewell. May we meet again one day." I move back, waiting for the inevitable. A minute passes before the man's body begins the final stages of life. His body begins to shudder and shake before it lifts into the air like a weightless feather floating softly. Small shimmers begin to cover his whole body, turning it into a constellation of twinkling stars. They hover there for a moment before bursting high up into the sky and dissolving into sparkling dust.

"May the light guide you, the darkness lead you, and the night welcome you a safe passage home."

I look down at my hand, seeing or feeling nothing unusual and wondering if I should be worried of any lingering effects.

A rattle startles me out of my somber mood, back to the present. Pulling my hood back in place, I check around for any prying eyes.

Finding no one but the unconscious Caligo guards, I join the darkness once more.

CHAPTER 5

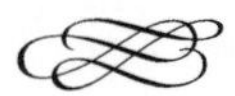

After last night's encounter with the strange orb, I inspect my body in the small mirror beside my bed, looking for anything out of the ordinary. After a few minutes of not finding anything unusual, I look inward, exploring my powers.

The cool, dark tendrils of my shadows bend and curl inside me, trying to reach out to my surroundings. I pull them back, turning to the light. Its warm glow flickers, a deceiving ember ready to ignite and burn like wildfire. I push it down, glancing back at my hand, thinking it will hold an answer.

What did the Sidus man mean about protecting the orb, and from who, the guards?

If he didn't want it to fall into the wrong hands, why then pass it to a stranger? One who might very well have destroyed it merely by touch. And if by some miracle it still exists, hidden somewhere deep within, how will I go about accessing and releasing it? I don't need the added complication to my already precarious abilities, but if it is inside me, I need to remove it in case it causes havoc.

Another thing to worry about but something that will have to wait for now.

Quickly changing into my dark clothes and long boots and strapping my daggers to my side, I throw on my hooded cloak before heading out, shadowing through the void to a building near the edges of the Sidus town.

It doesn't take me long to find them, even in the darkness of night.

Ryuu, my mother, and their close friends and allies Theon and Warrick are spread out among the small bushes and trees that sit before the forest-covered wall and shield.

Silently, they all watch and wait.

Theon is about the same height as Ryuu, his thin frame and build a deception many would look upon as weak. I would have assumed the same had I not seen him fight with such raw power and strength. Warrick is a half a head shorter than him, though his build is much bulkier and strong. I've seen him take out a man with one punch.

As if sensing the incoming creature, my mother shoots forward, Ryuu a half a second behind her, as they rush toward the wisps of dark creatures forming.

My eyes widen as I watch five—*no, six*—dark creatures nearly fully form. Twice as quickly as they did the other night with me.

It seems not only are they growing in numbers but strength too.

My mother attacks the nearest creature in swift, sharp movements while Ryuu covers her with brutal attacks only meant to kill. Theon and Warrick come up behind them to attack the two rushing toward them.

But unlike any other dark creatures I've seen, these seem to fight with a purpose. Their movements aren't as sloppy, and they look to one another every now and again as if they can communicate with one another.

It is as if they are starting to grow an awareness of themselves and their surroundings.

My theory seems to be proven when a dark creature that stayed at the back of the group moves forward and, in the blink of an eye, attacks with purpose. Its movements mimic Ryuu's brutal attack as it attempts to claw down Theon's back.

A light flashes from the corner of my eye; it's there and gone before I know it. But my attention is quickly brought to the flicker of shadows growing in the darkness, the others unaware of it as they still fight the dark creatures around them.

Without a second thought, I'm on my feet, swiftly moving toward my mother and Ryuu just as a half dozen more dark creatures show up.

Still too far away, I reach down and grab one of my daggers on my thigh to fling it forward. It lands directly in the center of a creature's head and quickly brings my presence to the attention of the others.

Ryuu's head whips in my direction, his eyes narrowing as he gives me a sharp look but says no more, continuing to fight as the dark creatures surround them all.

Once I'm close enough, I attack the dark creatures, my blades slicing through their limbs easily.

"Keep one alive," my mother shouts over to me.

I frown but do as she says, helping them until there's all but one creature left. Stabbing my long blade into its strange clawed foot, I pin it to the ground as Ryuu comes up beside me and whips out chains. Theon walks up beside him and shakes off his dark robe.

While Ryuu and Theon tie up and cover the creature, I walk closer to my mother.

"Seren. What are you doing here?" She raises a sharp brow and gives me a look of annoyance.

"Helping?" I reply, my smile innocent yet deceiving.

Both my mother and Ryuu have silently yet reluctantly given me their blessing to help but have yet to allow me entry into the workings of it. I took it upon myself to come tonight in hopes that my help was needed and they would drop any further hesitations.

Warrick moves over to us, dipping his head in greeting. "I did not realize you fought that well." He gives my mother a look. "Maybe you should join us—"

"*I* will decide that, Warrick." My mother gives him a glare that makes him immediately back down and agree.

Clearing his throat, he looks to the dark, rotting, and crumbling wall. "Let us keep watch for a minute to make sure no more come through tonight."

My mother's sigh is weary. "We can't be sure that will happen. The minute we leave, two dozen more could show up. We need guards out here at all times."

Warrick shakes his head. "We don't have that kind of manpower. You know that, Aloisia. Most Sidus can barely defend themselves with their abilities, let alone fight. Let us hope your plan works. It is all we have right now," he says, the worry slashed across his face as he glances to Ryuu and Theon. The creature appears to be knocked out; it's tied up, and the dark robes are wrapped around it tight. It could be easily mistaken for a bundle of weapons or a dead body.

"What plan?" I turn to my mother just as Ryuu steps up beside us. I ignore the agitated glare and focus on her.

Her face is filled with the same agitation but also with a small amount of acceptance.

"As you can see, the numbers seem to be multiplying quickly. Something needs to be done. The Caligo guards need to help," she says.

"They'll never agree to it. You know that," I reply. I don't even need to think about it, knowing it is a fact. The Caligo guards do not care about the Sidus.

My mother shares a look with Ryuu. "We're hoping after they see some evidence firsthand, they will have to move forward with a plan to secure the kingdom." She glances down at the tied-up creature, and it hits me what they are going to do. Or at least attempt.

They are going to take this creature straight to the guards.

"But how can you contain it? They move like smoke and are able to move through the wall."

"Iron," Warrick answers. "For some reason, they can't move through or beyond it. It is the only thing that seems to contain them."

"But—"

"Go home, Seren," Ryuu says, his tone leaving no room for question.

"*Straight* home," my mother warns, giving me a knowing look before placing a kiss on my head and turning to leave, Ryuu a step behind her.

They say their thanks to Theon and Warrick, warning them to be careful in their watch tonight, before heading toward the guard's watchtower nearest to the wall.

I turn and move quickly, heading into the shadows, and move into the void with ease before coming out on top of one of the old towers across from the watchtower. No Caligo guard enters it, as it now lies wasted to rot and is too near the crumbling wall and dark forest.

Using its darkness as cover, I keep an eye on my mother and Ryuu as they make their way toward the Caligo guards. As soon as they're a few feet away, a guard walks out, a snarl on his lips and an arrogant look on his face. His clothes are the same as most other Caligo—

black attire with soft leather and thin plates of gold armor over the shoulders and chest. Some have a small insignia woven onto the right upper shoulder, revealing their high rank among the guard. But their rank does not seem to matter to the Sidus, only themselves. They think us all beneath them anyway.

My stomach churns as I watch, knowing deep down how exactly this is going to go. Either the guards will think they are lying and this is just some trick or hoax or they will blame them for bringing such a threat into the kingdom.

I catch the look in Ryuu's eyes as he stares down the guard. Nothing but raw rage is there as he attempts to talk to him.

The guard laughs at something he says, and that rage only grows. Ryuu clenches his jaw before sharing a look with my mother. She nods her head, and he quickly bends down to slice his dagger across the robes that hide the dark creature.

The Caligo guard's haughty laugh is cut off at once as he jumps a step back in horror, his eyes not leaving the unconscious creature.

Ryuu says something again, making the guard nod a sharp reply, his face now ashen. But before any relief is felt, another guard appears and whips out his sword, slicing it across the creature's neck, effectively killing it. The iron chains drop to the ground as the creature disappears.

The new guard quickly turns on Ryuu and my

mother. I take a step to move toward them when I realize what I'm about to do and stop myself.

Going down there will only bring them more trouble.

I wait and watch, my fists clenched near my daggers as the new guard looks to threaten Ryuu, tipping his head toward my mother as if to threaten her too.

Ryuu gives him a thunderous look before taking my mother's hand and pulling her back toward the Sidus town.

Breathing a sigh of relief, I watch the new guard converse with the one who was shocked by the dark creature's appearance. The new guard looks to threaten him, using his sword to make his point before heading inside.

I pay them no more attention as I move quickly into the void and through the shadows to home.

My mother and Ryuu arrive a few minutes later, the tension and anger draped across them in droves.

"What happened?" I ask, feigning confusion.

Ryuu starts pacing back and forth in the small room, trying to cut off his rising temper.

My mother slides a hand down her face before turning to me, her face growing pale.

"They know."

"Who knows what?" I frown.

She gives me a pointed look, and everything in me freezes when I realize what she means. The Caligo guards know about the dark creatures. They know and still they... I shake my head, trying to clear the jolt of shock from my mind.

My mother nods her head as the impact of this and what it means settles in my veins.

"They *all* know?" I ask.

Ryuu releases a harsh breath. "I do not think they all are aware. The first guard was truly shocked upon seeing the creature. His reaction could not be faked, but the other guard..." He shakes his head. "It wasn't his first time to see one of those creatures. But some of them know, that much I'm sure of now."

A loud bang draws our attention to the door just as a group of Caligo storm through it.

"What is the meaning of this?" Ryuu shouts but is ignored as the Caligo guards start to upturn every piece of furniture in the house, ripping through the upholstery on the chairs and destroying any small keepsakes we've gathered over the years.

My mother pulls me toward her, and Ryuu reaches out and grabs one of the nearest guards. The guard stops and turns to him, a look of fear lighting his eyes.

"We're under orders... *sir*."

"Whose orders?" Ryuu snaps.

"The royals." Another guard walks in, an arrogant smirk on his face.

"You'll be happy to know that we have decided to look into your allegations. It seems there might be some truth to them after all. The royals have declared a curfew is to be put in place to protect the Sidus."

"A curfew? Then what of this?" Ryuu grits out as he glances around at our ruined home, his eyes turning murderous as he looks back to the guard.

The guard's smirk only grows.

I clench my fists by my side as my mother's grip tightens on me. A warning I will listen to. For now.

"This?" The guard laughs, and it crawls down my spine as heat burns through my veins. "This is but a warning. Know your place or we will show you. Bring the rebels, the *true* killers, to us, and your curfew will be lifted."

With one last look of contempt, he turns and heads out with the rest of the Caligo guards, leaving a path of destruction in their wake.

I turn to my mother as Ryuu checks the damage. "Were they faking it? Mentioning the rebels as the killers?"

A harsh exhale leaves her lips. "No. It appears as if some seem to believe the lie that was told to them."

"Do you think the royals know?" I ask.

A light dims in her eyes as she looks at me. "My hope is that they don't, for I fear what will come of the Sidus should they already be aware."

Ryuu comes over to us, shaking his head, a small furrow forming between his brows. "I don't believe the royals passed this curfew, nor that they know about these creatures. I think the guards took it upon themselves to act in their name. I have seen it happen many times before."

"How can you be so sure? You've never met them. No one has," I reply, forgetting for a moment who I am talking to.

Ryuu scowls at me, his frown deepening, but he doesn't call me on it. "I cannot tell you with complete certainty what the truth is, but my belief is that the royals are unaware. There has always been a veil of secrecy among the Caligo guards. But there is a shift in some of them lately. A distrust and secrecy even among their own. There is something happening here. Something we do not see yet." He shares a worried look with my mother before frowning at me again.

"It's late. Let's figure it out after some sleep." My mother sighs, the exhaustion now thick and heavy in her voice.

But my mind is twisting and turning, trying to figure out if what Ryuu believes is true. It makes the thought of sleep the furthest thing from my mind.

Jarek's conversation comes back to me, reminding me that this year's guard's competition is now held inside the palace grounds while all competitors also stay in the palace.

A spark of a plan begins to form with the thought.

If Ryuu is confident that the royals aren't aware of the dark creatures, maybe it is time they find out.

CHAPTER 6

I cleave a path through the darkness, through the night and rain and treacherous storm.

It's late. Too late for anyone to be out after the Caligo guards enacted their curfew.

They have already destroyed many Sidus homes under the guise of protecting them from the unlawful rebels. And even though many Sidus know the truth, the fear the Caligo evoke, the power they wield, and their abuse are more of a threat to them than attempting to provoke their wrath.

The heavy rain starts to ease as I slip into the shadows along the edges of the town to emerge near the river on the opposite side. The thick forest around it hides a peaceful small sanctuary, and among the darkness of night and threat of the guards, not another soul would attempt to visit it.

I move toward my hidden haven, the edge of a small riverbank, and think back to the last couple of hours.

With the first stage of my plan initiated, I can focus on how to deal with the more pressing fallout of my newest reckless decision: the captain and my mother.

They will not agree to what I just did, but there is no time left. With the dark creatures growing stronger and now the Caligo guards becoming more reckless, we need to move ahead with a plan.

The thick trees around the small river bring a small measure of protection from the rain, allowing me to pull my hood down and move closer to the water.

Taking a deep breath, I let my thoughts settle and my mind clear. A minute of serenity soothes my body and mind, giving me a fragment of peace in a moment of chaos. It aids my mental barriers, strengthening my will and intentions.

Our kingdom is struggling to survive, the bars on our cage tightening.

We cannot last like this. The Sidus people are already struggling with the rations of food we have. Jarek is right about one thing. We are all so busy trying to survive each day and minute that not one of us knows what it means to truly live.

I let my mind drift like the small current that seeps inward and attempt to shake my desolate thoughts.

My eyes trail across the glistening river as the moon above casts its light through the dark clouds and rain. My eye catches on something and I pause.

Stepping closer, I spot a sliver of darkness that coils and slithers through the river. More and more inky, dark strings appear, their origin seeming to be closer to the wall where the river seeps inward.

Moving around the edges of the river, I make it a couple of steps, noticing the dark taint growing outward, when I hear a terrified scream from somewhere behind me.

Turning around, I don't think; I move, running in the direction of the sound.

The wet tree branches snap against my skin as I rush forward. Another scream pierces my ears, and I move through the void without thought, coming out of it to the edge of a grove of trees and a small open center.

My eyes widen when I see the dark creature stalking toward an injured woman trying to escape it.

Reaching for one of my daggers at my sides, I shoot forward and catch it unaware, driving it into the back of the creature's neck and up into its head. It jolts as if hit by lightning before dropping to the muddy ground with a thump.

I look at the frightened woman now on the ground and reach out to help her up, but her eyes widen, focused on something behind me, the fear completely paralyzing her in place.

I spin around and my stomach drops as I watch a dozen dark creatures move toward us.

"Are you injured?" I ask her while keeping my eye on the incoming threat.

"A fff-flesh wound. N-nothing serious." Her voice trembles in fear, but there's strength beneath each word, convincing me she's in no immediate danger.

"When I tell you to run..." I don't finish my words as the group of creatures moves swiftly to surround us.

Unsheathing my sword from behind me, I wait for them to get a little closer before shooting forward and slicing the nearest creature's arm off as it reaches for me. Before it gets the chance to move, I behead it.

I remind myself of the Sidus woman behind me and pull back my shadows, which are trying to unleash and defend.

The creatures quickly surround me, caging me in. But I hold my ground and slam my elbow into the creature's neck on my right, dodging a claw from my left and grabbing the other dagger before twisting around to slice, stab, and cleave a path through them.

But more and more are appearing in place of those that turn to shadows and smoke. Their strength and movements are less staggered and sloppy than the last time I met with others like them, and there is a spark of light in their eyes, an intelligence that wasn't there before. It only makes my fears and doubts grow.

Dodging the next grasp from one of them, I use the nearest thick tree trunk as leverage to rise up and bounce off. Twisting, I land on top of one of the creature's shoulders. Using my weight, I wrap my legs around it and swiftly spin my body, breaking its neck before tumbling into a crouch beside it.

A cry rings out and I turn to find the Sidus woman scrambling backward. One of the creatures must have veered off and gotten past me.

I stand and turn to move toward her when a fiery burn slices down my back.

Gritting my teeth, I reel around and plow my dagger into the creature's stomach, ducking another clawed attack before turning and heading for the woman.

Ignoring the sharp, slicing pain down my back, I find my other dagger on the ground and pick it up, flinging it forward. My aim is slightly off, hitting the creature's shoulder instead, but it's enough to distract it and turn its attention on me.

My eyes land on a long vine on the ground, and an idea comes to mind. I pick it up and move quickly, wrapping it around the creature's neck, tightening my hold until it slumps and drops to the ground.

I head toward the woman when I hear movement from behind me. Whipping around, I find the last of the creatures moving toward us.

I try to think of another plan to get them away from her without using my shadows, when I tense up, hearing something rush through the trees.

Jarek appears, a sword in hand as if ready for battle, and a rush of relief fills me. His eyes widen when he spots me, and he rushes toward me and the creatures.

"Your sword!" I reach a hand out, and he throws it to me immediately, without question.

"Get her out of here," I shout to him as I twirl the

sword in my hand to test the pain in my back and shoulder, wincing when the burn intensifies. But the movement is smooth, which means there is no serious injury. Stepping forward, I slam the sword into the nearest creature's head and yank it out before ducking and avoiding a claw to the face.

"What about you?" Jarek shouts over to me as I evade another creature.

"I need to draw them farther away from town," I tell him. If any of them make it through the small haven here, there will be more than one death tonight. I thrust the sword into another creature's head before spinning and slicing another.

"Ren—"

"Go!" I evade another claw and surge forward, my blade impaling the next creature in front of me.

With a harsh sigh, Jarek leaves, taking the woman with him. Once she is gone and no one is around, I finally unleash my powers, letting my shadows out to become a weapon of darkness. I evade claw after claw, attack after attack, this time with ease. Using my shadows, I slip into them and appear in front of creature after creature, lunging forward and striking with aim to kill.

They drop one by one before disappearing quickly.

I move to find Jarek and see if the woman is safe when two more creatures arrive as if from nowhere.

Ignoring the sharp blaze of flames now sliding down my back, I let rage fuel my veins. Rage for those that would have died tonight because the Caligo guards have twisted their power to do whatever they want instead of guarding those who are weaker than them.

How many more must die before they listen?

With a renewed sense of energy, I attack the last two creatures with fury, my rage and wrath not only for them but for every Caligo guard who sits idly by and watches on while the Sidus cry out for help. Every innocent person that has died because of their negligence. And every death that will come should they continue to live in that ignorance.

The creatures are destroyed within seconds. Each breath is harsh as I try to leash my rage.

"It seems your friend was right." A deep voice comes from somewhere behind me.

I spin around, ignoring the slash of pain in my back, to find an older man about Ryuu's age, with dark blue eyes and a shaved head, looking at me with interest. A group of men and women move through the trees to surround me, all with weapons in their hands and more strapped across their dark clothing.

Their guarded eyes watch me as if anticipating a fight from me. Something they will get should they attack first. I tighten my grip on the hilt of my sword, ready for round three, when a rustle of branches draws my attention to it, soon revealing a distressed Jarek.

He rushes straight for me, not stopping until he has me enveloped in a tight hug.

The tight hold presses down on my wound, and I gasp as a bolt of pain shoots up my back. Jarek jolts away from me as if burnt and glances down at his hands and the slash of blood across them.

"You're injured," he accuses me as his face pales.

"I'm fine," I tell him and roll my shoulders as I try to eliminate some of the sharp pain now making itself known as the rush of adrenaline leaves me.

"But—"

"How is the woman?" I ask him, hoping to distract him.

But the expression on his face tells me this conversation is far from over.

"She's fine. A little frightened but happy to be alive, thanks to you. What are you doing out here?"

I glance around at the men and women and relax a little when I see that their weapons are no longer in hand but strapped at their sides or back.

I frown as they glance over at Jarek as if waiting on something from him, and I find myself looking back at one of my oldest friends in a new light.

It is not hard to deduce who these men and women are. There is no true leader among them, although they give a small look of admiration to the man who spoke to me first. Their appearance is haggard, with dark, mismatched old clothing, and there is a hard, calculating look in every pair of eyes.

They're rebels. And from the concealed glances

they're attempting to give Jarek, they know him. More than I would like.

"It seems you also have some explaining to do," I tell him with a raised brow, trying to invoke one of my mother's looks.

Jarek winces and the guilt seeps into his face, shadowing the worry he had for me a moment ago.

"I know. I'll tell you everything. I promise," he says with nothing but truth in his eyes.

"Come. Let's get out of here before the guards show up," a gruff voice sounds from behind me.

I turn to find a man with short, tight brown hair and a scar that runs down the left side of his entire cheek. His dark brown eyes stare at me, waiting for a reply. Eyes that have far too much knowing in them.

"This is Nikos. He is... a friend." Jarek dips his head to Nikos, sharing a look with him before he pulls me along with them as they move out.

I keep my eyes on the men and women around me as we move through the forest, most of them skittish, their eyes darting around them every couple of minutes. Jarek takes off his coat and drapes it across my back, covering my wound from the rain, which has lightened to a small haze.

"I'm fine, really," I tell him, more worried about the mess he seems to have gotten himself into.

"You're bleeding," he hisses, with a flash of anger in his eyes.

"It is a small flesh wound and will heal in no time." I

keep an eye on the rebels as we pass through the forest. Although the wound is painful, it is not my biggest concern right now.

He opens his mouth, most likely to lecture me on my foolishness, but stops short, thinking better of it. "They have a healer. He will see to it."

"Jarek—" I start, more interested in knowing what his involvement with the rebels is than dealing with my injured back. But after knowing me for so long, he already knows what I am about to ask and cuts me off with a glance that's full of guilt.

"I *know*, Ren. Let's just get you fixed up and I'll tell you everything."

Pushing down my impatience for now, I stay close to him as we move through the forest silently before making our way toward the end of the mountains on the opposite side of the Sidus town.

No one comes to this side. It's too far out and the terrain is too barren, the sharp, jagged cliffs and stone too harsh. And when the bad weather comes, the jagged rocky mountains are too open to protect against the treacherous rain and storms. So it makes no sense why the rebels are leading us toward it.

I frown at Jarek, the question on the tip of my tongue, but his eyes ask me to try and trust him, and so I do.

Until we reach the end of the mountain and turn into a passageway with two long, jagged cliffs overshadowing it. Both look ready to crash and fall upon us.

I open my mouth to ask the question that has been

burning at the tip of my tongue all throughout this little trek when Jarek pulls me sideways into the dark.

"Jarek..." My eyes slightly adjust, but I still can't make out anything. Silent seconds pass before light blares to life around me, flame after flame as the cave is dragged from the shadows to reveal a room full of small makeshift wooden beds and a long wall full of weapons.

"I don't have to remind you that anything you see or hear while here is not to be mentioned to anyone," Nikos says to the right of me.

The rest of his men pause, awaiting my reply. But I would never purposely do anything that would put another life in danger, nor ever put Jarek's life at risk.

"I can vouch for her," Jarek says, answering before I get the chance to reply.

Nikos looks to me as if waiting on some indication, but he must see something on my face, because he nods his head and leaves us be.

"Come on, let's get you fixed up." Jarek takes me through a series of passageways and narrow halls before coming to a small room with a small, raised bed at the center of it.

"Jarek, my boy. How did you fare tonight?" A man with short graying hair and soft brown eyes glances over at me. His clothes are less worn than the other rebels, his appearance well-kept and tidy. And something about the sincere smile that reaches his eyes sets me at ease.

"We fared well thanks to some help, but it seems she

isn't as invincible as she would like to think." Jarek narrows his eyes at me.

"Ah, so this is the infamous Seren I've heard so much about." A glint of joy sparks in his eyes, lighting up his entire face.

Jarek shakes his head with a small smile. "Ren, this is Matthias, our healer, and now, it seems, our old gossip."

"Hey now, away with that *old* part." He gives Jarek a playful swat before looking to me with a warm smile.

"Come take a seat," he says, patting the bed, "and I'll see what I can do for you."

I shake my head, ready to back out of the room and leave as soon as I can. He may seem trustworthy, but I do not know anyone here. And I most definitely do not trust them with Jarek.

"Honestly, I'll be fine. I can—"

"Nonsense. I have this gift for a reason," he says.

Some Caligo and Sidus have a rare ability to also manipulate the energy of the Sidus and Caligo. I've always been able to heal slightly faster than the norm, but I couldn't heal others, even with my dual nature. A Sidus with the ability to heal can also heal a Caligo, and a Caligo can do the same to the Sidus. I saw it with my own eyes when a Caligo guard managed to injure himself, and a Sidus healer came upon the incident. He healed him within minutes, but the guard only looked at him in disgust. It seems he would have preferred death over a Sidus' help.

Matthias steps closer to me, his manner telling me he isn't backing down on this anytime soon.

Keeping my sigh to myself, I move to the bed, and Jarek stands behind me and helps me take off his coat. He hisses through his teeth as he does.

"Why didn't you tell me it was this bad?" he snaps. But his voice is also laced with worry. It quickly halts any rising anger of my own.

I roll my shoulders, feeling the blaze of pain, but it has eased a little, my own accelerated ability to heal already kicking in.

It would have mostly healed over the next few days if I were able to cover it like every other injury I have had. But now that they've seen it, I will have to play along.

Matthias walks around the bed to take a look at my back while Jarek steps in front of me, his eyes filled with fear.

"It's not that bad," I tell him.

His eyes flash. "Your back looks like an animal has chewed on it. I can nearly see bone," he snarls, a panicked expression on his face. "I should *never* have left you. What kind of friend—"

I reach out to grasp his hand, stopping his spiraling guilt. "*I* told you to get that woman out of there. For which I'm grateful. The only reason I got this was because I was distracted. It was my own foolish fault."

"I should not have left you, and that is all there is to it," he fumes as he gazes off to the side with a conflicted look. "What would have happened if I didn't make it back in time," he mumbles more to himself than me, but I still answer him.

"Apparently, your rebels would have shown up to save me." I give him a pointed look. One he mirrors with a nod.

"We still need to discuss why you were out there in the dark, *alone*." He narrows his eyes on me.

"Only *after* you explain all of this." I glance around before my gaze lands back on his face... which is quickly losing its ire and shifting to guilt and concern.

A warmth brushes down my back, distracting me from our little disagreement. It quickly seeps into my sore muscles and tired bones, relieving each ache and pain. Within a couple of minutes, my back feels completely healed, no pain or ache left behind. I never experienced a healer's ability before, but it is not something I am ever going to forget. My entire body feels rested, as if I slept an entire night, and my muscles are relaxed and revived.

Matthias steps around me with an amused smile, and I wince. I had forgotten he was still here with us. I give him a sheepish look that only makes his amusement grow.

"Thank you," I tell him.

He dips his head to me. "Any friend of Jarek's is a friend of mine," he says.

I hop off the bed and move toward the door with Jarek.

"Don't be a stranger, Seren," Matthias says, wearing another warm smile.

"I won't," I tell him, meaning it. The type of involvement Jarek has with the rebels is more solidified than I had originally thought. I doubt it is something he would easily leave now. But the more I see and think about it, the less I would want him to.

I always thought the rebels to be nothing but misfits and troublemakers. But after tonight and seeing their willingness to help anyone in need, maybe it is time I stop judging people based on my narrow-minded experiences with them.

Jarek thanks Matthias and says his goodbyes before following me out into one of the empty hallways.

"How long?" I ask him as soon as we are alone.

Jarek swallows hard. "Three months."

I nod to myself, and he jumps to plead his case, as if he's afraid, thinking this is something that would break our friendship. But he is a silly fool if he thinks I would ever let anything like this come between us.

"I'm sorry. I should've told you. I just wanted to help, and they thought I would be of use. You're a league above me. You have the captain and Aloisia. I just wanted to find a place where I could fit in." His face is drenched in desperation, his voice full of dejection, making my heart clench.

"Jarek—"

A loud commotion quickly cuts off our conversation, drawing our attention to it. Sharing a look, we move through the stone halls to the main room we entered to find a group of men and women in a heated discussion spanned out across it.

"They are blaming those deaths on us," shouts a man who appears to be close to my age, his tawny eyes burning with anger. "My friend died, and they named us their killers!"

"We all know the truth," Nikos says, adopting a reassuring tone and a softer demeanor. "Every Sidus in this town knows who the *real* killers are, Andres." He gives Andres a look full of sympathy before turning to the others and continuing.

"We need to organize more teams to spread out throughout the day. I do not want anyone by themselves. The dark creatures are getting stronger and smarter. And we need to stay vigilant."

The others around him nod, waiting on his every word as he continues to set his rules. And from the admiration on their faces, it seems the rebels have a leader after all. One that sounds capable and fair enough to make deliberate and reasonable actions.

Once he's finished his speech, I set about asking some of my own questions, hoping they have some information that might help us.

"How long have they been getting through by the river?" I ask him directly.

The entire room turns to me with startled looks on their faces as if they had forgotten I was here.

"A fortnight," Nikos answers, not bothered by my

interruption. "We've kept them at bay, but they're getting stronger," he reveals, only confirming what I have learned.

"But you and your men and women have been killing them?" I ask while glancing around at their wearied faces. "While making sure they don't pass into the town?"

Their eyes tell a tale of some of the horrors they have seen and have had to deal with. My chest tightens when I realize that they have been protecting us a lot longer than I assumed. Which means the dark creature problem is a lot worse than even I expected.

"Who else will protect the Sidus if not us? The captain and your mother and friends are a small group and cannot fight them all. There are too many of them getting past the shield now. *We* are not even enough anymore. At this point, we need an army."

I glance around at the group as they nod in agreement, each one of them weary and bone-tired, but with a spark of determination to help their people. Something I did not realize would happen. At least not anytime soon.

If only that spark grew among the people around them. Maybe we might stand a chance after all. A seed of that dream starts to form as I look to Nikos.

"Then make one," I tell him, and he gives me a questioning look.

"Train the Sidus in secret if you must. They should know how to defend themselves, if anything. It is the best way you can help any of us."

Someone who can wield a sword has far better chances of defending themselves than one who waits on another to protect them.

"Many will not fight," Nikos says with a somber look as he shakes his head. But I see a spark of an idea in his eyes too. I latch on to it, hoping I can make it grow.

"But some will," I tell him. "Some will want to protect their families and friends. And *some* is better than none. Maybe that, too, will grow over time." And maybe one day we will have our own army who can protect the Sidus or anyone who is weaker or in need.

"You should join us," someone shouts out from behind me, but before I get the chance to answer, another replies with a chuckle.

"The captain would never allow it, and I, for one, do not want to end up on Aloisia's bad side."

I don't turn around to see who answered, but I smile to myself at his reply. It would seem my mother's reputation is still firmly intact.

"I will continue to protect the Sidus like you all," I tell them before looking to Nikos. "It looks like we are all on the same side after all."

Nikos dips his head to me in respect as I turn to leave with Jarek by my side. Once we clear the mountain, he reaches out to stop me.

"I should have told you. I know." His face is dejected and full of despair, revealing how much he hates that he hid this from me. And although I also dislike him keeping this secret, I know I have no right to. I have been keeping more weighty and dangerous secrets from him and for much longer too. Something that makes me feel exactly how he looks.

"Yes, you should have," I tell him, and he glances at me with a wince. "But... you are not the only one that has been keeping secrets."

"Ren?" Jarek frowns, giving me a questioning look. But one filled with worry.

"You have no idea how much I want to tell you everything. But I..." I swallow hard, hoping he won't hate me. Hoping I will not lose my truest friend.

Jarek gives me a soft smile and pulls me into him, wrapping his arms around me. "You're my friend, Ren, my *best* friend and family. We may not always tell each other everything at once. But I hope you know that I will *always* be here for you, if or when you choose to tell me whatever you need. And even if you don't, know that I will still always be here for you. No matter what."

The complete understanding and easy acceptance unravel the tight knot in my chest.

I pull back from his soothing warmth and glance over at the mountain where I now know the rebels reside. "I'm sorry if I ever made you feel like you couldn't tell me. The rebels are not what I expected, and I feel foolish for judging them so harshly. Forgive me?" I ask.

A wide smile full of relief spreads across his face as he pulls me back in for another hug.

"There is *nothing* to forgive."

"Thank you," I tell him, grateful to have such a friend like him.

"Always," he whispers, his arms tightening around me before he lets go and takes a step back, a look of mischief lighting his eyes.

"So... do I get a hint to any of these secrets?" he asks.

I look at him, trying to find any resentment or anger but finding only warmth and happiness in his eyes, bringing me nothing but relief.

A small smile dances on my lips. "Come to the town center tomorrow and you might find out one of them."

CHAPTER 7

"*Seren Solais.*"

Ryuu snaps to attention, his entire body turning to stone as my name is called out for the chosen participants in this year's guard's competition. Moving toward the center of the market square, where the Caligo guards set up their announcement, I attempt to act indifferent, knowing I will have to deal with him soon enough.

Ryuu isn't the only one shocked at a Sidus being chosen. The Caligo people that made their way down to the Sidus town to hear if their name has been picked also look at me with disbelief.

This is all just a game to the Caligo guards. Another way to degrade the Sidus and prove to every other Caligo how weak and incapable we are when we are not chosen. They could choose to have this up in the Caligo city, where nearly every last competitor has been chosen from these last few years. But instead, they go out of their way to come down here and do it.

And although none of this was my purpose when I slipped past the guards last night to swap my name with one of the already chosen participants, I secretly revel in the fact that they will not have any smug looks for the Sidus once they finish calling out the participants.

The Sidus murmur amongst themselves, all wearing shocked but happy expressions at finding one of their own is in the competition. The last one to be accepted was Ryuu, and it was over a decade ago.

No other Sidus has been able to be chosen for the guard's competition since then.

After Ryuu managed to beat every Caligo and win it, the guards made sure no other Sidus would ever want to attempt it again and made it known to those who were brave enough that they would be immediately overlooked and denied.

I take my parchment and stand to the left of Ryuu as the next few names of the competitors are called out. Time blurs as I focus on the guards to my right, their shocked stares now outright hostile glares.

I knew choosing this path would not be easy. I will have to tread carefully moving forward, watch my back and, from the looks of it, my sides and front too.

The announcement passes quickly, and I step off the stage and move toward Jarek and the wide smile he wears like a beacon of relief.

"So, your plan is to become rich and share your

winnings with your best friend?" he says the minute I step up beside him.

"Or maybe it is so I can destroy them from within." With a wicked smirk, I narrow my eyes on the nearest Caligo guard.

"Don't joke," Jarek says, his smile quickly dropping.

I chuckle, feeling light for once. "I have no interest in joining the guards, nor usurping them from their thrones. But I may have a *little* plan to try to help us with our mess."

Jarek straightens up as he fully turns to look at me, his face now shadowed with fear. "Now you have me worried."

"Don't be," I tell him.

"Seren—"

"You're using my full name? This must be serious." I turn to look back at him as he searches my face for something.

"I take it back. I don't want to be rich. I want you safe by my side instead." He takes my arm and quickly looks around. "Let's find one of the guards and tell them it was a mistake. A joke that someone played on you."

I pull my arm from his, forcing him to stop and look at me. "What has changed your mind? You were practically begging me to join the competition the other day."

Jarek fists his wavy brown hair. "In jest, *mostly*, because I knew you would never truly do it." He releases his now disheveled hair to look at me. "But I can see it in your eyes. You're serious about this. And whatever you are going to do will more than likely get you killed."

"You know I can take care of myself." I reach out and take his hand, hoping to ease some of his growing apprehension.

His fingers tighten around mine. "I *also* know that you are not invincible, and mistakes happen. Look at yesterday." He gives me a pointed look.

One that I glare back at him.

"Yesterday was my own fault. A foolish mistake that won't happen again."

He shakes his head at me, the worry clinging to every shadow on his face.

"Ren—"

"I *will* be careful. Trust me on this, please. You have my word," I promise.

Jarek sighs but soon relents. He knows I wouldn't do anything too impulsively. My plans are usually well thought out and conscientious.

"Seren." Ryuu's harsh voice rings out around us, making me stiffen and wince.

Jarek smiles at my discomfort. "Ah, maybe the captain can talk some sense into you."

"You are supposed to be *my* friend," I hiss, giving him a glare my mother would be proud of.

Jarek's eyes soften. "*Always*, Seren." His tone leaves no question about how much he means it. But then a glint of devilment enters his eyes as he opens his mouth to speak. "Even when the captain and Aloisia decide to lock you up and I have to visit you in your cell just to pass you some edible food."

"That's a tad bit dramatic, don't you think?" I frown at him.

Jarek leans forward, tilting his head at Ryuu. "Is it? Is it really?"

I chance a glance at Ryuu's face and instantly regret it. "Maybe not," I whisper just as Ryuu steps in front of me.

"Home. *Now*." Ryuu swiftly turns and heads in the direction.

"Good luck, Ren." Jarek starts walking backward, a small smile tilting his lips. "It looks like you're going to need it," he sings, chuckling under his breath as he disappears into the crowd.

Turning, I follow Ryuu home, leaving a few feet between us while I mentally prepare myself for the incoming battle with my mother.

Coming around the corner, I hesitate a moment, seeing half a dozen guards near the entrance of our small home. It sets my nerves on edge.

A couple notice me and glare or snarl as I pass them. It's nothing unusual, but something doesn't feel right. The guards don't pay social visits to the Sidus, even with the captain living here.

Stepping into the small front room of our home, I find Ryuu facing another man, whose back is to me, but his build and the insignia on his black coat inform me of a high-ranking position. Neither are talking but, rather, having some sort of tense stare down. The air in the room feels thick with trepidation.

Moving closer, I notice the tension radiating from Ryuu. His jaw is clenched, his arms crossed as I walk over to him. His eyes briefly flicker to mine before returning to the man in front of him.

"Seren, this is Lieutenant Amaro." Ryuu's face is unreadable as he introduces me to his commanding officer.

The man in question turns to me with no smile or warmth in his eyes. The lieutenant is not what I had envisioned. From Ryuu's brief description in passing conversation, I imagined a gruff older-looking man, stricter than the captain himself. And although his long hair is washed of any color, nearing complete gray, his face is youthful, only a few years older than mine.

It shouldn't surprise me. Most Caligo guards are corrupt and immoral. Why wouldn't they also have favors among themselves and skip the ranks?

The lieutenant is slightly shorter than Ryuu, but he holds his head high as if to look down upon everyone around him, and his expression shows nothing but arrogance.

I thought they might be somewhat amicable, having to work with each other, but seeing the two of them together suggests otherwise.

Amaro tilts his head as his cold glance examines me closely. "Seren. I have heard a great many things about you."

Keeping my facial expression neutral, I cast Ryuu a quick glance. I did not realize I would ever be a topic for discussion unless it was regarding some sort of dispute. Nothing about this conversation is easing my turbulent nerves.

Ryuu continues to ignore me, his complete focus on Amaro. I, too, face the lieutenant, giving him a tight smile, and wonder what it is he requires of me.

The lieutenant's cold face turns apologetic as he looks at Ryuu. "As you are aware, this year the guard's competition will take place in the palace grounds. Many of the guards have heard your... *worries* about strange creatures, and I thought it best to come collect your daughter personally." He gives Ryuu a vicious smile that makes my stomach drop to the floor.

The lieutenant knew. He knew Ryuu went to his men about the dark creatures, and it seems I am going to be a part of whatever payback he will receive for it.

I mask my face with one of indifference as Ryuu quickly realizes this too.

Ryuu clenches his fists at his side. "What is this about, Amaro?"

The lieutenant cuts Ryuu a sharp look. "It is *Lieutenant* Amaro to you, *Captain.* Do not forget that."

The look Ryuu gives him is terrifying. "Forgive me, *Lieutenant*. Explain... please." He grits his reply, his last word sounding like twisted thorns getting caught on each syllable and sounding anything but pleading.

Amaro, oblivious to Ryuu's silent rage, replies, "We

are simply protecting our own. Seren is... *special* to us. To have been chosen to enter the competition is a feat not many Sidus achieve. But not to worry, I will personally deliver her to the palace and make sure she is looked after with great care."

The glint in his eyes expands, and I can tell the exact kind of *care* he'll be administering the minute I enter the palace grounds.

Ryuu's rage explodes out of him at once when he realizes it too. "Seren entering the competition was a mistake. She will immediately rescind her entry."

Amaro whips his head toward him, his own rage burning like flames in his eyes. "That is not an option, *Captain*. Once entered and chosen, *all* entries must compete. And need I remind you which of us holds the power here?" I clench my fists tight as Amaro takes a step closer to him. Ryuu's whole body vibrates, his powers barely restrained. His eyes swirl with his Sidus power, waiting to be unleashed.

Amaro narrows his eyes, a cruel smirk to his lips. "Try it. I assure you it won't end well." He briefly glances over at me. "For either of you."

Ryuu snarls at Amaro before glancing away. Taking deep breaths, he tries to calm his tense body and pull back his powers from the brink.

Amaro turns back to me, his cold smirk still firmly in place. I pull my own powers back as they try to seep out to the surface to protect and attack the threat in front of me.

"Now, where were we? Ah yes, Seren, you will be coming with us immediately. The sooner we have you in the safety of the palace grounds, the better."

Amaro looks to Ryuu, a flicker in his eyes that quickly turns threatening before it is masked behind one of mock remorse. "I am sure you would not want any repercussions to befall your family should you not follow our rules. Would you, Seren?"

Although his tone is sincere, the final threat is unmistakable. The cruelty in his eyes reveals everything I need to know about what kind of man he is. He will get his way, one way or another. Now, it is down to me whether it happens quietly or not.

The look Ryuu gives me tells me not to trust him, nor even dare think to go with him, but if there were even a little truth to his words, attempting to prolong this would mean putting him and those I care about in harm's way.

It is a risk I would never be willing to take.

Seeing the decision on my face, Ryuu gives me a disappointed look.

"Seren—" Ryuu's tone holds nothing but fury.

Abruptly, the front door opens, revealing my mother. Upon seeing our guests, her calm face morphs into a controlled fury only years of training could display.

"Lieutenant Amaro." She speaks but two words. Two simple words, and I can already tell how much she despises this man. "What is it you need?" Her words are sharp and harsh even to my own ears.

"As sharp as a blade and straight to the point,

Aloisia." Amaro dips his head to her in greeting, one my mother does not return. She merely raises a brow, waiting for a response.

Amaro smirks. "On to more urgent matters, I see. You'll be delighted to know that Seren has been chosen to compete in the guard's competition and will be coming to stay with us in the palace. As a special guest, of course, until it is finished."

My mother's body turns stiff, her expression blank. "May I have a moment with my daughter? *Alone*," she says, her voice just as devoid of emotion.

"Of course." Amaro gives me a look of warning. "I'll be waiting outside. Do not be long." Amaro gives Ryuu a sharp look before heading outside, his guards following him closely behind.

Once they are gone, my mother rushes over to me, her masked fury no longer contained, bleeding out around her. "You are *not* going with that man!"

I swallow back the bile and pull on years of training to push away any emotions I feel right now. It would do me no good to regret what I cannot change. "I have to," I tell her.

"No, you don't." My mother looks to Ryuu for an answer. "We will come up with a plan."

Together, they start thinking of people they can contact to get me somewhere hidden and safe. But I know what I must do. No plan they will come up with will get me out of this. It would only make things worse. Amaro already holds a considerable amount of hostility toward Ryuu. It will not take much for him to turn on him and then my mother.

My stomach churns at the thought of what Amaro has planned for me, but I need to follow through with this. There is no other way.

"No." My voice cuts through their discussion, silencing them.

They both turn to look at me.

"It's too late. I have to go with him." I plead with my eyes, begging them to trust me with this, to understand.

"I will not allow you to leave with that... man! I'd trust a serpent quicker than I'd trust him."

I'd have to agree with my mother; there was something Amaro was hiding, something I know I will discover soon. But it might be better to be inside the nest of snakes than waiting on the edges for them to strike.

"Neither do I, but you know I need to go with him."

"I know no such thing," she says, her voice like a whip. Her stubborn nature is legendary. Her anger, a violent storm ready to be unleashed. But I was raised among her whirlwind of fury. Never fearing the raging turmoil, only feeling the strength beneath it. I will not yield on this. I can't, not with their lives at stake.

"Amaro has made it very clear how he expects this to go should we not agree to his terms," I tell her.

"He's going to make you pay, Seren. For *my* mistakes," Ryuu hisses, the fear in his eyes seeping onto his face.

"What mistakes?" I ask him. "All you did was try to make them listen."

Maybe revealing the dark creature to the lower guards *was* a mistake, but one that also ended up revealing their part in whatever they are hiding. It is time to find out if the royals are also a part of this.

"And because of it, you will pay for it."

I look to both of them. "You've both taught me how to fight. Taught me well. You know I can take care of myself. Besides, you said it yourself, the dark creatures are growing in numbers and strength. Apart from trying to keep them at bay, there is nothing more anyone else can do. I can enter the competition and try to meet with the royals to ask them to see reason."

"They will not listen to a child," Ryuu hisses out in anger, but I know it is born more from fear.

"Then I will *make* them listen," I tell him with complete certainty. I am not leaving that palace without the royals seeing the truth. No matter what I must do to show them.

I look at my mother. "You both believe that the royals are not aware of this? Then let's find out for sure. I will fight in the guard's competition and win if I have to. This will end one way or another. And after the competition, we will find out the truth once and for all."

A sheen of unshed tears glazes her eyes, causing a lump to form in my throat.

"You and Ryuu are all I have. I cannot lose you, Seren."

I step into her embrace, wrapping my arms around her, hoping she can feel some of the warmth and comfort she has always given me. "Trust me. Trust that I can do this. If not me, then in the years of training and support you've both given me."

I pull away and watch a lone tear fall from the corner of her eye. She wipes it away, furious that it escaped.

"We'll get through this, all of us," I tell them both with confidence behind my words, though feeling anything but. A storm of nerves swells inside me, ready to burst free at any moment.

"I can see this is something you will not relent on," Ryuu says with a sliver of hope in his tone, hope that I will hesitate.

But I nod my head, confirming my choice, and he frowns as that hope disappears.

Ryuu glances over at the door. "Amaro will test you. He will push you to your limits. This is not something I ever wanted you to experience. Fighting to defend yourself is all I ever hoped for."

He looks at me once more but finally sees it. Sees that I will follow through on this, whatever may come of it.

Ryuu sighs, shaking his head, and steps forward, his body tense and alert. "Are you sure about this? You are not used to being around so many Caligo guards. The palace houses most of them, and you will come across many... unsavory characters."

"I will be fine," I tell him, my voice confident and

assured. I look to my mother. "Watch over everyone while I'm gone. I *will* see you soon. I promise."

"You better," she warns, moving a step back before taking a hold of Ryuu's arm.

Ryuu reaches out his free hand and places it on my shoulder. "I will make sure to visit you as soon as I can. Stay alert and do not do anything too reckless."

"I will do what I must," I tell him, but I cannot promise him I will not do anything foolish. Although the competition provides an opportunity to reach the royals, I have no idea what I am willingly walking into. If I need to use force to protect myself or try something Ryuu considers reckless, I will.

He nods his head once more before letting go of my shoulder with a squeeze.

"I love you both."

Ryuu's eyes widen slightly. He swallows hard, looking away. My mother tightens her grip on his hand as she looks to me.

"As do we, Seren. Always. Come home to us soon, or I will go to the palace and get you myself."

My mother's words are warm and welcomed. I know she would do anything for me, but it will not be necessary. I will get myself out of this. One way or another.

Turning, I rush to my room and grab a few pieces of clothing and keepsakes before joining Amaro and his guards outside. Without question, the six guards form a circle around us both as they call on their shadows. Amaro crosses his arms and closes his eyes, waiting for the guards to perform their task of transport with no effort on his part.

I hide my own disbelief at his behavior. He is the perfect model for what is wrong with the Caligo guards. Just like the guards see themselves above the Sidus, he sees himself above even his own men, choosing not to help them when he can. The guards look to him for guidance, but showing them nothing but selfishness teaches them just that.

I feel their power, familiar yet different, as they work hard to generate the energy needed to transport us all.

Taking one last glance at my mother and Ryuu, I scan their somber faces and give them a small smile, hoping it will ease some of their dread.

The shadows slowly envelop us, quickly obscuring them as we are pulled into the darkness.

CHAPTER 8

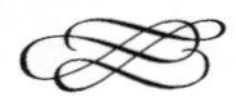

It takes the guards longer to pull themselves in and out of the void. When we come through on the other side, they're out of breath and their foreheads are beaded with sweat. Amaro spares them not so much as a glance nor thanks before stepping forward toward two monstrous dark gates. The size alone could fit two great beings the size of giants.

Tendrils of shadows swirl and coil around it like separate entities ready to strike and attack us.

I have never seen the gates this close, only heard of them in passing. They stand at the bottom of the mountains, guarding the entrance to the palace and adding an extra measure of security that would be useful for the Sidus when the dark creatures bypass the shield.

But as the royals have no care for the Sidus, only the Caligo will benefit from its neighboring shelter.

Although it is still not bright out, the light, even

amongst the murky gates, is a contrast I didn't realize would be so vivid when this close up. I look around, seeing shades and colors unlike anything I imagined. So bold and beautiful and rich.

The guards wait as more light filters through the large gates, groaning and grinding as they slowly creep open.

I had heard rumors that the Caligo could no longer shadow in or out of the void once they neared the palace grounds. An effort made to deter any intruders that would want to harm the royals.

A smart move, considering the reputation the royals have gained over the last decade with the Sidus.

The gates, now open wide, reveal a whole other world. Light that is so brilliant and clear impales the ascending steps like spears that sparkle and shimmer around me. The shrubbery housed at the sides of the steps have been transformed to emeralds and jewels, their alure bewitching me and catching me off guard.

"Move it," a guard barks out, breaking me from my stunned awe.

Walking up the steep steps, I notice an emerging gold trim beginning to form at each side, guiding our path. After a few minutes, we reach its top. I pause, seeing the long bridge that sits in front of a magnificent structure. Its shimmering golds and whites, which I have only ever seen from a distance, don't compare to its true beauty up close.

The pale bridge is worn with slight cracks and ridges

but easily holds its large structure and base. It spans wide enough to fit an army should it need to. Giant statues of old guards stand tall, as though in slumber, ready to come alive and protect. They spread out on each side, watching the people who dare try to pass its bridge without invitation.

Multiple Caligo guards are stationed beside and in front of the statues, acting as their watch and backup, and I feel their distrustful eyes as I pass them.

Ignoring them, I look out past the statues to see the hidden world below. A town covered by a night so dark it disappears among the shadows.

My home and a forgotten world for those who look down on it.

I wonder if this is all the Caligo ever see when they look down at us. A lost part of its kingdom that is too lost in the shadows to think about, as they live among the light.

Do they think about us at all and the hardships we face, or do they go about their lives living in sweet oblivion?

I turn away from the side and toward our impending arrival. At the end of the bridge stands wide arches that reach toward each other, forming a grand entrance. Stained glass with intricate designs spans out among the tall towers and bold walls around it. Passing through the entrance, I look upon a ceiling made from gold. Delicate carvings of ancient gods facing battles cover every inch of it.

Archways open up to a long corridor, and the sound of gushing water hits my ears as we pass through large open hallways that look out among the world of light.

The palace is in another world of its own. My own imagination holds only a fraction of its magnificence.

From the small view around me, I spot lush gardens with small fountains of gold and white. A courtyard sits in the middle of the palace grounds, housing every flower imaginable, with colors so bright and vivid they seem almost alive.

The structures around the palace are pieces of art. Vines of gold metal swirl and curve into designs so intricate only someone who has been blessed by the gods could create such a thing.

We pass structure after structure, each one just as beautiful as the first. Pale doors, rooms, and long hallways all pass by in a blur as we hurry along.

Abruptly, we come to a halt. A guard with wavy dark hair and piercing blue eyes walks up to greet us. His guard clothing is similar to Amaro's, with the same insignia revealing a high rank. Finding my gaze, his distant look turns to disgust.

"Were you able to procure the item?" Amaro asks the new guard.

The new guard nods his reply before walking toward me.

I smirk at the sneer on his face, and he continues to stare, waiting for a threat that would not reveal itself until ready.

"They smell like the excrement they live in. Vile creatures," he says.

I bite my tongue, holding back the foul reply on the tip of it while keeping my smirk in place.

Amaro chuckles softly. "I would have to agree with you, Levon. Vile creatures, they are indeed. Why we cannot just wipe them out and be done with it, I will never know."

Levon grunts an agreement before yanking my hands forward and placing thin gold bands that look like expensive bracelets on each one.

"What are these?" I try pulling at them, but they don't budge. It is as though they have molded to my skin. From the smug expression on Amaro's face, I know they are not normal bracelets.

"Just wait," Amaro says as his and Levon's faces reveal nothing but cruel contempt.

Their cruel natures are no longer concealed behind the mask they normally wear, and it sends an icy shiver down my back. I should have known they would have something underhanded arranged for my arrival. My heartbeat kicks up a notch, waiting for the inevitable.

I frown, feeling a pull deep inside me. Glancing down at the bands, I see a glint of strange symbols slither around it, disappearing and reappearing at random.

The pull grows, drawing upon any energy I have with force. I drop to my knees, the hard marble ground aiding my fall, just as the warmth abandons my very veins and leaves behind it a cool, empty vessel.

Trying to catch my breath, I glance down at the gold bands and the retreating glow of symbols.

What just happened? What are these things, and how are they able to make me feel this cold?

There is now a dark hole inside me. Something vacant in the place where the warmth once was.

A cruel chuckle pulls me from my thoughts.

"A nice little side effect these ingenious objects have." Amaro looks down at me with a smug expression.

"What... are... they?" My words puff out in labored breaths as I try to figure out why I feel so empty and drained.

Amaro's smug expression only grows. "An invaluable accessory. They mute those worthless Sidus abilities. They will, of course, stay on until I decide to remove them."

I grit my teeth, keeping my jaw shut to stop anything foul from leaving my lips. I will not let them get the better of me.

Two guards seize my arms, roughly yanking me up to my feet as Amaro steps in front of me.

"We need to take *special* care of the captain's daughter." Amaro gives me a cruel smile that is mirrored among the guards. "Tell us how you were able to enter the competition," he says, a glint of intrigue in his eyes.

Ignoring the sliver of fear that coils around me, I look at him with indifference. "I thought it was open for anyone to join?"

Amaro narrows his eyes on me. "Yes, but no *Sidus* should be able to."

My back straightens at what he is implying. And even though I knew it to be true, listening to him admit it is something else entirely.

"Are you admitting that it is fixed?"

His eyes flash with anger as he realizes his little slip. "Tell me who helped you," he grits through clenched teeth.

Quiet rage unfurls inside me. "No one helped me."

Amaro's eyes turn cold and calculating as he nods before composing himself and taking a step back. "A lie. Well then, I guess we will have to get a little *creative* to find out, won't we?" He shares a sinister smile with Levon and the guards before giving them a nod.

"Take our *guest* to her new accommodations. We cannot have her wandering about the palace." He casts me one last cold smirk before leaving with the new guard, Levon.

The guards around me shove me forward, but I catch myself before hitting the ground. Some of them chuckle, finding my forced clumsiness amusing. I whirl around, looking each in the eye, and memorize each sneering face.

Amber eyes with an arrogant smile; jaw-length muddy brown hair. Another with a shaved head and a square face. Brawny frame with a crooked nose as if it has been broken one too many times and not set right, and sandy-blond curls for the pretty boy in the back. He would be attractive if not for the malice seeping out of his glacial blue eyes.

A hand grabs me from the side, and thick fingers dig into my shoulder, pushing me back around before shoving my head down to the floor.

"Eyes downward, Sidus scum."

I glare at the white stone marble floor as we make our way down the curving hall. I commit to memory every bend and slight turn, not only to calm the rage bubbling inside me but to remember and retrieve when the time comes.

Descending a long stairway, I watch as the lights flicker and dim and shadows pave the way. Something inside me eases at the familiar shades of darkness.

Coming through a dark passageway, we walk along the cold corridor until I am abruptly halted by a heavy hand.

"This way." A guard pushes me down past empty cells that are enclosed with thick bars, to the very last one in the back of the room.

Another guard comes up beside me and opens the cell, while a third walks up behind me. I feel his torso as it presses up against my back. I hold my breath as stale hot air slithers across my neck, and the rage inside me reaches a peak.

"If there is anything left of you when the Breaker is finished, we will tear you apart, piece by piece, until the birds have only your bones to pick at."

I wait until he has finished his little speech before

slamming my head back into his face, hearing the crack I intended. I glance to my right and watch as the amber-eyed guard stumbles sideways and out of my way.

The other two guards grab me from each side, ripping my bag from my back and shoving me into the cold, dark cell before slamming its door swiftly behind me. I turn around, giving each of them a distant look, but on the inside, I feel anything but.

The amber-eyed guard I headbutted gives me a feral smile as he wipes the blood from his broken nose. There is a deranged look in his eyes. One that makes me wish I could break a few other bones to go along with it.

"Good to know you like it rough." He dips his head at me and shares a look with the guards before they leave.

Finally alone, I take in my new surroundings. The floor is full of dirt, the smell worse than the stables covered in manure, and the air is frigid with an icy chill. It is disgusting, but nothing I can't make do with.

I look down at my hand and the tendrils of darkness that swirl around it, a smirk tilting my lips.

Amaro might have muted my Sidus powers, but I still have my shadows.

Finding a suitable spot to sleep near the barred windows, I glance out at my new home for the next while, my smile growing as the shadows dance along my skin.

If they thought I would be a meek, frightened captive, willing to obey their threats and torture, they will quickly learn just how hard it is to bend and break me.

Because I bow to no one.

CHAPTER 9

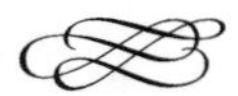

A shard of morning light breaks through the small rusty-barred window at the end of my cell. I stand up, stretching my stiff body from the awkward position I slept in while trying to stay warm last night.

With the absence of my Sidus power, the cold has turned bitter. A hollow space has taken up inside me, feeling unnatural, like a missing limb.

I glance down at the gold bands, fisting each hand.

Many Sidus view their power as a form of light that encases them like a cloak of protection, one that can also light up their way in the dark. While that is true for most Sidus, mine has always felt like white flames, ready to erupt out of me at any moment.

Reaching inward, I search for an ember of the wildfire that was once there but find only frozen, muted flames, the stillness and silence deafening.

I try to push past the strange suspended barrier holding my abilities hostage, and drag them up. But it's like pulling against solid rock.

I pull harder, my stubborn nature not giving in yet, when pain, sharp and electric, shoots across my body, forcing me to the ground. My breath comes out in sharp small pants as the jolt of pain slowly ebbs and eases.

Looking toward the small window causes me to wince, the slight shard of light now feeling like a hot spike against my sensitive eyes.

Glancing down at the bands, I watch a slither of glowing symbols move before disappearing once again.

Foolish.

I should have known there would be some sort of defense to inhibit someone from using their abilities. I will not be attempting anything so rash again, not until I figure out how to remove them without the guards finding out.

After all, I have to keep up appearances for what I have planned.

A few minutes pass with no sign of the guards. I have not eaten anything since yesterday morning, and my sluggish body is starting to feel the effect from lack of nutrition. But I know they need me alive, at least until I can compete in the first trial. They will come soon; of that, I am sure.

It will take me a couple of days to get used to their routines and watchful eyes before I figure a way around without them noticing my absence. I need to be able to roam the palace and find what I'm searching for, and soon. Every day I spend away from the Sidus is another day the dark creatures have a chance to attack and take another innocent life.

Everything has its weak point; I just need to figure out what and where they are and then use it to my advantage.

A clang echoes down the chamber, forcing me to my feet. Taking one last moment to myself before the guards come, I center my mind, feeling a wave of calmness settle over me, and the last edges of pain float away.

Heavy boots meander down the hall, getting louder each step. I listen intently, making out two guards.

They come into view, one holding a small tray of food, or at least that's what it is supposed to be. The slop is gray in color, and the smell is vile, but I cannot be picky in my precarious predicament, still needing nutrition, whatever form that may arrive in.

They are not the same guards from last night, both still tall enough to tower over me, though one is slightly shorter than the other. The one gripping the tray holds nothing but suspicion and disgust in his eyes, something I've come to expect from all the Caligo guards, so I am surprised to see a look of confusion and intrigue in the one behind him. The suspicious one has a small scar on his neck. The wound is still red, identifying it as a recent injury. His thin lips are pulled back in a sneer, and he's holding the tray so tightly he is possibly imagining flinging it over me.

His dull brown eyes and hair remind me of the murky sludge in the fields. Whereas his features are sharp and harsh, the other guard's are gentle, though no less hardened. His deep blue eyes betray a wealth of emotion, which I do not desire to discover.

The guard with the scar bends down and snarls at me, his sharp eyes never leaving mine as he slides the metal tray across the filthy floor. It stops a few feet in front of me, and the guard who deposited such a feast raises an eyebrow, waiting for some sort of reaction. One he won't receive, not yet at least.

Foul food does not bother me. I have lived on worse before, sometimes barely scraping by on stale bread and water alone.

I scent it for any poisons, not smelling any, and soon wolf down the slop, using the hard bread and water to wash down the lumpy texture.

The guard sneers at me, annoyed I have not given him an excuse for a beating.

"Be quick about it."

While drinking the last of my water, I keep an eye on both guards, mindful of their nature, especially the one who looks on intently. His curious glances carry nothing but trouble.

Once I have finished my meal, the scarred guard steps forward, ready to release me from my cell. I watch as he reaches behind his back to retrieve keys.

Just as he places the key inside the lock, he hesitates.

"Do not try anything stupid, or you will find yourself at the end of my blade."

I am not bothered by his threat but more interested in the fact that they have me trapped inside an average cell. One that opens and closes with a simple key, not sealed by any form of power. I had heard of the Caligo cells that could lock even the strongest of Caligo inside, their powers only useful as a parlor trick to pass the time.

With watchful eyes around my arrival last night, I didn't get the chance for a proper inspection to check the limitations of the cell I was in.

I keep my smirk to myself as he drags me out, while the other guard walks a step behind me. *Clever man.*

The scarred guard shoves me as he moves in front of me, effectively blocking me in with the other guard. We walk along the same corridors they brought me through yesterday but take a different turn at the end, coming out into a long entrance hall full of doors. I count each one as we pass them, finally reaching the end, where two big white doors with thick golden hinges stand closed.

The guard behind me steps forward, knocking on it twice before giving me a look. One meant to caution me to behave.

I ignore him, tracing my eyes over the pattern on the door. It takes a minute before they swing open from the inside.

A grand throne room, one impressive in size and luxury, greets me. The guard with the scar moves behind me and gives me a hard shove, jolting me from my perusal. The room is so long and wide it could house half the Sidus townspeople alone.

Gold chandeliers glisten above us, their jeweled decorations twinkling in the light, sending shimmers across the room. I glance around the hall, the detail and work that must have gone into its extravagance, with lush red fur carpets, lavish crystal ornaments, and a white marble floor leading up to a raised throne area.

The long hall acts as a parade to showcase its beauty and riches. Though impressive in structure, no amount of splendor could conceal its true foulness.

I glance around, noticing no one fitting the description of the Breaker is present, which is a small mercy.

Hushed whispers have seeped into the Sidus town about a special guard who enjoys inflicting pain and torture on those deemed traitors or disloyal, with a twisted ability that enables him to cause pain without touch. I only hope I can avoid him as long as possible.

Though I know he will seek me out soon; of that I am confident.

A few guards are stationed around the room, keeping watch. The only threat seems to be me, however, based on their harsh glares all directed toward me.

The rest of the competitors arrive, all Caligo, both men and women. They are dressed well, with luxurious coats and boots and look to have had the fortune of a good night's rest.

A few curious glances are aimed my way, but I ignore them to focus on the real threat that has just arrived.

Lieutenant Amaro strolls into the room with a smug expression on his face. He takes a seat beside a tall, lithe man with long black hair. The man welcomes the lieutenant before stepping up to the center of the throne area and calling for attention.

"My fellow comrades, this year's competition slightly differs from the rest. This year, the royals have requested that it take place in the palace. As I am sure you will all agree, it is a privilege to be here."

Murmurs of agreement sound out around me, with each competitor wearing a proud smile as if honored to be here. I hold in my scoff, desperately wanting to roll my eyes at their ignorance.

The lithe man nods, a smile on his face as he continues. "The first competition will be held in three days' time. This should give you enough time to sharpen those skills and train for the first trial, which will be hand-to-hand combat." He glances around the room, eyeing each competitor.

"Only the best have been chosen." He pauses on me, a small frown forming between his brows. Clearing his throat, he pastes on a fabricated smile and focuses on the Caligo to my left.

"The second trial will showcase your skills with weapons, which I hope will reveal some of your talents. And the third and final trial of the competition will test your powers."

A few smug faces glance over at me at the mention of powers.

"And what of those that don't have any *useful* powers?" a competitor to my right asks.

The look he gives me tells me all I need to know about him. I make note of him—his shaved head and bulky stature.

"All competitors will stay in the palace and continue on with all three trials. Unless"—the lithe man glances at me, a glint of malice in his eyes—"they are found to be too injured to continue."

Ah, so this is their plan to get rid of me. Beat me not only as payback for Ryuu's attempt to make them listen but also to make sure I don't make it through each trial to continue on. And from the savage looks from some of the competitors, they have figured it out too.

"This competition will not be easy. It will test you; push you to your limits and beyond that. We only want the best, after all." The lithe man chuckles.

"The best three competitors of all three trials will be rewarded with a meeting with the royals and a celebration in their honor."

A few of the men and women straighten up, a look of shock slashed across their faces.

It seems that little piece of information was kept secret. Jarek must have found out through the rebels. Which means the rebels have far more connections than I realized.

I push it to the back of my mind and try to focus on the lithe man now droning on about safety and rules.

"Use your time to train wisely, and rest and enjoy the amenities the palace has to offer," he says.

None of which I will ever see. Not as long as Amaro has his way, nor when I meet the Breaker. Something I have to look forward to.

"Lieutenant Amaro would like to say a few words."

The lithe man moves back to his seat as Amaro steps forward. The entire room grows silent and still as he quickly commands the attention of everyone here.

"As you might be aware, we have a *special* guest this year." Amaro spawns a serpent's smile as he glances over at me. "It is a strange happenstance to occur, considering how desperate the rebels have become to destroy everything we have worked so hard to build here."

I ignore the glares sent my way and plaster an indifferent look onto my face as Amaro continues his little speech meant to ensure all competitors distrust me.

"Therefore, for the good of the competition, we have made some slight adjustments to ensure your safety."

Some of the Caligo frown at me as Amaro causes a seed of doubt to grow inside their minds.

"I heard she is in a cell?" asks a woman with high cheekbones, short blue hair, and a beautiful black studded dagger.

"How do we know she is not a rebel?" another asks, though I ignore them all to stay focused on Amaro.

A spark lights up in his eyes as his smile turns to a sorrowful frown.

"I am afraid there's nothing I can do. Rules are rules, and all entrees *chosen* must compete."

"How do we know she can even fight?" someone sneers from the left of me. "She could be wasting our time here."

The lithe man jumps to his feet, an excited expression on his face. "Why don't we have a little display? Something to show us what she has to offer." He glances right at me. "Seren can prove to us her worth and show us her... *skills*."

I fist my hands at my sides as his eyes move down my body, his lecherous grin forming makes my skin crawl.

"Garath, you will be her opposition," he says.

"Yes, *sir*." Garath, a beefy man with pure white hair, steps forward, a savage smirk on his face meant to unnerve.

"No weapons. We do not know what unlawful tricks she has learned among her own," the lithe man says.

A sharp push from behind me sends me closer to the center of the room. I glance back and glare at the guard who shoved me. But he pays me no mind, instead sharing a knowing look with my opponent.

I turn to him and size him up. He's taller than me by at least a foot and a half. There are small scars all over his thick, muscled arms, telling me he's no stranger to a fight. And from the dark look in his eyes, I can tell he enjoys it too.

"You should learn your place, Sidus," Garath snarls, just loud enough for me to hear.

"Maybe you should show me." I smile at him, glad for a moment to unleash some of my building frustrations.

"Gladly," he says with a sneer before lunging forward.

I counter him, using my height and lightness to evade his attack. He turns, a snarl on his face as he rears up to full height, intending to use his brute strength to take me down. But he leaves himself open as he lunges for me once more. I use it to my advantage and punch him in his stomach before quickly jabbing his diaphragm. He bends forward, the wind knocked out of him from my hit.

Before he gets a chance to right himself, I reach out and grab the back of his head. His face meets my bent knee before slamming to the ground, knocking him out. The entire fight is over in seconds as his body hits the floor with a thump.

The silence in the room is deafening.

I turn to the throne area and finish off the little display I was forced to be a part of with a bow to them all, a small smile on my face that widens as I meet Amaro's eyes.

I know I will pay for it, and my theory is confirmed with Amaro's replying smirk, his eyes promising nothing but pain.

But pain is something I am used to. Pain, I can deal

with. It is the games I will have to learn to play in order to stay here.

Another competitor rushes to Garath, checking him over. "He needs a healer at once."

My body grows tense as a handful of the competitors move closer to me. Some now with looks of intrigue instead of outright hostility.

"She can fight." A man with unruly shoulder-length black hair glances at me with shock slashed across his pale face.

"She has been trained by Captain Ryuu. Of course she knows how to fight. Did you think she got in here on her looks alone? If that were the case, I would have won the competition already." A young male about my age, with short light brown hair and a friendly expression, grins over at them.

They shake their heads at him, some of them with small smiles or interested glances. But it does what he intended and breaks some of the growing tension in the room.

The group disperses with a few distrustful glances, but a couple nod to me in sincerity, one being the brown-haired male who spoke for me.

With a nod from Amaro, the same two guards pull me out of the room and down the hall.

"Foolish girl," the intrigued guard whispers fiercely while shaking his head. His face is full of disbelief and annoyance.

With their relentless pulling and pushing, we make it

back to my cell in half the time. They shove me forward, but I catch myself once more before swiftly turning around. The guard who holds nothing but cruelness in his eyes wears a smug grin. One that tells me he is up to no good.

He takes a step inside my cell, leaving it open behind him. "Bind her arms and legs. A few hours tied up might help shut that smart mouth of hers."

"Is this really necessary?" the other guard grits out. His arms are crossed, and he's avoiding looking me in the eye.

"She disrespected the lieutenant. She deserves this and more. Hand me some rope."

Gods forbid he be treated like another flawed being. His status holds no truth to his actions, nor does he get a pass for them.

I stand still, waiting for the guard to make his move, while the other guard continues to ignore him before glancing away.

"Fine, I'll do it myself." The guard huffs, getting the rope himself.

I watch him closely as he grabs a thin black rope from somewhere behind him and returns to the front of my cell, his cruel smirk firmly in place.

I give him a bland look, waiting for him to get on with this charade.

Stepping into the cell, he treads lightly as if approaching a wild beast. I know the moment he decides to whip forward, and counter him by stepping to the left.

Before he gets another chance, I use the cell bars as leverage to kick off and aim for his head. His body whips around, facing the other guard as his knees hit the ground. I quickly grab the rope that he dropped and wrap it around his neck, pulling tightly to cut off his air supply.

As he gasps for precious air, trying and failing to release the rope I hold tightly, my eyes find the other guard—and the smile he now wears.

I allow my bored look to fade, letting some of the wild rage bleed through my eyes, revealing a piece of my own true nature. A warning and a threat. One he should heed, unless he wants to end up like the foolish guard now in my hold.

But his smile only grows.

My eyes don't leave his as I pull the rope tighter once more before releasing the vile guard and kicking him forward out of the cell. While he is catching his breath, I slam the cell door behind him, walking backward while keeping an eye on them both. The other guard still watches on, a look of approval on his face.

After the guard collects himself, he spins around to face me. His whole face seethes with rage, his shadows seeping out around him, revealing his uncontrolled temper.

"We have been ordered not to use our shadows on you. But you will not always have that strength of yours or the fire behind your eyes." He spits out blood, sneering toward me. "The Breaker will strip you of your every strength, and when he has, I'll be right here, waiting."

I continue to watch him, knowing my silence and blank expression will rile him more than anything I could say.

But submitting was never something I would easily yield to, and they will have to go a lot further before I ever concede to their will.

He snarls once more before storming out of the room.

The silent guard takes a step forward, locking me in. "Nicely done."

His warm smile tries to elicit a reaction from me. I continue looking ahead and reveal no outward expression, but inside, all I feel is a burning rage of fire and flames.

"We are not all bad," he says softly.

I continue my silence, for fear that I will surrender to my anger and the control I work so hard to maintain. He thinks he did me a kindness by doing nothing.

After a minute, he frowns, dropping his fake smile, trying sincerity instead.

"I don't want to hurt you."

"No, you just prefer to watch." My voice is a whisper made from thorns.

He swallows hard before turning away but pauses with his back to me.

"Sometimes it is the only choice we have."

"A lie you continue to tell yourself."

With his back still to me, he dips his head once, acknowledging my words before leaving.

It is possible there are some guards who do not believe the same fabricated lies told of the Sidus by some of the other Caligo guards. It is considerably plausible that there are more who have a shred of remorse toward their mandatory tasks and duties, but I have no regret about my harsh judgment of them. Not when there are people dying by the very comrades who lead beside them. Not when they sit among food so generous in its quantity that not a thought is spared toward those who could benefit greatly from just a scrap of it.

In the end, there is always a choice. The one that is easy and ignorant or the one that is hard and challenging. The choice, like two paths, is still present. Choosing one that eases your conscience slightly is not a comfort, but rather an excuse.

Soft footsteps unlike the heavy thumps of the guard capture my attention, pushing my thoughts to the side as someone steps in front of my cell.

Eyes so dark the light itself denies them any regard, stare at me. His expression is otherwise indifferent, if not for those cold, calculating eyes. A skillful concealment of his true depraved nature.

I know whatever this man has planned for me will not be quiet. His eyes promise nothing but pain. But pain is temporary, and I will move past it. My mind will be the thing he will want to toy with and break. A true weakness, but it is something I will not allow.

I steel myself for what is about to happen, knowing I am stronger than anything he will do to me. Seeing the defiance in my eyes, a cruel smirk tilts his lips.

"I am the Breaker," he says, and a sliver of fear passes my defenses, making his smile widen.

"Good. I see you have heard of me." The cell door opens with a clang. "Let us commence."

CHAPTER 10

"I hear you had quite the sharp tongue with the lieutenant, no doubt acquired from your mother," he says, chuckling.

The Breaker's conceited look confuses me. I insulted his comrade, and yet I amuse him. It unsettles something inside me, taking root among my doubts and silent fears.

"No sharp wit or reply?" he asks with humor in his eyes.

I say nothing. My words will not aid me now. My stare is blank, stripped of any emotion. Nothing but numbness will be a companion.

The Breaker's smirk finally turns cold. "Take her."

No sound arrives from the two guards who have steadily slithered up behind him and step toward my cell. Their cloaks are as dark as the night, concealing most of their face and body. They don't bother looking at me as they pull me out.

I don't fight them.

I don't call on my shadows.

I let them drag me down the dark corridor without question.

We turn into a row of more cells, slightly different from my own; these ones with brick covering most of the cells and a small space only big enough to pass food through that is covered with thick bars. We pass half a dozen more cells before I spot a door off to the side. Its bare look makes it stand out among the rest, piquing my interest.

I had thought the only way into my cell block was the way they brought me in, but it seems there might be another, one that I might be able to exploit. Storing that thought away for now, I focus on the guards as we continue down the corridor of cells, reaching one at the end. They wait for the Breaker's permission before going any further. With the dip of his head, we move forward into the room.

Instead of a cell, it is a small hallway, one with another door at the end. Icy shivers slide down my spine at seeing the wooden door up close. Scratches scale their way up it, and chunks are missing, caused by what appear to be claw marks. Dark colors of every kind are splattered across it, soaked into the grooves.

They push the door open, shoving me inside.

Another prison, though one with no bars. One that is darker and colder, but not from any breeze, as there are no windows for it to pass through. The air itself is stagnant and stale, smelling only of death. The stench permeates the small room, making me want to vomit. I breathe through my mouth, trying and failing to prevent the vile odor from seeping in.

As the Breaker steps forward, the dark room casts shadows, concealing most of his body and face, making him seem otherworldly and more dangerous.

"Bind her," he orders.

I ready myself for an attack. Though they will try to break me, I will not make it easy.

But the fight never comes, nor do the guards move. Their shadows whip out, forcing me to my knees, stringing my hands up. I hold back my own shadows, which are begging to break free to aid and punish.

My plan is reliant on my stay at the palace. I can't afford to jeopardize my place here so soon. Not until I compete in the competition and meet with the royals.

Shoving down my shadows once more, I focus on the Breaker. The dim room casts shadows over his face that slither over his dark eyes as he steps closer. The guards' power forces my face up to look at him. His cold eyes stare back at me as the guards' punishing grip tightens.

I have come across many cruel people, their eyes always displaying their true nature. But never have I seen eyes so dark and empty of any remorse and light.

"This will hurt." No compassion or emotion is on his face nor in his voice. This is merely a means to an end. I am nothing more than another project he can attempt to break.

Around me, sound disappears as pain erupts across my body. Sharp blades pull and tear as something foreign moves about inside me, searching without care. The Breaker spares no thought to my torment as it continues on a constant loop. It rips and tears at my soul, agony just as afflicting as physical pain.

I breathe through my nose, the putrid smell doing nothing to distract the torment.

Looking forward, I find a jagged brick that has shifted in the wall. The muddy slab is barely visible in the dark room, but it captures and holds my attention. The cramped cell dissolves around me as I fixate on the chipped edges and surfaces, counting each scratch, each furrow and groove, until I am no longer in my body but someplace far away. The numbness, like a warm cloak, wraps around me, pushing the pain to the far reaches of my mind.

My purpose here is bigger than myself, bigger than my pain. If I follow through with my plan and make it through the competition, I might be able to bring light to the endless torment the Sidus have been living through.

Just like hope is so capricious when darkness appears, it can grow if lit by a single entity. The Sidus desperately need some form of hope to continue on. We cannot keep going the way we have been. It will not be long before that small light dwindles and is forever extinguished.

The moment of peace is quickly stripped from my mind and body as a burn, so intense, slices up my back, shaking my focus. I try to push it back, picturing Meira and her warm smiles. Natasa and her unyielding will. My mother's embrace, and Ryuu's strength. I take their warmth and let it guide me out of the dark pain and hold on to the slight reprieve. I grab on to that feeling and embrace the numbness as it settles over me once more.

But the freedom from affliction is fleeting. And a violent tug pulls me back to my body and reawakens the agony once more. The sharp pull grows, clawing its way into my skull. It passes in waves as it moves throughout me. I hold in the scream that wants a release to ease some of the torment.

"It seems this one is not going to be as easy as I had expected." The Breaker's voice is a distant echo as I fight to stay conscious, though the displeasure in his tone is evident.

My eyes blur as sharp needles splinter every nerve, the torment growing more intense. They burn hotter than any fire, spreading to every inch of me. I clench my jaw shut, not willing to give them any sound. Not willing to show them a moment of my weakness.

I hold on even when the room slips away, becoming patches of darkness and hazy figures. I am about to slip into a peaceful darkness, when the pain begins to ebb and release.

Barely conscious, I sway sideways. The only thing holding me is the guards' shadowed chains.

The Breaker takes a step back, a frown on his blurry face. What felt like hours was possibly only minutes.

The sweat clings to my face and body as my breath rushes out in sharp pants, and I fight against sweet oblivion and dark's warm embrace.

"Tell me how you managed to enter the guard's competition." The Breaker's harsh words are searing.

I try to form words, any sound, but nothing comes out.

"Tell me and you will be free."

A lie. One so clear I can taste it on my tongue.

"Again." The Breaker chuckles before moving back a step, not waiting on a reply any longer.

The guards pull their shadow chains tighter, and pain once again becomes my friend and tormentor.

Just as the pain reaches a peak, a sweet darkness embraces me.

What feels like a moment later, I wake to slices of pain scraping down my back as the Breaker's men drag me along the harsh ground, back to my cell. Every bump and knock sends a jolt of sharp pain throughout my tender body. The rough ground and small stones run along my taut skin, pulling it tight. I clench my jaw, concealing any gasps. They continue on, their handling having no softness or care, their grips hard and punishing.

They dump me on the cold ground and discard me without so much as a glance.

A moment of peace settles over me when they leave my sight, and a stolen gasp escapes my lips as I drag my body into a sitting position.

Though the Breaker did not cause any physical injury, his form of infliction feels exactly that. I glance down at myself, looking for any substantial evidence, but find nothing. My body feels drained, similar, if not worse, to the aftermath of too many training sessions and nights out guarding the Sidus town. Though one where I have lost every single fight.

The Breaker has shown me exactly what I will be spending my time doing here between the trials and how far they were willing to go to stop me from succeeding.

I know I can't keep up his form of torment forever. I need to figure a way to come and go from the palace, and soon.

CHAPTER 11

Night creeps across the small cell, gliding over the last of the daylight to blanket it in night's dusk. I wait a few moments before complete darkness encases my cell.

Standing up, I stretch my tense muscles, loosening the phantom pain from the Breaker's cruel administrations. Testing my body, I notice the pain is quickly disappearing. It must be because the Breaker's form of torture is not physical. I can only hope that any further *sessions* will bring about the same result. It will make getting through them a little easier.

Bringing my shadows to the surface of my skin, I pause when I remember the shadow void block in place at the palace. Using the void would be easier than having to sneak in and out of my cell. And I wouldn't be surprised if the guards used it purely as a fear tactic to hoard over all those who believed it.

The cool, dark tendrils of my shadows curl inside me as I reach down to the deepest part of them. Beginning to take a step into the center of it, I imagine myself on the other side of the cell.

But the minute my foot hits the floor, I feel it. A solid barrier that obstructs my way through the void to the other side. I try to push against it, hoping to feel the rush of cool ice flood my veins, but I can't reach beyond the barrier to get to it.

I open my eyes and sigh as I glance around my cell. Although I'm disappointed that the barrier is not a lie fabricated by the Caligo guards, I'm glad that they also cannot use it.

After listening for a few minutes and hearing nothing but silence, I form a small shadow in my hand, pushing it through the lock and manipulating it to open my cell door. A low click brings a smile to my face.

While I slept and healed from the Breaker's session over the last couple of days, I made sure to give the guards no entertainment and to ignore them completely. They quickly grew bored with me and soon left to do whatever they usually do when not attempting to watch me.

Today they showed up as usual to give me my slop of a meal before checking on me once more. If my presumption is correct based on the last two nights, I should have most of tonight to search for what I'm looking for.

On limber feet, I ease the cell door ajar and slip out,

closing it softly behind me. I listen again for any sounds before moving down the hall to where the guards brought me before.

I pass the empty brick cells, and my gaze falls on the odd door from when the Breaker paid a visit. Making my way over, I listen up against it for any sound on the other side. But only silence greets me.

I hesitate before pushing it open as a sliver of doubt creeps in. This door could be deceiving, containing any noise behind it. For all I know, the entire guard could be concealed behind it, ready and waiting.

But I have no other choice if I want to find a way out of here.

Shaking my wayward thoughts aside, I step forward, ready to see what lies beyond it.

After waiting another moment to listen for any sound, I push it open slowly, releasing a sigh of relief when I spot an empty stairway with no guards in sight.

My ascending steps are hasty yet silent while I stay alert. Halting at the top, I face a plain brown-and-cream door, one a lot more ornate than the prison below. A small shard of hope makes its way into my chest.

Not allowing myself to worry over what may lie behind it, I push it open and smile to myself when I spot the familiar large corridor of the main palace.

Arches with shimmering lights hanging on each side guide my path.

Stepping forward, I glance around, keeping my

senses open and alert for the slightest of noises. All I need is the guards to catch me, and then this will all be for nothing.

The shimmering lights along the arches shine bright as I make my way past them. At night, the palace looks like something the Sidus would create. A land full of twinkling stars that drift along the darkness of the cool night.

After a few moments of following the long arches, I come to a large open area with three other long halls trailing off in different directions. None of them give me any hint as to what may lie ahead of each.

Taking a deep breath, I follow my instincts and start my way down the corridor on my left.

Passing the long hallways, I ignore their decorative features, making sure to keep watch for any guards coming my way. Moving to the spiral staircase, I peek over, and my gaze is immediately drawn to the expanse of extravagance below.

Although extravagant and eye-catching, it gives me no clue as to how to find another way out.

Sighing to myself, I continue on, but time starts to blur as the halls become a labyrinth. One so endless that any hope for finding a hidden way out of the palace is slowly waning. I come to another hall with rows of doors, each closed, with no sound from behind as I edge past them.

Coming upon another corridor that opens up, I veer

to the right and decide to give it one last shot before I make my way back to my cell.

After a couple of minutes with nothing but more grandeur and doors, I'm about to turn around when I hear a loud chuckle echo down the hall, halting my search.

I whip around, looking for someplace to hide. Choosing a door to my left, I silently open it and slip inside. Glancing around, I see it's another hallway with a small staircase. A sigh of relief leaves my lips as I descend the stairs, which bring me out to an open corridor.

Large paintings hang on the walls. Portraits of what must be the royals who have come before me. Their eyes follow me as I make my way down the hall when whispers and a familiar light draw my attention.

There is no mistaking what type of light it is nor the draw I feel toward it.

A Sidus light. Which must mean there is another Sidus in the palace.

I quickly follow it, but when I turn the corner, I freeze and my entire body grows taut with what lies before me.

The brown-haired man from the throne room, the one who stood up for me, has his hands outstretched, one wielding shadows while the other directs light. A *Sidus* light.

A wielder of both light and dark, and something that I never thought was possible. The thought that there may be more than just me and now him out there starts to unravel something inside me.

His light grows, expanding around the door from the other side. A gasp slips past my lips at how easily he wields both abilities together at the same time. He whips around, his shadows and light quickly dispersing, his eyes widening in fear when he spots me.

"It's not what it... I mean, what you saw..."

There was no denying what I saw. "I saw you using a Sidus light and Caligo shadows."

"Yes... but, I mean, no." He shakes his head as his face grows pale. But I am the last person he needs to worry about finding out his secret.

"How are you both?" I ask, needing to know everything about him and where he came from. Are there more of us?

"Both?" he asks.

"Both Sidus and Caligo. Were you born with both abilities? Or did they show up later?"

I was born with mine, but maybe they manifested differently in others.

He swallows hard, glancing at the door before slowly nodding his head. "Yes. I was born with both." He moves to take a step forward but thinks better of it and steps back, fisting his hands at his side.

"But you can't tell anyone. They'll kill me," he pleads.

"I know." It has been my own fear for as long I can remember. "I won't... I won't tell them," I promise.

He runs a hand over his face, a frown now marring

his brow. "How can I trust you? This secret is... It means life or death to me."

"I'm a Sidus. Who would believe me anyway?" I ask, reminding him with a raised brow.

He winces at my reply but realizes how true it is. They think him to be a Caligo. If I were to tell them he is both, they would simply laugh at me and then punish me for lying about him.

I should despise him for choosing the Caligo side of himself. Choosing the easy way, full of comfort and protection. But in truth, all I feel is hope. Hope that I am no longer alone in this world. That what I am is not some form of abomination but an evolution of our kind.

"I would never tell them," I promise him again. He has no reason to trust me, nor I him, but knowing what he is, that he's like me, makes it hard not to want to.

"I will keep your secret," I tell him. But his eyes narrow on mine, searching my face for something. A lie, perhaps, or some form of distrust. But he will find neither.

He seems to think so too, when he releases a harsh breath and nods. "Thank you, Seren. I'm Oryn."

"You know my name?" I ask, quickly forgetting he was the one to mention I was trained by Ryuu.

A small smile tilts his lips. "I've heard about you. You're one hell of a fighter. You could have entered the guard's competition any other year. Why now?"

Realizing I don't have much time, I ignore his question and tilt my head toward the door. "What were you trying to do?"

Oryn glances back at the door with a frown. "I wanted to unlock a door that seemed to be locked by some other means. I thought I could use both abilities to break it open, but I wasn't having much luck." He rubs a hand down the back of his neck and gives me a small smile.

"What did you think was behind it?" I ask.

He glances around the hall, frowning. "I thought there might be a clue."

"A clue?" I step toward the door, leaning against it, and I listen for any sound on the other side but quickly find none.

The guards could have it shielded somehow, blocking any sound from within. But I have a feeling there is nothing inside it, as we would have both been overheard by now and caught. I tell Oryn as much.

Oryn nods as if it is something he might have already been aware of but also hoping it was not true. His face grows grim.

"I thought so too." Oryn releases a harsh breath, staring at me once more. "I don't know why I'm telling you this, but something tells me I can trust you. That you have enough of your own problems to deal with rather than try to turn around and betray me." He sighs before turning to me completely and looking me straight in the eye. "My sister was taken three days ago. It's the only reason I'm here. And I need to find her before it's too late."

Everything inside me freezes. "Taken by whom?"

"I don't know. But it wasn't a Caligo." He says it with complete certainty in his voice.

I raise a brow. "Do you think it was a Sidus?"

His eyes widen as if he's only now realizing what he has implied. He quickly shakes his head. "That's the thing. I don't think it was either."

The dark creatures flash across my mind. "How do you know your sister was taken and not...?"

"Killed?" he says, finishing my question. "There was a... residue of some kind left behind." His frown deepens. "A silver film that glimmered in the light. When I touched it, it felt... off. Like it didn't belong in our world." He shakes his head again, but more to himself. "I know it sounds crazy, but I *know* my sister is alive." He brings his hand to his chest. "I *feel* it. Here."

I have no reason to help him, with the list of things I should be trying to figure out myself. But the sadness in his eyes makes me want to at least try.

"What is your plan?" I ask.

He gives me a grateful look for not questioning him on his strange hunch, but who am I to judge him and what he feels is right? Many of my own decisions are based on my gut instincts rather than knowledge. If he feels his sister is alive, then she is alive.

"I wanted to search the palace. I assume that

whoever has taken her has to be powerful. That the royals may know something... But—"

"You thought they may be in on it?"

He nods. "I thought it may be a possibility. I decided to search the palace first. So far, I've found nothing that would—"

Something clatters around the corner, making me freeze. Oryn doesn't think twice as he grabs my arm and pulls me down the hall in the opposite direction.

We move quickly, finding ourselves in another dark, quiet hallway.

"I think we lost them," Oryn says, glancing back.

My mind mulls over what he just told me, realizing that maybe there is a specific reason why they took his sister.

"Is your sister a Caligo?" I ask, and he immediately understands what I am asking.

"Yes, *only* Caligo. I'm the only one that's a little... *different*." He gives me a quick look before glancing away.

"Does anyone else know about you?" Maybe they found out about him and thought his sister was the same. Or maybe they are using her to lure him out.

"No. No one knows. Not a soul," he says before frowning.

"Then why would they have taken her? Why her? Why not—"

"Others?" He nods. "She's not the only one. There's more. More women going missing. My sister was not the first, and I fear she will not be the last."

Ice fills my veins. This changes everything. How long has this been going on? Is it just Caligo women and women in general, or is it males too? I'm about to ask him when I hear footsteps sound out down the corridor from us, and it forces us to get moving.

Finding a small black spiraling staircase, we move swiftly down it, only to come to another damp and dark hall similar to the passageways I was brought through to the cells.

Halfway down the passageway, Oryn stops and turns to me. "I know you have no reason to trust me, but I need to know why you are here."

I stay silent, wondering what he has deduced so far.

"My only reasoning is that you have also come here under a guise for something else. That you do not care for the winning position of a guard, and that whatever it is that forced your hand means a great deal to you."

I search his face for any ill-intent or deceit but find nothing so obvious. And I decide to give him some of my trust for now and hope it does not come back to bite me.

"There is something killing the Sidus. Creatures that are slipping past the shield," I tell him.

Oryn's eyes widen in shock and fear. "Why haven't you told anyone? The Caligo—"

"Already know." My words stop him silent. "They know and they do not care. At least not about the Sidus."

Oryn's mouth drops open in shock. But then a spark of dread fills his eyes.

"These... creatures? Do they leave any residue?" The fear seeps into his face, turning it ashen.

I shake my head, stopping his downward spiral. "Nothing. It is as if they are made from smoke. They kill and leave no evidence behind."

He releases a harsh breath, rubbing his chest. "Then it can't be them." He looks at me. "Taking the missing women, I mean."

"No, it doesn't sound like it," I tell him, hoping we are right.

He nods his head again, more to himself, before his eyes land on my bracelets.

"What are those cuffs you wear? I have a feeling they are not your normal attire."

I glance down at them, still feeling the lack of warmth from my missing abilities. "A gift from the lieutenant. One that inhibits me from using my Sidus abilities."

Oryn winces before releasing another harsh breath. "I understand why the Sidus see us as nothing but their enemy when you have people like the lieutenant making it look like we are."

We start moving again and turn into a room full of empty cells. Cells so old the bars are rotting from within, and the stench of blood and death still fills the air.

"Do you know where we are? Maybe we took a wrong turn?" I glance around, trying to figure out where we ended up.

"It's one of the many prison cells that are located

underneath the palace. This one seems to be one of the older ones." He walks down to the end of the room and glances around as if double-checking it is empty before turning back to me. Scanning my face for something, he nods when he seems to find it, a determined expression now on his face.

"Maybe we can help each other? The palace is endless in size. Too large to search individually. I can help you with whatever you're searching for, and you can help me with mine."

I look at him closely and try to sense anything off before revealing what I am searching for. Still not sensing any deceit or anything malicious, I decide to reveal it.

"Do you know a way to come and go from the palace? Some hidden entrance the guards leave unguarded or unused?"

Oryn frowns. "I—"

Chains rattle as movement comes from within the small cell beside us. Moving a step back, I notice strange silver symbols carved into the ground around the cell, swirling and slithering up and along the bars.

Oryn gasps as he reaches out to touch it.

"I wouldn't do that if I were you." A man with wavy shoulder-length dark brown hair and striking blue eyes steps from the shadows. One of his ears is pierced with a small blue gem that matches the color of his eyes. But it is the energy around him that draws most of my attention. It feels different and otherworldly.

Goose bumps break out across my skin as he glances from me to Oryn.

"Who are you?" Oryn asks but heeds his warning and pulls his hand back from the bars.

That is when I feel it. *Him*. His power. It reaches out, searching, his eyes landing on mine as a wide smile spreads across his lips.

"*What* are you?" I ask, and his smile grows wicked.

"Veles. And I'm what you call a Fae."

CHAPTER 12

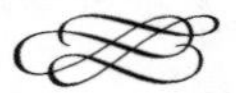

Fae.

Fae are myths. Immortal legends that I thought no longer existed. How is it that one now stands before me?

"Well, technically I'm half," Veles says with a twisted smile. One that does not put me at ease.

"You can't be Fae," Oryn says, sharing a look with me. "They don't exist."

"And yet here I am," he says.

Oryn frowns, gesturing toward the silver symbols. "What are these symbols?"

"Fae enchantments," Veles reveals.

It's as if something snaps inside Oryn on hearing Veles' words. He takes a step toward the cell without thought. "What do they do? Do all Fae use these? Are there more of you?"

"Oryn?" I give him a questioning look.

He fists his shaking hands. "The silver." He tilts his head toward it. "It looks like the residue left behind."

Oryn's previous theory could be right if Veles is what he says he is. And if that is the case, it means that the Fae might be behind this. Immortal beings we thought were long extinct could be the culprits behind the missing women.

"Do you really think the yearly competition was the guard's idea to find more precious guards?" Veles asks with a smug expression. One that hides a glint of knowing.

"What do you mean? What else is there to find?" I ask.

Veles sighs, giving us both a look full of pity. "There is so much you don't know. So many things I could tell you."

"Then tell us," I push, and Veles focuses his attention directly on me.

"Free me from here, and I will tell you anything you want to know," he vows.

Anything... I share a look with Oryn. He looks just as wary as I feel, but I can also see it in his eyes. He is willing to do anything to find his sister.

"Why are you in here?" I ask him, needing to know more than the scraps he has told us.

"I am half of what they deem perfection. My existence sullies their line, and for it, I deserve a swift death." Veles shrugs and glances around his cell, but the look he attempts to hide reveals just how much it bothers him.

A pang of sympathy hits me, understanding exactly how he feels.

"Do you know a way to come and go from the palace without the guards finding out?" I ask him.

He turns back to face me with a wicked smirk. "That I do."

"And how do we know we can trust you?" I ask with a frown, knowing damn well I won't be able to trust him in the slightest, even if we do come to some type of agreement.

"We make a deal. One that is binding." His eyes light up with a flicker of hope concealed beneath them.

"Binding?" I ask.

"It cannot be broken until both parties have upheld their end of the bargain. The deal will be binding until death."

He must see the glimmer of doubt in my eyes, as his expression turns desperate.

"The guard's competition brings more Fae here," Veles says, attempting to mask his desperation as he leans back and twirls his chains around his fingers. But I am too distracted by what he just revealed.

"How are they getting in? The shield—"

"Was created by the Fae. They bring it partially down once a year to enter the kingdom. Only a small passageway, enough to fit a handful of people."

My stomach drops, twisting and churning at his words. It can't be true.

If that's the case, then... "Are they also letting the dark creatures in?"

Veles frowns. "Dark creatures?" He leans forward and hisses when his hands graze the bars.

"*What* dark creatures?" His tone is sharp, his question filled with alarm.

"I thought you knew everything," I reply with a raised brow.

He moves back, a contemplative look on his face. "If it is what I think, we are in far more trouble than I initially thought."

He glances between us both. "Help me escape this cell, and I will tell you everything I know and help you where I can. I can promise you, you both will need it."

I glance at Oryn, but I can see that he has already made his choice; he is just waiting on mine.

I sigh, regretting the decision I am about to make, knowing deep down it is somehow going to come back to haunt me.

"Fine. Let's make a deal," I tell him, watching a devilish grin slide across his face in triumph.

"A blade. I need a blade," Veles says with haste and excitement.

Oryn whips out a small dagger and passes it to him without question.

"Ladies first." Veles chuckles softly before reaching out toward me. "Your hand."

Hesitantly, I reach my hand through the bars and

hiss as Veles slides the blade along my palm before quickly doing the same to his and joining them together.

"Your name?" he asks with a smile that does nothing to ease my nerves.

"Seren," I tell him reluctantly.

"Seren, I vow to help you in any way I can," he says with complete conviction in his voice.

"I promise to help you gain your freedom from this prison," I reply, the words forming without thought.

A brush of energy sweeps around our hands, settling inside my palm. I pull my hand back and he releases it as a small tingle slithers through the wound, instantly healing it. All that's left behind is a small scar.

"It is done," Veles says, pocketing Oryn's dagger.

"What about me?" Oryn moves closer to the cell bars.

Veles raises a brow. "I only need to bind myself to one of you. The deal still stands."

Oryn clenches his jaw. "Now, wait a minute—"

"How do we set you free?" I ask, trying to move this along. It will be a miracle if the guards have not noticed I'm missing yet. I need to get back, and soon.

Veles ignores Oryn to focus on me once more. "This cell is enchanted by another Fae. The only way I can escape is to acquire the blood of the one who imprisoned me."

I narrow my eyes on him, already regretting our little deal.

He smirks at me, a glint of amusement in his eyes.

"Don't worry, you won't have to kill anyone. Unless you would prefer it?"

My narrowed eyes turn to slits.

"No? Well then, I merely need a drop of blood."

"Whose blood do we need to acquire? Please tell me it is not the lieutenant's?" Oryn asks.

"No. The lieutenant would not shed even a speck of his precious blood for anyone. That is something that is beneath him. The person I need the small drop of blood from goes by the name Levon."

Veles's smile widens at my frown. "Ah, I see you've already had the pleasure of meeting him."

Oryn gives me a questioning look.

"He is Amaro's right-hand man. I met him upon my arrival. He's just as foul and ill-mannered as Amaro." I glance back at Veles. "How are we supposed to get his blood?"

A look full of mischief spreads across his face, making my stomach churn.

"I have a plan. An old friend has a bottle of wine with my name on it which you will need to acquire."

"Wine? You want us to steal wine?" Oryn frowns.

"It is *special* wine," he says with a smirk. "Extremely potent. Slip some into Levon's drink, and you should be able to get his blood without him noticing anything amiss."

"And *how* exactly am I supposed to get this drink to Levon? I doubt he will take anything from either of us," I point out. He will immediately think it is poisoned.

"That is where you will have to get a little creative." Veles glances between us. "I can't do everything for you."

Oryn scoffs at him, opening his mouth to surely curse him, when Veles's expression grows serious.

"You have three days before I'm out of time," he says with no amusement. Just a dead look in his eyes that is filled with fear.

Three days to stay out of the guards' way, try not to be killed by the Breaker, make it through the first trial, and acquire a bottle of wine from somewhere in the palace. All while I am supposedly locked up in a cell.

Maybe I should have tried to slip through the shield and take the dark creatures on myself. It might have been less trouble than whatever I have managed to get myself into now.

"What happens should I fail?" I ask him.

Veles's eyes cut to mine. "*Don't* fail. Believe me, neither of us will like the outcome."

* * *

Glancing around, I listen for any sound before slipping back into my cell. As I close it firmly behind me, I think over the last few hours and glance down at the small scar now on my right palm.

Don't fail...

Veles explained where I was to go to get the wine. It is a room on the east wing of the palace, the complete opposite side to where my cell is. It isn't impossible to get to, but I will need to be quick.

Starting the first trial tomorrow doesn't make things any easier, but it might just come in handy. Levon seems like the type to flaunt his achievements for all to see. He must have a favorite among the Caligo competitors.

Maybe I can help him along and make sure a celebration is needed.

A celebration that might require a *special* bottle of wine.

With a small smile on my face, a plan slowly starts to form.

CHAPTER 13

In the dead of night, the air is dragged from my lungs as something hard slams into my right side and then stomach. Pain explodes up and across my chest as a crack sounds out, and I know instantly that my rib is broken.

Deep chuckles sound out as a hard boot hits my thigh, making me grit my teeth against the shooting pain. I yank myself away from the hands attempting to hold me down, and scramble backward to put my back against the cell wall as I glare at the two guards smirking at me.

Using the wall to steady myself, I clutch my side and get to my feet with a wince.

"This beating will not be your last," says the guard with the scar on his neck.

The new guard beside him, one I have not had the pleasure of meeting yet, throws a tray of slop on the floor in front of my feet, most of it hitting my boots, before chuckling.

I guess neither of us are going to be friends. How unfortunate.

"Eat up," he says with a smirk. "The first trial begins soon. You wouldn't want to miss it now, would you?"

With their warning, the two guards back out of my cell with savage smirks, locking the bar door before making their way out, chuckling to themselves.

I wait a couple of minutes after they have gone before testing my injuries. The burning pain slicing across my side and into my chest is painful but manageable. My thigh probably has a bruise the size of the boot that slammed into it, and my stomach still churns with the impact of the fist that hit it, but I have worked with worse before. And with my innate ability to heal a little faster than normal, I will be able to move around without pain quicker than some.

With a wince, I bend down for my tray of food and try to force down the tasteless slop. Their attempt at trying to weaken me through beatings and starvation will not be something that breaks me. Nor will the cuffs that bind my Sidus abilities.

After consuming what I can, I check the bag that one of the guards must have thrown in while I foolishly slept hard and find it still has some of the clothes I packed before coming here, though many of the small keepsakes are missing and most likely destroyed.

It was foolish of me to have even attempted to bring them here.

Glancing around, I quickly get changed, using some of the extra fabric I have left to pad the lining around my chest and stomach.

Throwing my boots back on, I hear the familiar thud of the guard's arrival. Quickly getting to my feet, I ignore the pain of my injuries and focus on getting through the first trial and making sure everything goes to plan.

Two new guards come around the corner to my cell. Neither seem interested in talking or hurling insults, which suits me fine.

Opening the cell door, they step back and wait for me to walk through.

Bracing myself, I step through the entrance, only to be met with an unexpected hard shove to the ground.

"Know your place, Sidus scum. Don't try anything stupid in the trials, or you will pay for it dearly."

Fisting my hands on the ground, I push down the urge to slam one of them into the cocky guard's face, and push myself up with a wince.

Looking ahead, I ignore their mumbling threats but stay on alert for any more sneak attacks. I can still fight with the injuries I have, but it's best not to push it.

They shove me forward through the long passageways and halls and up through the palace to a large outdoor arena.

The entire area is nearly the same size as the throne room, with small spaced-out seats most likely suited to the guard's needs for training and not for any public audiences.

The seating around nearly all of the square-shaped arena is mostly empty if not for the odd guard here and there, while the top space is cloaked behind shadows.

With one last hard shove, the guards leave me at the entrance and edge of the arena.

The feeling of someone watching me crawls down my back as I make my way over to the group of competitors who are spread out in the center of the arena.

Glancing around, I find no one staring directly at me, but my eyes are drawn to the stage, which is covered in shadows.

Shaking off the strange feeling, I spot Oryn and move toward him but stop when I realize this... *friendship* could be a means to an end, and he might not want to associate with a Sidus in public.

But my doubts are unwarranted as he sees me and gives me a friendly smile before walking the rest of the way over.

"Seren." He dips his head, finishing off the rest of his sandwich with some type of meat in it. The smell of the fresh bread hits my senses, making my stomach rumble. But the feeling quickly turns sour seeing the looks the other competitors are giving us both.

I lean closer to Oryn, and he dips his head down to me. "Your carefully built Caligo image might be ruined if you continue to associate with me in public."

Oryn frowns down at me before following my line of

sight and scowling when he sees the others disgusted faces.

"If I were to choose my friends based on what others think, I would only ever be surrounded by my enemies." He glances down at me. "Ignore them. They are not worth our time nor energy."

"You truly don't care?" I ask, feeling slightly stunned by his reply.

"Not even a little." He smiles as he looks at me, but that smile quickly fades the longer he stares.

"Are you not getting enough sleep? You look unwell."

I glance away quickly, reminded of my early morning visit. "I'm fine."

"If you're worried about the plan, I can—"

"I'm not worried about it," I tell him with complete certainty. He stares a little longer, but I don't back down, and soon enough he nods, agreeing.

"If you're sure?" he asks, but with a wary expression.

"Positive," I mumble, done with this conversation and happy for a change in subject.

The change of subject comes in the form of a tall, lean man who makes his way over to us, a scowl slashed across his face like it's a permanent fixture. He is at least a head taller than Oryn and has dark, choppy hair that seems to mirror his bad mood.

"I hate it here. When can we leave?" the new man asks Oryn, as if they are familiar with one another.

I raise a brow at Oryn, and he chuckles. "Seren, this is Nevan. Nevan, this is Seren."

Nevan's eyes widen as he clears his throat. "My apologies for my rudeness. Being surrounded by so many Caligo seems to bring out the worst in me."

"Being surrounded by your own kind makes you miserable?" I ask, wondering if I heard him correctly.

Nevan straightens up, wincing a little before looking at me. "I realize how it must sound, but I'm well aware of the reputation the Caligo have and prefer not to be grouped together with the small-minded few who ruin it for the rest of us. Not all of us are like that."

"I will have to take your word for it," I tell him.

"You must not have met many good Caligo, then?" he asks with a sad expression on his face.

"Before you two, I had not met any," I tell him truthfully. With the exception of the guards, most, if not all, Caligo stay in the mountains, where the Sidus are forbidden to enter.

Nevan and Oryn share a look, but I ignore it to watch the lithe man from my first visit to the throne room moving from the shadows to a small dais at the top of the arena. It confirms my little hunch that others are watching us behind the shadows.

Oryn follows my line of sight and dips his head closer to me. "That's Alderic. He is a powerful Caligo lord not only because of his wealth and influence but also because he has the backing of the lieutenant and guards. I would stay away from him if I were you," he warns.

But it's not needed. The way this man makes my skin

crawl anytime he is near is warning enough. I do not trust him or his malicious smile. Staying away from him will not be a hardship, especially if I have my way.

"Today marks the first day of the guard's competition," Alderic announces with a smile.

Cheering sounds out, with the competitors and guards joining in. An overenthusiastic roar blares out, followed by laughter and chuckling.

"Yes, yes. It is all very exciting," Alderic says.

I squint, trying to hold back the twitch of annoyance wanting to be set free at their fawning.

"You will be paired off against chosen competitors suited to best showcase your skills," Alderic continues, quieting the crowd down. "All pairs were individually handpicked by the guards, so make sure you all show us your best."

I could bet that the competitor they handpicked for me is no doubt meant to maim and kill rather than showcase any type of skill.

"Those who win their match will face off against another winner and so on until the final winner is announced. Should you be knocked out of the round quickly, don't be too discouraged, as you will all have another chance to redeem yourselves in the next trial." Alderic claps his hands together and a Caligo guard with a bald head and hard expression stands up beside him to start calling out pairs.

The lieutenant isn't here, which is a small mercy, but

Levon is. I spot him eyeing a tall, bulky man with short brown hair.

"That is Haddon. Levon has personally chosen him to be here," Oryn says.

I share a look with him before glancing back at Haddon, this trial's first winner, no doubt.

"Oryn with Koa. Peyton with Triston. Seren with Ward." The guard continues with more names, but Oryn's eyes widen as a towering, stocky man with short black hair and a vicious smile walks over to us, setting his sights directly on me.

"I don't think they have chosen your partner based on a suited skill set," Nevan mumbles next to me.

"I wasn't expecting them to," I reply.

Oryn frowns as Ward moves closer, the glint of excitement in his eyes looking more deranged the closer he gets.

"Maybe we can talk to them and—"

"Sit down and have a quiet conversation with some tea and biscuits?" I turn to Oryn. "I knew coming here would mean I would have to fight my way at every step."

"You shouldn't be treated unfairly just because of what you are," he grits out, giving Ward a murderous expression.

"I'm used to it," I tell him.

Oryn turns to me, his anger quickly deflating as his expression grows sad. "You shouldn't have to be."

His words warm something inside my chest, giving me hope for a future where our kingdom is no longer divided. That is, until reality comes crashing down as Ward pushes him aside and steps in front of me.

"I'm going to thoroughly enjoy breaking every part of you," he says with an ugly smile.

I don't get the chance to reply as Ward attacks before we are given the go ahead, slamming a fist into the exact spot of my broken ribs. Pain blossoms inside my chest, making the previous broken rib feel like a bruise in comparison, and each intake of air burns as I try to catch my breath.

Alderic quickly announces to begin, covering Ward's sneak attack.

Ward steps back, but the callous smile growing on his face makes me think he knew exactly where to aim to injure me further. The look he shares with one of the other guards seconds later only confirms it.

Spitting out the blood from what is most likely a punctured lung, I ignore the tight, stabbing pain spreading across my chest and focus on the ruthless beast of a man in front of me.

A girl with dark hair in a blunt cut and sharp features turns around after I spit the blood out and scrunches her nose in disgust rather than showing any type of sympathy.

"She is wild and savage. She does not belong here," she hisses.

Tracking Ward's movements, I block his next attack, duck his next punch, and use my elbow to aim straight at his throat.

He chokes, attempting to catch his breath, and stumbles back.

Stepping forward, I grab hold of his wrist, twisting it before slamming my head into his nose, instantly breaking it.

Ryuu's methods were built on structure and precision, but he also had a side to him that was molded from the depths of despair and the ruthless world we live in. He taught me to be brutal and savage, and it seems it has come to my aid today.

Ward drops to the ground, on his knees as a pool of blood pours down his face and chest from his now crooked nose.

Cradling his wrist, he sways sideways, his eyes rolling to the back of his head before he falls to the ground with a thump.

The girl who turned to me with disgust now looks at me in shock and horror, her mouth and eyes wide open.

"How is that for savage?" I ask her with a smirk.

She snaps her mouth shut and quickly turns back to her fight, ignoring me completely.

I glance around, catching the guards' glares and snarls, and my smile widens. I will not let them think I am afraid of them, nor that I will back down so easily.

Oryn catches my eye and smiles at me, mouthing a "Nicely done" before ending the fight with his opponent and knocking him out.

My next few matches all seem to be similar to Ward.

All large, brutish, and with skill sets completely different from my own.

But they all fall just as hard as the first.

Ignoring my pain, I use it to fuel me, fighting without mercy. If they think a couple of broken bones and beatings will break me, they really don't know what the Sidus are made of.

After a few minutes, all that is left to continue competing is Nevan, Oryn, Haddon, and a few others.

Waiting on my next opponent to be called, I stand to the side and watch Oryn's fight. He is paired with someone who has the same build as him, his moves just as quick and impressive.

But whereas both seem to be evenly skilled, Oryn doesn't charge in blindly trying to gain an upper hand; he reads his opponent well, blocking and evading any attacks before spotting a weakness and striking it with force.

I glance over at Nevan and his opponent. His fighting style is a little sloppy, his attacks more personal, and they drain his energy quickly. One small mistake is all it takes to force him to forfeit any further fights.

My gaze finally lands on Haddon. His level of skill seems to be on par with Oryn, his ability to access weaknesses and attack similar. But that is where the similarity ends. Where Oryn uses his opponent's main weakness to take them down, Haddon seems to use every single one he spots. He leaves his opponents bloodied, broken, and completely destroyed.

My next opponent is called, a short stocky male with nothing but hate in his eyes. But just like every other competitor before, he underestimates me, and the fight ends quickly.

A heavy exhaustion settles over me as I push myself to move through the next couple of rounds. Time passes quickly until all that is left is me, Oryn, and Haddon.

"Oryn and Seren," the guard calls out. It means whoever wins between us will have to fight Haddon.

Oryn quickly moves in front of me, a worried expression shadowing his face.

"Let me do it," he whispers low enough that no one else can hear.

I give him a sharp look, but he doesn't back down.

"I have watched you favor your left side the last few hours. If I have noticed it, so has Haddon."

I glance over at Haddon, watching as he wraps his arms around his opponent's neck and slowly squeezes, his opponent's face quickly turning red and then blue. He doesn't let up, even when his opponent passes out. He catches me watching and winks before dropping the man to the ground.

"I'm not afraid of him," I tell Oryn as we attempt to look like we're sizing each other up.

"I never said you were, but I thought you were smart. Neither of us is trying to win this," he reminds me before he advances on me.

"I can take a hit," I snap as I dodge his poor attempt at an attack.

"So can I," he says.

I raise a brow before striking, hitting him in the side. He grunts and moves a step back but doesn't let up on his incessant need to be the one to sacrifice himself.

"I think you have taken enough hits for today. Besides, *you* need to be the one to follow through on the plan."

My rising ire quickly disappears when I realize he's right. I'm injured, and from the look in Haddon's eyes, he will make sure I will not be leaving my cell for a few days. And unlike the other competitors, who seem to have healers at their beck and call, I will not be so lucky. He will leave me too beaten to continue on with our plan, and Veles will also suffer because of it.

"Fine," I grit out. "But you have to make it look real. They won't believe it otherwise."

Oryn swallows hard but nods. "Just know that I do not want to hurt you."

"If you don't shut up and hit me, I *will* take Haddon on myself," I hiss.

My words are all it takes for Oryn to strike, hitting my broken ribs just hard enough to hurt before twisting and swiping my feet from under me, knocking me down.

My head hits the ground hard, and the world tilts and spins around me.

"Stay down," Oryn whispers, believing me to be faking it. But he doesn't realize I have broken ribs. The hit on them was hard enough to keep me down without having to fake it.

I turn and cough up blood, knowing he will feel guilt for something that he had nothing to do with.

"Oryn wins and will fight against Haddon," the guard calls out, and the others cheer around us.

Ignoring the smug looks from the other competitors and guards, I force myself to my feet. Moving to the nearest wall to help me stay upward, I hold my head high and conceal the pain from my injuries, not allowing any of them to see me weak or to try to use it against me.

Each rattling breath feels like flames of steel, but I force myself to watch the fight, hoping it will take my mind off the sharp pain.

The fight is vicious and brutal and over in minutes. Haddon leaves Oryn completely destroyed, not finishing the fight until Oryn is blackened and bloodied, completely passed out on the ground.

I can't tell if Oryn is faking it, playing along like we planned, but one thing I do know is that he was right. Had I fought Haddon, I would have been too broken to do anything, let alone follow through with our plan.

The two guards who brought me to the trial appear and take me back to my cell. Their shoves and pushes are a welcome distraction that helps me make my way through the palace and back to my cell without passing out from the pain of my injuries.

One last hard shove has me inside my cell, with the steel door slammed shut and locked behind me. I force myself to stay awake long enough to watch the two guards leave before darkness completely envelops my vision and I pass out.

* * *

Waking with a jolt, I sit up straight without thinking, quickly realizing my mistake when my broken ribs protest in pain.

I push myself up, preparing for the trek across the palace to find a bottle of wine, when I hear movement coming toward me.

Listening intently, I notice there are no thumps of footsteps like when the guards announce their arrival to me.

Whoever this is likes their arrival to go unnoticed.

Slowing my breathing, I take stock of my injuries should I need to fight my way out of this.

My ribs are still sharp and painful, but the punctured lung must have nearly healed, as each breath no longer feels like I am swallowing flames.

My body aches and is probably blackened with bruises, but I can move it, which tells me it isn't too broken and it won't be long before I feel like myself again.

Just as I finish inspecting my injuries, the newcomer reveals themselves.

"I hope you have not missed me too much." The Breaker smiles and it slides down my back like ice.

Two men in dark cloaks open my cell and drag me out as another session with the Breaker begins.

CHAPTER 14

Pain holds no favor over one part of my body. It encases it whole, tearing through me like a tidal wave.

The Breaker left hours ago, discarding my crumbled body and splintered spirit on the floor of my cell, his session a payment for my performance in the first trial, which will only worsen should I continue.

They don't want me to fight. They want me weak, feeble. They want me to portray the Sidus they have built up in their twisted minds.

To them, I should not be strong nor a fighter. I should be beneath them, *always*.

The thought alone makes me claw my way to a sitting position.

I may be weakened right now, but not broken. *Never* broken. I will make it through this like I have every other obstacle I have faced before it. With the stubbornness my mother gave me and an unyielding will.

On shaky legs, I force myself to stand, breathing through the phantom pain left behind from the Breaker's session.

With one step in front of the other, I get moving, using my shadows to aid me, unlocking my cell and moving through the passageways up to the palace above.

Clenching my teeth against the sharp pain in my ribs, which are still healing from the trial, I make my way as fast as I can to the location Veles gave me.

Moving through the hallways, I use the hidden coves and dark shadows as my cloak, concealing me when any guards or palace people are near, and swiftly move into the east wing, where the room should be.

It takes longer than it normally would to make it there. But when I arrive, I immediately find myself in a slight predicament.

The hallway along the entire wing seems to be heavily guarded, with a handful of guards stationed throughout it. And the only other way in seems to be through the balcony that sits outside it.

The balcony that sits on a mountain that is a straight drop into the black sea and its dark, tainted waters that bring nothing but death.

I will have to use the nearest ground floor and archways to climb up the side of the first floor and then up again to the small walkway to reach the balcony. All without slipping or falling to my death.

Moving outside to the ground floor, I push every ache and pain in my body out of my mind and focus on moving upward.

Climbing up to the first archway leaves me breathless and my injured ribs throbbing. Glancing upward, I note that I will at least have the trees and vines to conceal me and aid the rest of my journey, but it will not be easy.

From my slightly higher vantage point, I also notice that not many guards are outside. Maybe they thought only a fool would attempt something so dangerous.

A small chuckle leaves my lips. A fool indeed.

Every nerve in my battered body is still tender and painful, so I prepare myself for how hard I will need to push myself to continue upward.

Taking one last moment to gather my strength, I move to the vines and push my body beyond its limits right now to climb up the side of the palace. Each haul upward feels like I'm dragging double my body weight.

My trembling arms grow weaker, forcing me to take another break halfway up.

A rattle starts in my chest with each breath, and I curse myself for most likely further injuring my broken ribs.

With no other choice, I push through it and continue on, making it to the small walkway in double the time it would usually take me. Sitting for another moment, I try to catch my breath once more before dragging my body over the balcony and to the door that leads inside the room.

Finding it slightly ajar, I listen for any sound or movement from inside before moving. After a moment of hearing nothing but the crashing waves below, I head inside.

Taking in the room, my eyes widen at the luxury and extravagance around me.

Thick rugs are laid out on every piece of the floor. There is a huge four-poster bed with a heap of white silk pillows that look like a small haven. The golden embroidered blankets draped over it make me wish I was wrapped within them.

I understand now why Oryn would choose to remain with the Caligo when the luxury the Sidus are afforded is even a fragment of what they see.

Realizing how much time I have wasted gaping at the extravagance, I ignore the rest of the room and glance around for the wine Veles described. He said it will be in a glass bottle, but not like any glass I have seen before, and the wine itself will be shimmery, revealing its uniqueness.

Glancing around, I spot at least a dozen glass bottles placed haphazardly throughout the large room, most of them empty and on their side.

With a sigh, I start searching through any cupboards and dresser. My hand lands on a flimsy piece of silky fabric that looks to belong to an extremely small woman, and I start to wonder what type of room I've come to find myself in.

Placing the flimsy material back where I got it, I move

to the wide oak armoire on the opposite side of the room. But upon opening it, I find it filled with weapons rather than clothes.

Dragging myself away from the beautiful collection of blades and swords, I turn and spot another small chest on the other side of the bed. Moving over to it, I open it and find a case full of glass bottles filled with what I hope is wine.

Picking one up, I raise it to the light and watch with glee as it shimmers.

Feeling a small measure of relief, I turn, ready to head back the way I came, when my gaze is drawn to a pair of golden-brown eyes. His hair is the same color as mine but cut short against his head.

"Well, hello there. What have I done to meet such a beauty this fine evening?" His voice is deep, almost a raspy growl. It is a complete contradiction to his relaxed posture and easy-going expression as he leans against the wall. His shirt pulls tight against his chest, revealing a muscular build, and the look he gives me is anything but innocent, making me think the move is intentional.

He glances from my face to the wine in my hands, his smile only widening. "Or maybe it isn't me you were looking for?" he says, amusement toying with his lips.

I clear my throat, scrambling to think of something that will get me out of this. "I was told this room had the best wine in the palace."

He nods, the amusement now a growing glimmer in

his eyes. "You would be right, but *who* may I ask informed you of this?"

I tighten my hold on the bottle of wine. "A... *friend*." Veles isn't someone I would call a friend yet, but our blood vow made sure we would have to help each other until the deal was complete.

The man straightens up, and I notice that he's at least a head and a half taller than me. His frame is much larger than I initially thought too, having the physique of a warrior.

"This *friend* sent you here. Alone?" he asks as a small frown furrows his brow.

I narrow my eyes on him, wondering where he is going with this. "And if he did?"

"Then *he* is a fool not to have kept you to himself." He steps toward me slowly, the frown clearing from his face as his easy smile reappears.

When he gets close enough, I start sizing him up, my years of training already spotting where I should aim to take him down.

He seems to notice my perusal for exactly what it is, and his brows raise as his entire face transforms into something I can only describe as delight.

"I remember you. You were part of the first trial. You fought with passion and great skill." He clicks his fingers. "Seren. A name and face I should not have forgotten."

My eyes quickly scan him again. He was most definitely not in the arena, nor in any of the seats that surrounded it. I would have remembered someone of his size, his wolfish presence not something I could forget. But I did feel watchful eyes in that shadowed stage.

"How is it that you have no issue with someone slipping into your room without your knowing?" I ask him, wondering why he has not called the guards on me or thrown me out yet. Or at least attempted to take the bottle of wine from me.

He moves closer, and when I don't move a muscle, he continues until he is right in front of me. He studies my face, his eyes growing hooded.

"I find Sidus women to be the most beautiful women I have ever met. Add a woman who knows how to fight, and you have no idea of the power you wield."

I raise a brow. "I am only interested in the wine in my hand."

His smile grows wicked. "Then how about I make you a little offer? A trade of sorts."

I narrow my eyes on the suggestive look he gives me. "What kind of trade?"

"You can have the entire bottle of wine to do with as you will."

"And in return?" I ask.

His eyes dip to my lips, and I know instantly what his request will be.

"In return, all I would ask for is a little... *kiss*."

My spine straightens. "I would rather a different kind of trade, or maybe a deal?"

His chuckle rumbles from his chest as his eyes light

up. “You would choose a deal that could end up being anything over a small kiss with a handsome man?”

“That you would conceive yourself handsome tells me I should instantly choose the deal.”

A peal of laughter resounds around the room, his entire body relaxing as he shakes his head at me with a soft smile.

“Seren. What a joy it is to meet someone who—”

“Doesn’t constantly feed your ego?” I finish his sentence with a mischievous smile, feeling lighter than I have in days.

“How did you manage to get past the guards?” he asks.

“Who says I passed any guards?” I give him my own wicked smile, letting him deduce it himself.

His brows raise as his eyes dart to the door balcony and back to me. “You climbed up the side of the palace? For a bottle of wine?”

“I like a challenge,” I tell him, and that smile of his turns sinful.

“Stay and have a drink with me.”

I shake my head. “I can’t.”

“This friend of yours does not deserve a moment of your time if he made you get him a drink. Stay and I will make it worth your while,” he promises.

“You’re inconceivable.” I move too quickly and wince, hastily trying to cover it with a forced smile.

He quickly loses any amusement. “You’re hurt?”

I tighten my hold on the bottle and shove down the pain once more. "I'm fine."

He frowns and turns to find something in a small drawer in his armoire before moving back to me and placing it in my free hand.

"What is this?" A small dark stone the size of half my hand sits in my palm. On closer inspection, I see hundreds of small glittering colors at the center.

"Just wait," he says and gazes right at me while he grows quiet.

I open my mouth to ask him what he means when I feel it. A soft brush of energy that moves through me, growing warm near my injuries.

My eyes widen as they lock on his when my ribs slowly start to heal, and the aches and pains quickly leave me.

It's a healing stone. A rare gem that is usually hoarded by only those who are lucky enough to find one or trade a hefty bargain for it. The ability to heal the person that holds it will never expire and can heal all types of injuries as long as they are not too close to death.

How he came across one only proves to me how wealthy he must be. I reach out to hand it back to him, but he shakes his head.

"Keep it."

I am not one to accept gifts so easily, but with my last few visits from the guards and the Breaker, I will need all the help I can get. But I am also not willing to pay for it in the manner he may require of me.

"And what would I owe you for this? We have yet to come to a deal for the wine."

"You deserve the wine after the fight and level of skill you displayed earlier, and the stone is a selfish need to ensure you give me another fight." He gives me a wolfish grin, and the look in his eyes tells me he is sincere.

But it still makes no sense for him to give me a healing stone. Something that is not easy to come by and extremely valuable, even among the wealthy.

"Why?" I ask.

His expression turns contemplative as he silently stares at me. "Maybe I would just like to be your friend."

"*Just* my friend?" I ask with a pointed look. He has made it obvious just what type of *friend* he would want in me should I allow it.

A glint of devilment enters his eyes. "I am always open to other suggestions. But for now, yes. And as a gesture to our new budding friendship..." He moves over to the door and speaks to someone outside. I can't hear what they are saying —he's too far away to make it out—but once he is finished, loud thumps sound down the hall, quickly reminding me of the guards stationed directly along this hallway.

He walks back to me with a youthful expression full of recklessness. "Your coast is clear, milady."

"You..." I freeze, glancing over at the door with a raised brow.

"Got rid of the guards?" He smiles with a nod.

"How?" I ask.

"I told them there was a wicked thief attempting to steal from the floor below."

A small smile spreads across my lips. "And they believed you so easily?"

"I can be *very* convincing when I want to be. And if I were to take a guess, by the time they eventually figure out it was all a ruse, I would assume it would buy you enough time to return to your room. Hopefully *alone*." He gives me a hopeful yet pointed look. "With a new bottle of wine in hand."

"I could have just left the way I came." Especially now with most of my injuries healed thanks to the stone.

"But I would hate for anything to happen to you. Especially when I can't wait to see your skill with a weapon in your hand."

I feel excitement bubble up inside me at the thought. "You'll be watching?"

"I wouldn't miss it," he says with a husky voice.

I move to the door, peeking out to find the hallway empty before turning back to find him right beside me.

"Does my new friend have a name?" I ask.

Warmth seeps into his eyes as he watches me. "Asra."

Feeling bold, I lean forward and place a kiss on the side of his cheek. "Thank you, Asra."

I quickly turn and head out, the bottle of wine safely in the palm of my hand.

"Make sure you give them hell," Asra shouts out from behind me.

"Oh, I intend to," I assure him without looking back, and his deep chuckle follows me down the hall.

CHAPTER 15

The halls are left vacant after Asra's little gesture, ensuring I have time to do what Oryn and I had planned.

Stealing a cloak off one of the guards' chairs in the hall, I move with haste, halfway to the other side of the palace when I overhear a guard being invited to a celebratory occasion in Haddon's rooms, and I silently thank the gods for my luck.

I thought I would have to wander the halls for a while before finding his room, but maybe the guards might lead me to it instead.

Following them, I keep my distance and eyes watchful as they make their way to what I hope is Haddon's room. We pass the entrance to the arena before coming to an open corridor.

Loud, boisterous shouts echo across the area, giving me hope that I am exactly where I need to be.

With no way to conceal myself from them, I wait a moment and stay in the hallway, giving it a couple of minutes for the guards to pass through before pulling my hood over me and following them down a dark brick stairwell.

It opens up to a large common room with tables spread out around the space. There are four doors, two on each side of the room. One is open, revealing a sleeping quarter.

There must be over two dozen men and women celebrating, but only some of them are faces I remember from the competition. But there are also guards and many other faces I have not met nor want to if their treatment of the servers is anything to go by.

Some of the servers are dressed in scanty clothing, rushing around tables, quickly refilling drinks and trying to fend off wandering hands. And if the stench of ale permeating the room is anything to go by, I would say most of these people are drunk too. Which should only aid my plan.

I move into the shadows under the staircase, and no one takes notice of me as I disappear from view and glance around the room, looking for my intended target.

My gaze falls on a group of familiar guards and the small scar on one of their necks. His little promise comes to mind, and a small plan to buy me some time starts to form.

A couple of tables over from them, I spot my mark. Levon sits in the middle of the room, with Haddon on his left and a female with long brown hair and revealing clothing to his right. He ignores her completely, while she tries her best to gain his attention. It seems his sole focus is on whatever intense conversation he is having with Haddon. He doesn't look as drunk as the rest, but maybe that is something I can help him with.

I wait and watch for a while longer, letting the light in the room grow dim and the people grow more intoxicated and foolish.

Stealing some bread from the table closest to me, I fill my stomach with it, chewing slowly so as not to make myself sick after not getting the chance to eat in a while.

Pocketing the rest for later, I watch as Haddon stands up and starts swaying clumsily, an obnoxious smile on his face as he and Levon slowly become enraptured by a new dark-haired beauty dancing around them, slowly removing her flimsy clothing.

Seeing an opportunity, I make sure the cloak and hood cover me as I head for the makeshift bar, purposely bumping into one of the servers and mumbling an apology. She drops her tray on the counter and quickly moves to one of the rooms to change.

Glancing around to make sure no one is watching, I take the discarded tray of drinks and swap it out for the wine.

With my tray of wine in hand, I turn to head over to my targets when I notice a discarded small empty vial on the side of a table.

Quickly pocketing it, I move around the tables, coming up behind Levon and Haddon.

While their complete attention is on the practically naked woman, I swap out their drinks and move over to the other table and do the same to the guards' drinks before quickly moving back to my spot under the staircase.

The dark-haired woman seems to have garnered not only Levon and Haddon's attention but the entire room's. At least for those not already passed out across the tables and on the floor.

The female continues to bewitch and seduce them with her beauty and sway of her hips, and the men finally reach for their drinks, knocking back the entire glass as she slowly takes off the last piece of her clothing.

Veles said they would only need a small amount for it to work. But even with the blood bound vow, I didn't trust him. Giving the men an entire glass ensures the plan will work and hopefully make Levon so intoxicated that he will not wake upon feeling my blade against his skin.

My doubts and worries, though, are unfounded when minutes pass and Levon, Haddon, and my newest targets end up so inebriated that they are stumbling about. A few minutes later, they're practically comatose.

The rest of the room slowly dies down. Some of the women move to one of the four rooms, with men who still have some of their senses, while the rest steal the coin owed to them for having to put up with such vulgarity most of the night.

They quickly leave, paying no mind to what lurks between the shadows of the stairway.

I wait until all have left and the only sound around me is the rumbling snores from the passed-out men. Using my shadows, I cast them out around the entire room, blanketing it to near complete darkness before moving.

Moving over to them, I swipe a blade I spotted earlier from a passed-out competitor and pull the vial out of my pocket. Building my shadows around me, I conceal myself among the darkness in case anything goes wrong.

Placing the blade to one of Levon's fingers, I quickly slide the tip of it across his fingertip and pause for a moment, waiting to see if he reacts. But he doesn't move an inch.

I quickly squeeze a few drops of blood into the vial before pocketing it along with the blade and stepping back.

Glancing around, I make sure no one is watching before moving to the table of guards.

It is going to take me most of the rest of the night to carry out what I have in mind for them, but I suppose it is a small blessing that I no longer have to worry about them catching me returning to my cell.

I am also lucky Haddon's rooms are so close to the arena, or this may not have been possible.

With the help of my shadows, I carry the first body to

the staircase and release the rest of my shadows around the room. I keep my quick pace, making sure all the guards get the attention they deserve before making my way to Veles's cell.

Three days is all he said he has left. With nearly two days already passed, it is better not to push our luck and fulfill our side of the deal before anything happens.

Moving down the familiar dark passageways, I walk quickly to the last cell. Veles is already standing in front of the bars, a knowing smile on his face.

"I knew you could do it," he says, his voice assured and full of ease.

I narrow my eyes on him. "Tell me what to do and quickly. I need to get back before anyone notices I'm missing."

"Of course. Pass me the blood and I will do the rest." He reaches a hand out for the vial in my hand but pauses when he remembers the painful bars.

"That's it?" I ask.

"Did you think I would need you also for a sacrifice?" He smirks at me in jest, but it has been a long night already, and I am so tired that I am starting to look forward to the floor of my cold cell.

I pass the vial of blood to him, careful not to touch the bars should they have a similar defensive reaction.

Veles immediately takes the vial and places it to his lips, swallowing every last drop of blood in it before throwing the empty vial against the cell wall, smashing it.

His eyes fill with amusement when he spots my look of disgust. Ignoring me, he starts mumbling something in a strange, lyrical language that soothes something inside me. Quickly becoming entranced by it, I jolt when a loud clang of chains hitting the ground rings out.

The silver carvings on the bars and ground grab my attention as they begin to glow and swirl, getting brighter and brighter. I raise a hand to my eyes to cover them just as a burst of light shoots out around the room before completely dispersing at once.

The cell door grinds open slowly, and Veles steps through, a wide smile on his face.

"They brought me through a hidden tunnel below the cells on the other side of this one," he says, quickly gaining my interest.

"The other side of the palace?" I ask, wondering if it is the same one I am in.

"There is a brown-and-cream door with ornate carvings on one side, then go past a stairwell and another hall before coming to a room of cells. The entrance to the tunnel is a cell itself. It is the first one to the right."

My eyes light up at the mention of the carved door and his description. It sounds too similar to be a coincidence.

"The tunnels lead far enough away from that little block they have on the palace grounds. Your Caligo friend should be able to shadow jump you to and from there, allowing you to come and go as you please."

Hope fills me as my original plans come back to life. I

don't need Oryn to help me shadow jump, but I don't need to tell Veles that either.

Veles takes my hand, and I look up at him to find nothing but gratitude in his eyes.

"I owe you more than you know, but I'm afraid it will have to wait until we meet again."

"But—" Oryn and his part of the deal. "Wait," I call out, but he's already gone, disappearing between the shadows and moving too quickly for my eyes to catch.

"Damn it," I whisper. Oryn isn't going to be happy with this outcome, especially since we are no closer to finding out anything about his missing sister.

Still, I feel hope that this news will aid us both.

I head back toward my cell with renewed vigor. Maybe I will have time to investigate if the hidden tunnel Veles revealed is where I think it may be.

I make it out of the lower-level cells and up into the palace hall where the portraits of old kings and royalty hang, when a tutting sound reaches my ear.

I turn to find a tall stout woman with graying hair glaring at me.

"We are normally here to be seen and not heard," she says as she swiftly walks toward me with purpose.

I glance around, wondering if she has confused me with someone else.

"I—"

"But I can no longer stand that foul stench another moment." She takes hold of my arm and drags me with her.

I'm too shocked to do anything but follow. When I eventually snap out of my stupor, I notice I'm already in a room full of maids and servants. They dip their heads to me, not one bit surprised to see me here.

The woman continues to drag me into a smaller room with a large white tub in the center. It sits beside a large open fire, and its crackling flames are a warm welcome.

Another woman with soft brown eyes appears with a large basin of steaming water. She pours it into the tub and smiles at me before leaving me with the older woman.

"In you go," she says as she shoves me toward the tub while pulling at my clothing.

"What are you trying to—"

"I am trying to wash that foul smell," she says, frowning when I take a step back away from her and her attempt to undress me.

She sighs harshly. "Give me those filthy clothes, and I will wash them while you clean up."

I glance at the steaming tub of water and back at her. "You want me to have a bath?"

"For the sake of the palace, I am willing to beg at this stage." She gives me a genuine look, making me think she is serious.

I raise an arm and wince when the smell hits me, and my eyes begin watering.

Through the tears, I see her nod, a small twinkle in her eyes. "In you go."

I glance over at the tub with longing, its warmth and clean water a luxury not many in the Sidus town ever see. And an opportunity I should not look down on.

Forgoing my sleep for this rare moment will be worth it. Quickly stripping, I slip the healing stone from my pocket and pass my clothes to the woman before stepping into the tub. A gasp of pleasure slips past my lips the moment my feet hit the steaming water.

Once I'm completely inside and the stone is safely hidden in my palm, I submerge myself and bask in the warmth enveloping me whole like a warm hug.

Forgetting about the woman beside me, I am reminded of her presence when she sniffs my clothes and gags.

"Would you rather I burn them?" She gags again but asks sincerely, and I wince at her reaction.

"If you can save them, I would be very grateful." Considering I have nothing else to wear.

She glances at me with a weary sigh. "I will see what I can do." She turns and heads out of the room without another word, leaving me to have this strange yet wonderful moment by myself.

Once I've enjoyed the feel of warmth, I hide the stone in the water by my leg and start scrubbing the grime off every inch of my body, reminding myself of the cell and small hole I have to freshen up in. I scrub harder, knowing the only water I will have after this is the small cup the guards give me each morning with my slop. And with basic needs coming first, I will not have this luxury again anytime soon.

I make sure the foul stench is completely gone from my skin before moving to my hair. It takes double the time to attempt to untangle and clean it, but its pale blonde color soon returns.

Once I'm completely clean, I glance around the room for something I can throw over myself while I wait for the woman to return. But I don't need to wait long, as she returns with a robe and plate full of warm food in her hand. It reminds me of the bread I stole earlier, which is most likely wet now or has been thrown out.

My stomach rumbles as I imagine the taste of the meats and fruits on it. I feel for the stone and hide it in my palm once more.

The woman places the food aside and helps me out of the tub and into the robe.

"Eat and one of the girls will be in to sort out that hair of yours." She frowns while glancing at my head, but all I can think about is the plate of food that I am allowed to eat. I slip the stone into my robe and head straight for it as she leaves the room. I devour it as if it is the first and last thing I have ever eaten. Every bite is heavenly, and I decide that I am not leaving here without finishing every last morsel.

The girl with the soft brown eyes from earlier returns and smiles at me before motioning for me to turn around on my seat. I do as she says, too engrossed in finishing my food to question her motives.

But they become clear when I feel the bristles of a brush attempt to slide through my mangled hair. It takes a few tries, but eventually she manages to detangle the mass of knots in my hair.

"Your hair is beautiful. I can braid it if you would like?" She moves around me, and I look up at her own beautifully braided brown hair before nodding.

"If it is not too much trouble?" I ask, wanting to stay in this moment a little while longer.

"Not at all." The woman starts braiding my hair quickly, her soft temperament not bothered by my silence. The older woman returns just as she is finishing up.

"Thank you," I tell her, and she smiles and dips her head to me before leaving.

The older woman steps up to me, a look on her face that demands I listen to her.

"My name is Visha. Should you ever need food, come here and tell them I sent you. A plate will always be ready for you should you need it."

She glances down at my body as I stand up. "You are too thin. You need a bit of meat on you if you are to continue on in the competition."

My spine straightens at her words. "You know who I am?"

The woman gives me a knowing smile. "The Sidus competitor?" She nods. "Yes. You are a great fighter and deserve your place here. Do not let anyone tell you otherwise." She pats my shoulder and hands me my clean and mended clothes before heading toward the door.

"Thank you, Visha," I whisper, hearing a soft "You're welcome" as she disappears.

After a warm bath, clean clothing, a full stomach of food, and a healing stone tucked safely in my pocket, I head back toward my cell with a renewed sense of energy.

Passing by a long hallway with large columns, I spot a view of the outside sky, and it draws me to it.

Moving to one of the columns, I lean against it and watch the upcoming sunrise and first signs of dawn slowly rise in the sky, casting its light across the darkness and bringing with it a sense of hope for the new day.

It's tranquil. Serene. The silence a soft reminder to not take moments like this for granted. I'm so lost in my own thoughts and the alluring view that I don't notice someone else in the hall until he is right beside me.

My eyes clash with ones so silver and gray, it's as if a storm is swirling inside them. Wrenching my gaze away from the pull they evoke, I take in the rest of him. He is young, possibly only a few years older than my nineteen years. He has short black hair and sun-kissed skin, and his clothes are plain and dark, as if he is attempting to conceal himself and blend in with everyone around him. But nothing about him blends in. From his strong jawline to his broad shoulders, it is clear he is every inch the warrior. And someone I should clearly stay far away from. Even if he is the most attractive man I have ever met.

"You are the Sidus competitor," he says with a deep, husky voice that sends a warm shiver down my spine.

"Is that all I am to be known as? Not just an average competitor?" I quirk a brow, in too good a mood to fight with anyone unless absolutely necessary.

"From what I hear, there is nothing average about you, Seren." He says my name with a familiarity I do not understand.

"And do you also have a name, or should I just call you a Caligo lord?" He can't be a guard. There is an air of wealth, power, and gracefulness that the Caligo guards could never imitate.

"Kestral," he says. "Besides, not many Sidus enter the competition; I meant it more as a compliment than anything else."

I wonder if he knows the real reason not many Sidus ever enter the guard's competition, especially the last few years. But I find no deception in his eyes, just a spark of interest and warmth.

I turn back to the view, and a glint of light catches my eye, drawing my attention further to my right and over in the direction of what must be the Caligo city.

"What is the Caligo city like?" I ask him, wondering if there are more kind Caligo people like Visha and Oryn. Would they let the Sidus come to their city if they knew the truth? Would they stand by or join us in the fight against the dark creatures or watch on like the Caligo guards?

Kestral moves a step closer to me with a small frown on his face.

"You've never been?" he asks.

I shake my head with a small smile, not willing to reveal the truth to him if he doesn't already know. There is already a deep sadness in his eyes that I do not wish to add to.

He glances in the direction the glint of light came from. "It is bright. Similar to the palace with its white and gold. There are bakeries, bookstores, and many clothes shops with every type of fabric you can imagine." His eyes travel down the line of my body, leaving a trace of warmth behind as his voice trails off. He blinks and frowns as if just realizing something that bothers him.

"You have lived here your entire life. You should see more of your kingdom," he says.

"Maybe one day." One day when the shadows and light join together and become one. Until then, I will just have to enjoy these moments as the sun rises high above the mountain to shine its light among the shadows.

"Don't leave it too long," he says, a hint of warning in his tone.

It makes me turn to him.

"Life is short. You should enjoy it as much as possible," he says with a soft voice and sadness in his eyes before glancing down at his hands.

It draws my attention to the item he is holding. "Is

that a book?" I haven't gotten the chance to read many as of late, but I have a small collection beneath my bed at home. One my mother spent years trying to attain for me.

"Just some silly old rhymes." He clears his throat, closing the pages, and it immediately piques my interest.

"Read me one?" I ask.

He glances up at me with a raised brow. But there is a glint of amusement in his eyes that wasn't there before.

"Is that a request or a demand?"

"You choose. But read it either way," I tell him with a smirk. He shakes his head at me, but whatever sadness he felt moments ago is no longer visible in his eyes. And he starts to read.

But the more he reads, the more somber I feel. The rhyme is sorrowful, dark and full of despair. There is no happiness or hope to grasp, just a never-ending torment of suffering and pain.

I'm still waiting for that sliver of hope and happy ending when he stops all of a sudden and looks up at me.

"That's all of it?" I ask, feeling stunned.

He smiles at me, but it's not a happy smile. It's filled with sadness once more, making my heart twist. He glances down at the book in his hand and swallows hard before closing it.

"Not all endings are meant to be happy. Some just are. Some just exist to *be*."

“That sounds very dark and extremely sad,” I tell him, my sliver of happiness shriveling up after hearing it.

“There is beauty in sadness and among the darkness,” he says, and I can see in his eyes that he believes it too.

“There is also hope and new beginnings. Try not to forget that,” I tell him, and his eyes widen a fraction. It is the only acknowledgment I get as I take one last glance at the view.

I turn to head back to my cell, even when his presence draws me to stay. But as soon as I turn away from him, I immediately spin back around.

He pauses with a frown. “What—”

“Ah, there you are. I was wondering...”

My eyes widen, and something in Kestral’s eyes flash as if in understanding. He quickly moves, using his body to block me from view, his back to mine as he acknowledges Lieutenant Amaro.

“Lieutenant, I will discuss anything you need in a moment, once I finish up here.”

“Of course,” Amaro says, and I hear the irritation in his tone just before his footsteps move farther and farther away.

I turn when I hear his footsteps disappear, but another moment passes before Kestral turns around to me. Not realizing how close he was, I’m a step closer, leaving just an inch between us. My eyes find his once more as they draw me in and hold me captive. The silver in them swirls, and something warm jolts through my chest.

As if he's just realizing how close we are, his eyes widen, and he quickly moves a step back before clearing his throat.

"I could see you didn't particularly want to run into the lieutenant," he says as he searches my face for something.

Shaking off the strange moment, I give him a forced smile. "I seem to have ended up on his bad side."

"He has another?" Kestral raises a brow and gives me a wry smile.

A small chuckle leaves my lips. "What type of position do you hold that allows you to dismiss the lieutenant so easily?"

His smile only widens, a glint of amusement filling his eyes as he stays silent. When it is obvious that he isn't going to reveal anything, I take a step around him.

"I should get back." The cold cell is the last place I want to be, but my time here was a means to an end and nothing more. No matter how much those stormy eyes call to me.

"Good luck tomorrow," he says, bringing a smile to my face, but I don't turn back around as I leave the hallway or when I disappear into the shadows of the palace. But the smile never leaves my face the entire journey down to my cell.

Now that I don't have Veles's life on the line, I can focus back on the trials and my original plan. I just need to find that hidden tunnel Veles described. Everything now hinges on finding it.

I move down below the palace to the strange door that lies not too far from the stairwell and my cell room. I take a closer look at the carvings that crawl up it and hope that my instinct is right and that this is the door Veles recounted.

Moving down the stairway and through the hall, I head inside my cell block, ready to inspect the first cell on the right, when I hear movement from behind me.

Quickly making my way toward my cell, I lock myself inside and check to make sure the healing stone is still in my pocket before I turn and silently wait for the newcomer to reveal themselves.

CHAPTER 16

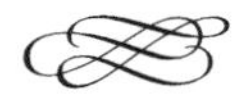

The guard with interest in his blue eyes from before comes with a plate of food and water, and not just gray-looking slop. He dips his head to me before unlocking the cell and reaches a hand out to pass my tray and drink to me rather than throw it to me on the floor.

I eye him warily before reaching out to take it. Once I do, he steps back and out of the cell, giving me my space.

"Finish what you can, and then I will take you to the next competition." He turns and looks ahead, attempting to give me some form of privacy.

"*Straight* to the competition?" I ask, wondering if maybe his kindness comes with a catch.

I spot the frown from his side profile before he turns to look at me. "I have no hidden agenda, nor do I wish you harm. You may choose not to believe me, and I wouldn't blame you, based on your ill-treatment here.

But I, for one, hope you continue to do well and succeed." With a dip of his head, he turns back to his position, leaving me to think on his words.

I never truly assumed all Caligo were bad, but I didn't have the greatest opinion of them. After all, I only met the ones who were cruel, rude, or outright hostile.

But after coming to the palace, I've realized that some Caligo are just like the Sidus, warm and welcoming.

The Caligo guards have become a completely separate entity to that realization. There is not one of them that has proven to me they have an ounce of compassion or kindness in them.

Until him. The blue-eyed guard in front of me.

I doubt I will ever be able to fully trust any Caligo guard, but maybe I can try to not assume the worst of all of them based on the ones I have met.

"I don't see a friendship ever forming between us, but maybe we can start off being allies of sorts," I tell him while starting to dig into my food, not wanting to waste it even though my belly is still full from the meal Visha made for me.

"I am not one to sit and braid hair, though yours looks particularly nice this morning." He turns his head and gives me a small pointed look. "Visha wishes you a good day and good luck in the competition."

My smile widens as he turns back to gaze ahead, but I spot his expression as it slightly softens.

With a seed of trust, I sit down and eat another delicious meal, knowing I will not be offered good food like this often.

Once I'm finished, I thank him, and he gets rid of my tray before we head up into the palace above.

Just before we come to the arena, he slows down. "Good luck today. They might try to push you. Be on your guard at all times."

His warning is not needed, but this time it is appreciated, knowing he means it. I thank him once more as we turn into the open arena, and he freezes.

There is already a commotion, with groups of people either laughing toward the little display or frowning in disgust.

We move a little closer, and I get a better look at my handiwork.

The guards are all wearing the women's flimsy clothing I acquired around Haddon's common room and are all tied up in precarious positions. Still in slumber and unaware of their predicament, they're positioning themselves a little more provocatively as they reach toward one another in what I can only assume is a search for warmth.

The guard beside me dips his head as he moves closer to me. "Remind me never to get on your bad side," he whispers with amusement in his tone.

My answering smile is all the reply he needs as he shakes his head and leaves me with one more "Good luck."

One of the higher-ranking guards pushes his way

through the growing crowd and freezes with horror when he finds his precious guards wrapped around one another.

Quickly snapping out of his frozen state, he moves swiftly and kicks the guards awake. They rouse with a grunt, bleary eyes, and a slow growing panic that is quickly followed by revulsion once they realize what they are wearing and where they are.

The guard who woke them calls on some of the other guards to drag them out of here. The looks of chagrin from each of them as they are yanked and shoved out of the arena, their heads bowed in shame, is worth the lack of sleep and every aching muscle from moving their bulky bodies around.

Once they are gone, the guard calls for order as Alderic and a group arrives.

My stomach drops as I realize the lieutenant will be watching the second trial today. They take their place in front of the shadowed stage.

I glance around, catching a few looks from the competitors, some with disgust and abhorrence in their eyes, but many with a glint of respect. Some even nod to me in greeting, making me wonder if I should be worried with this newfound regard.

Oryn and Nevan arrive just as Alderic takes to the small dais. Oryn glances around and spots me, quickly making his way over.

“Welcome. I hope you all are well rested and ready for another trial,” Alderic starts. “You will be paired up again, but this time based on how well you did in the last trial. This trial will test your level of skill with weapons. Try not to kill your opponent, but everything else goes."

I ignore the rest of Alderic's speech to check Oryn for any of the injuries he had the last time I saw him. But there are no cuts or bruises anywhere on him.

"You look much better than the last time I saw you," I tell him as more of a question than a statement.

He glances down at his body with a frown. "Oh, I had a healer look after me."

"Good," I tell him and mean it. I consider him a friend and would not like to see him in any pain.

Taking a deep breath, I prepare myself before I break the news to him about Veles.

"I managed to achieve our little goal last night," I tell him.

Oryn's eyes widen as he turns to me. I keep my head faced forward so as not to draw any attention to us.

"And?" he asks, the impatience in his voice evident.

"And he thanked me and said he would be in contact. That there were many things he needed to do first." I chance a glance at him and watch as he turns ahead, clenching his jaw and fisting his hands.

"I knew we shouldn't have trusted him," he grits out.

"*You* are not the one who did a blood-binding vow with him," I remind him, and he winces.

Shaking his head, he sighs to himself before moving a step closer to me and lowering his voice.

"I have been searching the palace every chance I get, but I have yet to find anything."

"Maybe we are looking in the wrong place?" I tell him. The palace is a labyrinth of halls and passageways. I doubt we would be able to search them all in the time we have here.

He glances ahead with a faraway look on his face. "I just need a clue or a lead. *Something*."

"What you need is to focus on this trial. Let us figure out the rest after," I remind him, hoping he doesn't get inside his head too much and end up maimed because of it.

He nods his head as a reply, heeding my warning, and we both catch the end of Alderic's speech as a wall of weapons is laid out to the side. He wishes us good luck before moving into the shadows.

A guard goes around dividing the large group into two. The strongest fighters are told to take a seat, while the less skilled fighters are paired up and told to gather around the edges of the arena.

The group I end up in is the less skilled one, making me chuckle quietly to myself. The competitors around me frown, glancing from one another over to the other group.

Only one is bold enough to question the guard's decision.

"Sir? I think there has been a mistake. Seren should be over there." He points over to the stronger fighters. "Should she not?"

"She will fight who we say," the guard growls out, giving him a sharp look that quickly shuts him up.

"Yes, sir," he replies before moving off to the side with his pair.

I glance over at Oryn and his group and catch his frown as he watches me, but I expected some sort of foul play. They were never going to make it easy for me, or equal for that matter.

If I were to guess, their hopes would be to attempt to exhaust and weaken me by forcing me to fight the less skilled fighters, hoping when they make me fight the stronger ones, that I will make a mistake and fail.

But what they don't realize is the gift they have just given me. A day of fighting is something I will always look forward to.

The first pair from my group choose their weapons. One chooses a long wooden spear with a steel tip, while the other chooses an axe. They take their positions and begin.

Sizing each other up, they give each other enough distance before attacking. The one who chose the axe is larger than the one with the spear. He quickly gains distance on him, his size giving him an advantage to push his opponent back.

Though their fighting is clumsy with an attempt at brutality, they make too many mistakes to show any real level of skill.

The smaller man manages to gain some distance from the other, and with the spear in his hand, he directs it with a force and strength I didn't think he had inside him.

A scream of pain rings out as the spear pierces the other competitor's thigh, bringing him to his knees.

"Seren will fight the winner," a guard announces.

Without question, I head to the wall of weapons and choose a long sword, testing its weight in my hands before moving to the center of the arena.

The man retrieves his bloodied spear as a couple of guards cart the injured competitor away. He stands across from me, his face growing ashen.

"Begin," the guard shouts out.

From watching the previous fight, I can tell his plan is to try to get me at a distance, his only true skill to wield the spear at a long range. Before he gets the chance to move, I whip forward and slice the wooden shaft in half before sliding my blade across the arm that holds it.

My aim is precise, just deep enough to make him drop the head of the spear and reach for the wound to try to staunch the bleeding.

A guard quickly shuffles him off before another two are paired off and another fight begins.

Both use long swords, their skill slightly above the last pair, but both focus on the strength of their attack, not thinking beyond it. It makes it a quick fight, with the bulkier one managing to catch the other unaware.

Instead of giving him a slice across his skin for warning, he chops off his entire hand with a savage smile. The screams from the man bellow out around the arena while deep chuckles follow it.

The man is carted off without so much as a blink of sympathy from the others.

"Seren will fight the winner."

Again, my name is called to fight. But I already know the game they are playing and assume it will continue on until they deem otherwise.

I choose a short blade this time and move to stand across from my new opponent. I eye him a little more thoughtfully. He didn't have to maim the other competitor. A healer cannot fix something that has been completely severed, and it will more than likely remove him from the competition completely. He chose to make this personal, and because of it, so will I.

His bulky form towers over me as he gives me a toothy grin full of arrogance. His dark brown eyes size me up like he thinks he can easily break me, but he has forgotten that the bigger you are, the harder you fall.

He lunges forward with his sword, but I bend low to avoid it, spin my blade, and use the hilt to slam into his left knee. A resounding crack follows a grunt of pain as he drops forward. I twist my blade to my other hand and slam it into his back just where one of his kidneys sits. An unlawful howl of agony bellows out as he curls into a ball on the ground, and a pool of blood begins to form around him.

The man will be passing red for a while until the healers figure out how to fix him.

The guards snarl at me as they remove him, while a couple of the competitors dip their heads in respect.

Seren... Seren... Again and again, I am called to fight another winner, but again and again, they quickly fall, the guards growing more and more agitated while the lieutenant looks on with a murderous glare.

"Stay where you are," the guard growls at me before he heads over to the last of the group and says something to them that makes them frown, but they nod, abiding by whatever order he has given them.

A dozen competitors choose their weapons and step in front of me, all ready to fight.

I throw my last weapon to the ground, and the guard gives me a smug look.

"Giving up already?"

Without a word, I walk over to the wall of weapons, choosing two curved daggers before moving back to my spot.

Twirling them in my hands, I give the guard a wicked smile. "Not even close."

Around me, the competitors grow pale as the guard clenches his jaw.

"Begin," he shouts, and they all attack at once.

I slice, thrust, and slash my way through half of the group while lunging, ducking, and swirling around the rest. I work through the rest of the group with ease, my body moving from muscle memory to do what it is trained to do.

As the last competitor falls, I am greeted by complete silence.

Minutes is all it has taken to finish the fight as I pluck my dagger from the thigh of the fallen man beside me. He grunts in pain as I move past him and take up my spot once more, with a raised brow aimed at the lieutenant.

Instead of more fights, a break is called, with the lieutenant meeting his men for a heated discussion.

Oryn makes his way over to me. But before he gets to me, three guards block him, their focus directly on me.

CHAPTER 17

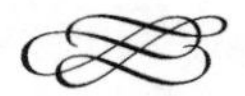

"Come with us."

Nothing about their smug looks eases my twisting stomach, my instinct telling me something isn't right.

They quickly bring me back to my cell. Before I get the chance to figure out what they have planned, a boot slams into my back, and shadows slash out and encase me. I guess their little warning about not using shadows will be overlooked this time.

"This is for your little display."

Their shadows raise me up off the ground before slamming me into the cell wall, and the air is ripped from my lungs just as I'm thrown to the ground.

While their shadows hold me down, boots and punches slam into my chest, stomach, back, and legs. The only place they don't touch is my face, leaving all evidence of their attack anywhere my skin is clothed.

I try to focus on my raspy breaths, each inhale and shaky exhale, and not on the sound of their punches as they hit my skin or the burn and agony they leave behind. Nor how their thick boots slam into my back and legs, surely leaving an imprint. By the time they start to ease up, my entire body throbs with pain.

"That should be enough." One last final boot slams down on my leg, and a whimper escapes my lips.

"Five minutes and we'll be back to collect you for your next round in the trial. Enjoy your *break*." Chuckles echo around me as their footsteps move farther and farther away until I'm left on my own.

With a trembling hand, I reach for the healing stone in my pocket, but my heart drops when I find it missing.

My stomach churns when I realize that I am going to have to fight the other competitors, those more skilled and rested, while I'm injured and in agony.

I want to break. To split open and seep out onto the floor. But this pain will pass, and I will rise like I have every other time. I can't let them get to me. Not now, nor ever, and definitely not when I am at my weakest.

I claw a hand into the dirt and then another before pushing up on unsteady hands. A sharp bolt of pain slices down my back, ripping the breath from me once more. But I take my time, breathing through it, and it passes.

I push to my knees next, grateful when neither is broken or seriously injured, just heavily bruised and battered. Crawling over to the cell door, I use the bars to drag the rest of my body upward.

Eventually I get to my feet and nearly fall once more as a jolt of sharp pain shoots up through my right foot and pulses around my ankle. I test it again, putting a little pressure on it when it happens again, making me gasp.

I glance down and see the swelling forming around it and realize with dread that it must be broken or severely sprained.

Holding on to the cell door, I test my other foot, but it's not as bad as my right.

Thudding boots and deep chuckles move toward me. I push away from the cell door and straighten my body, gritting my teeth against the pain from my broken ankle.

"Time is up, Sidus," the guard sneers.

I move slowly and with a limp to avoid putting too much pressure on my right foot. But the guards seem to dislike my slow movements, as one shoves me forward.

I gasp, catching myself with my bad foot and most likely injuring it further.

Clenching my fists, I dig my nails into my hands and move forward, one step at a time until I arrive at the arena.

I ignore the guards and their whispered warnings before they leave.

Oryn spots me at the edge of the arena and comes straight over to me.

"Do you have tape?" I ask him, knowing what I must do if I want to make it through this alive.

"Yes, I think—"

"Get it for me... *please*." I grit against the pain and push it down once more.

"Seren—"

I shake my head at him as my eyes blur. "Don't. Just do as I ask."

With a frown, he gets me the tape and I quickly get to work, wrapping it around both ankles to make sure they don't assume my weakness.

"Cover me," I tell Oryn.

"What—"

I pull up my shirt and he spins around.

"I'm sorry, I..." He clears his throat before growing quiet.

I wrap my stomach and quickly pull down my shirt before anyone comes in from behind me.

"Thank you," I tell him, and he turns around. I throw him what is left of the tape and hope he doesn't mind that I used most of it.

"Seren, what happened—"

"Round two will begin soon." Alderic claps his hands to gain everyone's attention. "As these competitors are more advanced in skill, the winner of each fight will continue on to the next one. If your name is called, come to the center and choose your weapon."

"It doesn't matter. Let us just get through this," I tell

him and ignore his deepening frown and growing worry to focus on the guard as he calls out the first pairing.

"Vardan and... *Seren*."

My stomach drops and my gaze finds the lieutenant's as he smiles at me. A vicious, cruel thing that only adds fuel to the burning flame slowly building inside me.

They have planned it so I must fight each skilled competitor, should I win each one. But they have also attempted to weaken and break me to ensure I don't.

But I will *never* give up fighting, and it is something they will all come to learn.

The first fight doesn't last long, and even though I end up with more injuries, I win. The next four fights are the same, each one more draining than the last, but my foot holds along with my other injuries.

But the longer I am forced to fight with my injuries, the more foolish mistakes I make.

I fall to the ground a third time but push myself up once again, blocking another attack before giving myself some ground to try to gain some footing between us.

With my injured foot, I am slower than normal, so I counter it by attempting to be smarter than the other competitors. I watch my opponents, finding their weaknesses and countering their moves before they get a chance to cause any true damage.

It works well for me, but I know I won't be able to keep this up and block out the pain for much longer.

"Finish her," someone screams from the sidelines, their voice filled with nothing but hate.

They do not know me. Not one of them. And yet they aim their complete and utter hatred directly at me. They *want* to see me in pain. To suffer and watch on with glee.

A numbness blankets my every pain and ache, my body becoming something other. A blinding rage slides over me as something snaps inside me.

No more games. They want to take me down, then I'll drag them with me. Everywhere already hurts, the pain having no bounds or limits over my body, but my soul and spirit is still intact.

Covered in blood and with more injuries than I can count, I manage to make it through as one of the last three competitors. Haddon chooses to go up against me next, a savage smirk on his face, and the guards allow it without question.

Haddon fights with a skill not many have. But his bloodthirst for hurting others and his savage cruelty will only be his downfall.

He lunges forward and attacks me with purpose, but I manage to intercept him. He tries to maneuver me into a tight spot, but I duck low and slash his thigh, moving back to the center of the arena. It barely deters him, only making his savage smile widen.

He lunges forward again, but I miss my stepping and he grabs hold of my arm and twists it, snapping my wrist and quickly unarming me, throwing my blade to the side.

I stumble away from him, grabbing my wrist as it throbs. Hissing through the pain, I readjust my grip and quickly unwrap some of the tape from my good ankle to use it on my wrist.

Before I get the chance to prepare myself, he attacks without mercy while I defend with everything I have. But he manages to shove me to the ground once more.

Not ready to give up, I grab a handful of dirt with my good hand and wait until he is close enough before throwing it straight into his eyes.

While he's momentarily blinded, I roll to the side and grab my sword from the ground before getting up and spinning around to him. I barely manage to block the blade aimed for my head but luckily manage it.

Before he aims his sword toward me again, I slice mine across his back and spin it before slamming the hilt of it into the back of his head. Just as he falls forward, I move in front of him, grab a handful of his hair, and slam his head down onto my bent knee as hard as I can. A crack sounds out as I break his nose, and he drops to the ground with a thump.

The silence in the arena is deafening as everyone's gaze veers from Haddon's passed-out form to me.

It takes a minute for the guards to collect themselves, and I use it to refocus and center myself, pushing my injuries and pain to the back of my mind for just a little longer.

"Oryn and Seren," the guard growls out before they take Haddon away with more care than any other.

Oryn steps up in front of me, and his gaze trails over me, his eyes widening in shock the more he looks.

"Fight," I tell him, readying my stance.

"You're injured." He moves a step back, and the look in his eyes tells me he is about to forfeit and ruin everything.

"Fight me or lose and you will *never* find your sister," I grit out, reminding him of our purpose here.

A spark of determination enters his eyes as he finally attacks. But I misjudge my stepping, foolishly letting my guard down with him, and he twists, sliding the blade straight through my stomach before yanking it out.

His eyes widen in horror as I drop to my knees and fall to the side, darkness quickly clouding my vision.

He drops the sword and starts toward me, but the guards come quick and pull him to the side to congratulate him. I watch on, no longer able to move as the guards drag my body carelessly back to my cell, my entire body blanketed in pain.

Slamming the cell door shut with a lock, they leave me to my torment and suffering.

Wave after wave of thick agony envelops my body. It slowly tries to drag me into its darkness, but I fight to stay above the surface.

A small glint of a light catches my eye, drawing me to it, and my eyes widen slightly when I spot the healing stone on the other side of the cell.

It must have fallen from my pocket when the guards attacked me earlier. If I can just reach it, I will soon be free of this agony.

I try to move a single finger, but no part of my body

will listen. Everything is too painful, too sore. The numbness has completely left me, only to reveal the piercing slash and burn that radiates throughout every part of me.

My body grows heavy, and I know I need to move it, the warning thrumming through the air around me before crawling down my spine like ice.

Clawing my fingers through the dirt, I get one arm steady under me before doing the same to the other.

Using my arms to crawl, I slowly make my way over to the stone, my body giving out just a foot in front of it. Not ready to give up just yet, I reach out and push myself, my fingertips sliding off the stone before it moves toward me.

I wrap my fingers around it, drawing it closer to my body just as the darkness drags me under.

CHAPTER 18

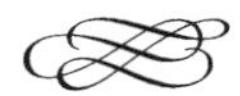

I jolt awake, my body still on the floor of the cell but now in a curled position. I should be aching from the awkward angle alone, but with the smooth healing stone still tightly encased in my hand, I'm completely painless, my injuries fully healed and my body well rested.

Unfurling from my spot, I place the healing stone in my pocket and sit up, testing my upper body before moving to a stand to inspect my injured foot.

No shooting pain begins when I put full pressure on it, and everything seems to have mended well and back to normal.

Untying the tape from my wrist, I twist it to ensure the tape wasn't the thing that was making it feel better. But just like everything else, it is thoroughly healed.

Removing the rest of the tape from my ankle and upper stomach, I check my body over and find not one bruise, the only evidence of my previous injuries, the dry blood now caked all over my clothes and skin. That and the large hole in my shirt.

Oryn's face flashes before me, his look of horror reminding me of our last match. I hope he knows that I take none of this personally, and it was only through my own foolish mistake that I managed to get hurt.

Pushing it to the side of my mind, I unlock my cell with my shadows and slip from it, heading straight for the small enclosed cell on the right side of the room. I listen for any other sound before pushing the door forward and pausing, my stomach dropping.

It is just a normal cell. There is no other door or way out. Just a simple dirty space similar to my own. I mentally curse myself for blindly trusting in Veles.

Moving into the cell room, I glance around it, making sure I thoroughly search everywhere before I assume my last piece of hope has completely gone.

I turn to check the side of the cell when my foot catches on something. Bending down, I wipe some of the dirt away, only to find a line of dark steel about an inch in width.

Swiping away more dirt, I follow it and it leads me to the back of the cell, where it meets the wall before disappearing.

Reaching out, I search the brick wall for any other steel lines or clues to what it is, when one of the bricks loosens and begins to move on its own.

A rumble sounds out as the bricks on the floor

beneath it shudder and slightly shake. I jump back a step as they gather together and roll under to reveal a tight small passageway downward.

Relief seeps through me as I glance down into the passage and spot what looks to be the start of a tunnel.

But before I make my way down it, I need to ensure that the guards are not going to find me missing from my cell or figure out that I am aware of this secret tunnel.

I glance around, trying to figure out how to reseal it first. I start pressing random bricks across the back wall before moving to another until eventually something clicks and a brick in the corner moves. The soft rumbling starts again, and the passageway quickly closes up.

Slipping out of the cell room and up into the palace, I spot a mirror and freeze, shocked to find the person staring back at me. I have fully healed, but my pallor and blood-streaked face make me look like I have been to battle and back.

I need to clean off this blood, but I can't afford the luxury of a bath now or the time it would take to have one.

Heading toward Visha's quarters, hoping to ask for some wet cloths and a jug of water, I run into the girl who braided my hair. She stops in her tracks, her mouth dropping open when she spots me.

"Oh my," she whispers as she makes her way over to me before walking around me.

"Are you badly injured? Should I call a healer?" she asks with alarm in her voice.

"No. No, I'm fine. I have been healed already; this is just..." I glance down at myself, frowning when I do not know what else to say to her that would not reveal the situation I'm in without wasting more time. "If you have a change of clothes I could borrow, I would very much appreciate it."

With a sad look in her eyes, she nods and takes my hand, pulling me into a room down at the end of the hall. There is a small bed to the side, a chest of drawers, and a long mirror, but nothing else inside.

"Let me run you a bath," she pleads.

"I'm afraid I don't have the time for one," I tell her and hope she understands with the look I give her.

She nods at me before turning and leaving. A couple of minutes pass, and I decide that it is better to have the time I do than worry about how I look. I still need to check on the guards.

I head for the door when she rushes in with a steaming hot basin of water in her hands, small white cloths draped across her arms, and dark clothing thrown over her shoulder.

"Here. Wash and change out of those. Whatever it is you must do, I can see it is important. I will make sure your clothes are cleaned for you."

Emotion clogs my throat, burning my eyes at her kindness. "How can I—I have no way to pay you. But if there is something I can do to thank you—"

She shakes her head, stopping me, and places the basin and cloths on the chest of drawers before coming over to me. She starts sizing the dark clothing up against me, nodding when it looks like they will fit.

"No payment is necessary. I know the guards do not treat you well because of what you are. I want you to know that not all of us are like that. My name is Isolde. Come to me whenever you need anything, me or Visha, and do not be a stranger."

Warmth expands in my chest. "Thank you, Isolde."

She gives me a soft smile before leaving me to it. Stripping out of my clothes, I place the stone beside me as I quickly scrub my body of all the blood and use the floral-smelling soap she left for me, smiling at her thoughtfulness. I change into the new clothes, slipping the healing stone into my pocket, noting how they fit my body like they were made for me, before placing the dirty pile on the chest of drawers.

Slipping out of the room, I head to the guards' normal spots but eventually find them passed out in Haddon's quarters once more, the entire room stinking of ale.

Haddon still made it to the top three, with Oryn coming out the winner and me second. Even though it wasn't a fair fight, I managed to stay in the top three, hopefully ensuring my place in the next trial.

I grab a discarded cloak on the back of one of the chairs and make my way back to my cell, hoping that the guards think I am too injured to move and that a visit is the last thing on their minds, especially in their drunken state. I should be able to leave for a few hours before anyone notices my missing presence.

Using the dark cloak as my decoy, I stuff it with dirt and place it at the back of my cell, hoping anyone sent to check on me would not bother to get too close to see what it is.

Locking my cell behind me, I head for the secret tunnel. Pushing the bricks reveals the passageway, and I quickly enter it, following it down to the tunnel, which opens up into a cavern entranceway, the ceiling a death-trap of large spiked structures ready to fall on any unsuspecting visitors.

My steps are soft and mindful as I move through it to another smaller opening that leads into a wide oval chamber, the ceiling high enough to fit a dozen giants.

A glint of gold hits my eye, and I move toward it, finding a line of it carved into the wall. I follow the line with my fingers and around a large rock, coming to a stop at the sight before me.

Nine large crumbling statues stand in large hollow spaces in the walls of a huge chamber. Each one looks as if it is carved from the wall itself.

I don't know many stories of the old gods, but if I were to take a guess, I would say I am in the presence of them now. Or at least their statues.

At the center of the statues, raised higher than the rest, is a female goddess. She holds a basin in her hands, filled with water. It overflows out to the gods and goddesses around her before falling into a hole in the center of them all.

To her left is another goddess, her beauty something that radiates out around her. To her right, a god that looks more like a warrior ready for battle but with kind eyes.

The others are spread out around the room. A god with an oval eye above his head, a female with a crow on her shoulder, a horned god that looks more beast than man, a goddess with three great birds surrounding her, a god with a flaming sword that sits upon a huge horse, and the last, a god with an instrument of some kind in one hand and a book in the other.

With one last glance around, I make my way past them, but it is as if their eyes follow me, and a chill slides down my back as I move on.

The room next to it opens up to another cavern large enough to hold an entire army. There are no statues with eyes that follow me, but there is a circular carving of a tree with deep roots. The branches reach upward and twist and turn, forming a knot.

With one last look, I move past the cavern, coming to a small path and bridge. And that is when I feel it. My connection to the void and the rush of cool ice as it floods my veins. As easy as breathing, I let my shadows envelop me. The familiar depths to my Caligo powers awaken and brush against my skin like an icy breeze that quickly rushes over me.

With ease, I jump through the void and come out to the edges of the Sidus town.

The town is quiet, too quiet. It is late enough that the curfew has long been enforced, but there is a stillness that feels wrong.

Without thought and needing to see my mother for at least a moment, I jump through the shadows and head for home.

Arriving outside, I see no light is on, and any hopes of seeing her slowly start to disappear. I move into the shadows once more and slip inside, my shoulders dropping when I realize no one is home.

With a sigh, I double-check all the rooms before moving back through the shadows to the other side of the town, to where I am sure to find a dark creature.

After an hour wasted of finding nothing but the odd bird, I give up and shadow to the river, hoping I will find one there. But just like the town, all is eerily quiet.

I move closer to the river and freeze. It looks like a mirror of the night sky above, but with no glimmering stars. The entire river is black, as if someone has dyed it.

I reach toward it when something rustles behind me.

"Don't touch it," a familiar voice shouts out as I whip around.

Jarek stands as if ready to move toward me, but his eyes widen when he realizes it's me.

"Ren." He rushes forward and pulls me into a hug. One I didn't realize I desperately needed. He holds me a bit longer before pulling back and checking me over.

"You are unharmed? I heard only too late what happened, and before I knew it, you were gone, swept away into the palace where I could not reach you."

"I'm well and it was all planned," I tell him with a smile.

He gives me a hesitant look before frowning. "I heard whispers of a certain Sidus making it to the top three in the first two trials. So how is it that you are here?"

"My entire plan is heavily weighted on retrieving what I need tonight. I'm going to need your help," I tell him.

"Anything, Ren, you know that."

I give him a smile with thanks.

"How is everyone?" I ask before turning to the black river and pointing to it. "And what is that?"

Jarek sighs, giving me a sad smile. "A lot has happened in the time you've been gone. Come on, I'll explain everything soon."

Jarek brings me back through the forest to the base of the mountains and through the hidden passageway to the rebels' base.

Bustling noise hits my ears as we move into the large carved-out stone room. No one notices us as we enter, with more people spanning out across the room, all tending to different things. Some are injured and taping their wounds, while others strap on weapons as if preparing for battle.

I turn to Jarek as my stomach drops. "Has something happened?"

"*Seren.*"

My head whips toward the sound of my mother's voice just as she rushes toward me, enveloping me in a hug that has every muscle in my body relaxing.

Pulling back, she checks me over just like Jarek did, her eyes panicked and full of worry.

"As you can see, I'm perfectly fine. Not a mark on me," I tell her, attempting to ease some of her worries.

But she continues to stare at me, and despair shadows her face. "But your eyes tell me a different tale."

I swallow hard, giving her a brittle smile. I never was able to conceal my true emotions from her.

She pulls me back into a hug meant to heal. I hold her tighter for a moment before releasing her.

"I hear congratulations are in order." Ryuu steps up beside us, a small unsure expression on his face.

I glance around at the rebels in the room before looking back at Ryuu and then to Jarek.

"The captain is here," I say to him, more in shock than anything else. I never thought I would see the day when he would be in the same room as them, no matter how much they proved how helpful they could be.

Jarek attempts to cut off his rumbling laugh at my facial expression, but his entire face transforms to one of amusement.

"We tied him up and dragged him here under duress, of course."

Ryuu gives us both an exasperated look, shaking his

head before focusing back on what he was saying. "You made it through the first two trials."

"I plan to do the same for the last one." The lieutenant and his guards will have to do a lot more than beat me to try to force me to give up. There are too many people depending on this.

I glance around the cold room, the heavy despair thickening over. It makes me pause.

"Why are all these people here? The entire town is quiet."

I spot the look of reluctance Ryuu and my mother share with Jarek and realize they are keeping something from me. Most likely thinking they are protecting me.

"Tell me," I demand. I need to know they will be safe down here when I go back to the palace, or I will not be leaving.

"I will not ask how you have come to be here when no competitor is supposed to be able to leave the palace while the competition is taking place," Ryuu says. "So instead, I will ask why you are here."

"I was planning to go back soon. I came with hopes to get what I need for the last of my plan," I tell them truthfully, hoping they will do the same.

"What is it you need?" my mother asks, the look on her face telling me she is ready to get me anything I want.

"A dark creature."

CHAPTER 19

No further questions are asked as my mother and Ryuu immediately start planning and discussing the best place to find a dark creature at this time.

While they are distracted, I pull Jarek aside to find out what they have been keeping from me.

"Tell me everything, now," I demand.

He looks at me, and whatever he finds makes him relent instantly. He is well aware of how stubborn I am and knows only too well that I will not let this go.

Jarek sighs, his face aging in minutes. "Ryuu and your mother joined us a few days ago. But most of the people in the town have already moved up here. We work in shifts, and it has worked well for now. A handful of people stay in the town, and all are trained, but the guards are no wiser. Nor do they seem to care. Though, that was to be expected. The Caligo guards have never cared about us. Why start now when we are all dying?" Jarek shakes his head, his eyes burning with rage but also pain.

"Jarek..." I move in front of him to force him to look at me.

He glances down at me, his anger slowly loosening to become a wearied frustration.

"The dark creatures now slip through the shield in multiple places at the same time. It is no longer predictable, but it is a certainty they will show up." He glances away from me as his eyes glisten with despair.

"They're strong. They have killed so many already that I..." He shakes his head, stopping himself as if just realizing something. "You shouldn't be worrying about this. You have enough on your plate." He says it with more worry for me than him. But I was the one who left them. I left them just when everything got worse, and they have suffered. I can see it in his eyes, in my mother's and everyone else here. I can feel the despair and hopelessness that seems to be slowly draining them all.

I've wasted too much time with a plan that may not yield anything. The royals may already be aware of all of this and still not care, and then my time away will have been for nothing.

I glance around the room, seeing nothing but my doubts and fears. Maybe I could have been here fighting instead. I may not have been able to stop what has happened, but I would have been able to fight. To protect. Maybe so many lives might not have been lost.

"I would never have left. If I had known, I would—"

Jarek shakes his head, taking my hands in his and giving me a look full of resolve. "No. No. This is why they didn't want to tell you, Ren. They knew you would try to blame yourself. And although I hate that you are in that wretched palace with all of those loathsome guards, I can now see that you are well capable of taking care of yourself."

I narrow my eyes on him. "You should have known that well before I went into the palace."

He chuckles and it lights up his entire face, quickly clearing the sadness and despair. He pulls me into him, pressing a kiss to my head.

"I know how strong you are—envy it, in fact. And how you are able to face any issue head-on. But I also know you are not invincible and need reminding of it daily."

I lightly punch him in the stomach and step back as he chuckles harder. His laughter and good humor bring me a sliver of relief, easing the tightness from my chest and limbs.

"You have to go back, Ren. You have to because you give us all hope. Hope that maybe this will not last forever. That we will not have to fight each day just to survive the next. You give us hope for a future, and it is something we all desperately need right now."

I swallow hard at his intense look of complete faith and trust. Something I do not feel I deserve. But I will do my best to ensure his trust in me is not unwarranted.

"You will watch out for them?" I ask, not needing to tell him whom I speak of. Although my mother and Ryuu are extremely capable fighters, they still need someone to keep them on their toes, to distract them from the heaviness of their daily tasks and the things they try to shoulder alone.

He gives me a soft smile, his eyes full of warmth. "It is not something you *ever* need to ask. Aloisia has always been like a mother to me, and the captain..." He squints, as if thinking. "A disapproving uncle who likes to frequently remind me of all my faults and flaws."

A laugh ripples from my throat. "That makes two of us, then."

Jarek gives me a strange expression, but there is something soft and longing to it that makes me give him a questioning look.

"He tried to go to the palace soon after you left, to check on you."

My spine straightens as amusement quickly falls away. Jarek gives me a sad half smile.

"They wouldn't let him in. He may or may not have insulted a few higher-ups. He has been placed on leave and was told his privileges are stripped until they deem otherwise."

I try to let Jarek's words sink in, but I still can't wrap my mind around it.

"He considers you his daughter, Ren. In every sense of the word. He loves you, but I suppose that isn't a hard thing to do."

"I love you, too," I tell him, reminding him that he is part of that family too.

"As you should." His eyes narrow on me.

I shake my head at him, a soft smile on my lips. If anything were to happen to him...

My hand falls against my side and the small bulge there, my eyes widening when I remember what it is. Reaching into my pocket, I grab Jarek's arm and open his hand to place the small stone in it.

"What is this?" he asks, opening his palm.

"A healing stone."

"A healing—" Jarek looks at me with wide eyes. "How did you manage to find one?"

"It was a gift." Asra might not be happy that I gave it away, but Jarek needs it more than I do right now. He might be able to use it, with everyone here.

He inspects it in awe, turning it over in his hand before something snaps him out of it.

"No, you keep it. You will need it." He tries to hand it back to me, but I close his hand over it.

"They have fancy healers in the palace. Please take it. Keep it on you at all times, and be safe while I am gone. Give me this small measure of peace," I plead and mean it. I need to know they will be safe once I go back.

Jarek scoffs but gives me a small smile, pocketing the stone before pulling me into a hug before releasing me.

"Now off you go. Catch a nice big, ugly, dark creature for whatever you have planned in that strange mind of yours. But don't keep it."

"Worried I might replace you?" I jest, trying to get a rise out of him just to see some light back in his eyes once again.

He doesn't fall for my joke, but he does smile, and it lights up his entire face.

"There is nothing in this world that *can* replace me," he says.

"I didn't realize big, ugly, and dark was not so easily replaceable."

"You little brat." He reaches for me, but I sidestep him and spin out of reach, laughing to myself.

He shakes his head with a soft expression on his face. "I've missed my friend; come home soon, Ren."

"I will," I promise. With one last hug, I turn and leave with Ryuu and my mother.

She walks with us until we reach the start of the forest before stopping with a harsh sigh.

"I should be going with you both," she says.

"You're needed here," Ryuu tells her.

"I should be here too," I tell them both. I didn't think this through before I left. I didn't realize how bad it would get for them. Now they are all left here to struggle while I play games in the palace.

My mother turns to me, a determined glint in her eyes, one that is filled with endless love.

"Do you know why I called you Seren?" she asks. "Because the minute I laid eyes on you, I found serenity among the chaos and turmoil. You brought me peace and hope in a moment of darkness. And I truly believe that the gods sent you just for me. You are doing something none of us can. You are giving us hope for a future. And that is more important than anything else." She scans every inch of my face as if trying to memorize it before pulling me into another tight hug. "Please be safe. Both of you. And come home to me soon, Seren." She gives me a warning look as if demanding I do so, before placing a kiss on Ryuu's cheek and turning to head back.

We both wait until she is out of view before we start moving through the forest.

"I haven't seen Warrick or Theon. Did they choose not to join the rebels?" I ask, trying to make some small talk to fill the silence.

Ryuu's body grows tense beside me "They're dead."

I stop in my tracks, and time seems to slow down. Ryuu stares down at his empty hands, but I see the anguish as it seeps across his face.

"It happened a couple of nights after you left for the palace. There were too many of them, the dark creatures. We didn't realize..." He releases a harsh breath, shaking his head. "Many have fallen since. And the guards..." His somber expression disappears as anger rises up to slash across his face.

"Is that why you joined the rebels?" I ask.

He clears his throat before looking at me. "They at least listen and try to help. Though their ability to follow rules seems to be lacking."

"Under your guidance, I'm sure they will become great fighters." Ryuu is one of the best fighters I have ever seen and also has an innate ability to teach others. The rebels will be better fighters because of him.

He gives me a small smile, something not many are privy to.

"Let's find you a dark creature." He turns and moves to the forest and town with stealth.

With his keen senses, it doesn't take us long to find one. It just happens to be right beside one of the guard stations. I glance around, but there don't seem to be any guards about.

"The guards abandoned it days ago under the guise of moving to a better one. But..." Ryuu gives me a look. One filled with fury and violence.

A look I agree with.

They knew... The guards knew either that the creatures would come or that there was a possibility of them breaking through the shield right here. And instead of staying and helping or even warning those closest, they left it to the Sidus people and moved aside.

"Prepare yourself," Ryuu warns as he scans his surroundings.

My gaze finds the wall and the dark smoke that forms around it as if on fire with blackened flames.

My stomach drops when I realize what it is. But surely not...

"How are they moving past the wall?" I ask, hesitant to hear the answer.

Ryuu nods his head toward the black smoke. "They move *through* it now. They no longer need a break in it to get through. Once the shield is down near it, they can enter."

My hand tightens on my daggers as I focus on the wall, but instead of one or a couple of dark creatures forming, an entire group spills through all at once.

Ryuu dips his head to me before rushing forward. I follow him and as soon as I'm close enough, I behead the nearest one.

Ensuring Ryuu's back is covered, I spin around and attack any who get too close. But we quickly get overwhelmed with more coming through the wall to attack us. Surrounded, with a group advancing on us, I let go and attack without limitations, the only restraints left on my powers.

Without any confines, the fight is exhilarating. Instead of tiring me, it refuels me, feeding the part inside me that craves battle and bloodshed.

Ryuu snags one of the dark creatures and pushes it against the wall before pulling out his iron chains to secure it. With his back turned, another comes up behind him.

Twisting the dagger in my hand, I throw it, my aim directly hitting the middle of its head. I catch Ryuu flinch, but my focus turns back to the handful of creatures around me. I duck a clawed attack before twisting and sliding my other blade across its neck.

I quickly move through the rest, slashing across their bodies and using the wall as leverage to twist and rise, slamming my body weight into my next target before moving on.

Before I know it, they're all gone, disappearing into the black smoke they formed from.

Ryuu stands off to the side, a creature at his feet already wrapped in chains and covered.

"I don't think I was needed," he says with a small smile on his face, and it mirrors my own.

"A fine compliment from one who helped train me."

"I only added to your already large skill set, nothing more." He turns around and picks up some more chains, handing them to me. "Should you need it."

I take them with thanks.

"How will you get it inside the palace without the guards finding out?" he asks.

With my eyes firmly on the chains, I answer him as best I can without revealing something that would only provoke further questioning and a possible lecture.

"I have something arranged," I tell him and glance up to catch his frown.

"I don't think I want to know," he says, but his frown deepens as he looks at my wrists.

I glance down to see what has caused the look and find my sleeves pushed up, revealing my cuffs. I quickly pull them back down, but from the worried expression on Ryuu's face, he has already seen them.

"What are those?" he asks carefully.

"A little... *gift*." Technically, they were given without payment, so it isn't exactly a lie.

"Seren—"

"Trust me?" I whisper, needing to leave soon and not wanting to fight. Tonight was a good night, seeing them all.

"I do," he says quickly.

I look at him, shocked to hear the sincerity in his voice.

"I should have trusted you long ago when you first asked to join our fight. Trusted your capabilities and strength. I trust you now even when my instinct is telling me to keep you here, safe and away from anything that can harm you."

He steps forward, moving in front of me. "I know that I have not been the best... role model to guide you, but I will always be here for you, Seren. Sometimes I... worry."

"It is a father's right to worry," I tell him. And mean it. Jarek was right. And only now, when I am not so blindly absorbed in my own thoughts and perspective, do I see it too.

He swallows hard, his eyes widening a fraction before he nods his head.

"Be safe, Seren."

Grabbing hold of the chain, I use it to pull the dark creature along. With one last nod to Ryuu, I turn to head to the palace, forcing myself not to glance back and knowing that if I do, I won't ever want to go back.

Once I'm far enough away and with no prying eyes, I shadow to the cavern and find a place to hide the dark creature until it is time.

Once it is tightly secured with the extra iron chains Ryuu gave me and hidden, I move back through the caverns, the gods chamber, and up the tunnel to the entrance in the cell.

Pushing the brick to close it, I stop for a moment and listen for any sounds. Finding none, I head to my cell and undo the cloaked body of dirt before sitting down and letting my mind drift to thoughts of today.

The third and final trial starts soon. A trial meant to test our powers. Powers I have not used in so long that I am beginning to forget the warmth of them.

But seeing my mother, Jarek, and Ryuu today helped. It fills me with a warmth that only fuels the quiet rage now burning throughout my veins.

There is more at stake now. More lives that count on me. I need to get through this trial and be in the top three, no matter the cost.

There is no other choice.

CHAPTER 20

The guards are not shocked to see me healed. Instead, they are angry that a healer has slipped in and apparently helped me. I go along with their assumptions, threats, and vows that no other healers will be allowed near me, until finally they bring me up into the palace to the next trial.

But instead of heading toward the arena, we move through the palace to the outside where the rest of the competitors are. The guards leave me there with a vicious warning I instantly ignore to focus on Alderic and his little speech. I glance around and note not all competitors are here, and even some who were not seriously injured are missing.

"For the final test in the competition, we have decided to do things a little differently. Please follow me," Alderic says.

We move along a long, open pathway that encases

most of the side of the palace. Just when I think we're about to stop, we are brought through another entrance and led through a guard watch station, though this one is far more capable looking than those that are placed in the Sidus town.

With passing glares and looks of disgust from the guards there, I move on past them and out to the side of the mountain, following a jagged stepway of large stones.

The tension is thick in the air as we move in silence farther from the palace to a carved pathway around the mountain, the edge not railed off. Should you fall, you fall to your death.

The competitors around me grow more and more uneasy the longer we move into the mountains and away from the palace grounds.

We move around a huge rock, and that is when I see what they have planned for us today. Or at least the opening of it.

A colossal structure, made from the mountain rock itself, sits before us. It looks like the start of a stone maze with a wide opening and no way else around it.

Alderic and his group of guards come to a stop. He turns to us with a wide smile on his face. A smile I have no trust in.

"As you can see, we have decided to change things up. The final trial will not be in the arena, and instead, placed here." Alderic shares a look with the guards. "The guards have been gracious enough to allow you to use their training ground and obstacle course."

Training ground... From my viewpoint, all I can see is the entrance to what looks to be a maze. But for them to have something so grand to potentially grow their skills and still not use it to help those in need fills me with disbelief.

It is a waste of a structure. No advantages have come from it for the Sidus, and the only benefit I can see is it adding to the grandeur of the palace.

I knew the Caligo guards were trained and somewhat skilled. But it is detestable to think they have an entire training ground to grow those skills and yet still sit back and watch as the Sidus die.

My stomach churns as the lieutenant and Levon arrive, moving up beside Alderic as if they were always there.

"A few rules to note," Alderic continues, his eyes wide with anticipation, making my churning stomach drop. "As this is a trial to test your powers, no weapons will be given; you are to rely on your abilities alone."

A few smug expressions slide my way, but I ignore them to listen to whatever else they have planned for today, knowing that they will have something up their sleeves. The last two trials alone confirm it when they tried to break me. I doubt today will be any different.

In fact, I'm expecting it to be worse.

"There will be no pairs today. You will each go into the maze alone and face each obstacle. There is only one entrance, and it is the same exit you see behind me."

Alderic points at the wide stone entrance before turning back to us.

"Once you enter, you will need to pass through each obstacle to move on. If you attempt to turn back, you will forfeit immediately. That is *if* the obstacles have not already killed you."

Alderic shares a chuckle with the guards. It crawls down my back like ice.

And there it is. Their last attempt to make sure I do not make it through this final trial.

Murmurs and looks of disbelief fill the crowd of competitors around me as I prepare myself for what I will need to do.

I no longer have the healing stone Asra gave me, so I will need to be smart. Alderic said this trial was filled with obstacles, and although I can only see the entrance to a maze, I'm sure there are places I can use to evade and escape. I work best on my feet and should be able to set about a plan and fend off when needed.

I can make it through this; I just need to have my wits about me and not let the guards get the better of me.

"No one said there was the possibility of death!" a male competitor shouts out.

Alderic gives him a sharp look with a cruel smile. "When you are a guard, you face all dangers. Death is always around the corner. Especially when it comes to unlawful rebels." Alderic gives me a pointed look, one that I ignore, before continuing. "One final amendment. You all will be fighting one another for the top three spots once again to meet with the royals. Any recent top three competitors can still be knocked off their spot."

I catch some of the competitors sizing me up, and I know that I am going to have my work cut out for me today.

Oryn comes up beside me, wearing a frown.

"What about her abilities?" he calls out to Alderic, bringing a look of disappointment to his face.

Oryn ignores it to continue on, pointing to my bracelets. "She will need her powers if she is to compete."

With a reluctant nod from Amaro, Levon walks over to me with a snarl and grabs my wrists, yanking me forward. I bite my tongue and glare up at him as his hands tighten painfully around my wrists.

Oryn takes a step to move toward me, but I slightly shake my head, and he stops, clenching his hands at his sides.

Levon's grip tightens further before he releases my wrists with a yank, taking the bracelets with him.

The minute they are gone, I feel it. The warmth. It pulses from my chest, spreading outward before encasing me whole.

"What the—"

It rushes out of me, the warmth igniting to flames that burn and seek out all those who have shuttered it out.

Blocking out the murmurs and horrified gasps around me, I try to shove it down, focusing on each inhale and exhale as I center myself and calm the wildfire inside me.

Beads of sweat slide down my face as I manage to drag it back beneath the surface. Opening my eyes, I catch the end of my luminescent strings floating out around me, captivating the competitors nearest to me. I pull them back into me, and the competitors shake off their enthrallment. It quickly morphs into a collection of varying glares, all aimed at me.

"When your name is called, you are to enter the maze. Those who did well in the previous trials will get to go first," Alderic announces.

Oryn bumps my shoulder with his, a happy expression on his face. "Finally, a trial in your favor. We shall get a head start and buy ourselves another chance to find what we're looking for."

I give him a small smile as my reply, not having the heart to tell him that I will not be joining him. I have no doubt that the guards will leave me to the end before allowing me to enter the maze.

"*Oryn.*"

"See you in there." Oryn dips his head to me before turning and running into the maze. And just as I had assumed, the guard waits to call my name until the very end.

"Seren." The guard gives me a savage smirk. It is mirrored on the rest of the guards' faces, including Amaro's, Levon's, and Alderic's.

Their watchful eyes follow me as I move toward the

entrance. I keep watch, my gaze following their every move as I head inside, but they don't move, nor do they try to stop me. Though, I can tell from the look they are giving me that most of my troubles will be *inside* the maze of obstacles.

Once I'm clear of them, I rush forward, moving around the dead ends and through the large stone pathways, when a scream sounds out, cut off a moment later by complete silence.

The rules said not to help another competitor. I've never been one to follow rules. At least not blindly. But there are also a lot of people counting on me succeeding here today.

Damn it. My foolish conscience wins out, and I get moving in the direction of the screams, hoping to find someone alive. But the maze is a twisting nightmare of dead ends and tight paths that stop me from getting anywhere near it.

A rumble brings me to a stop, and I watch as the wall beside me detaches and rolls to the side, cutting off my path. I turn, ready to go back and search for another way, when two competitors block my exit.

One with shoulder-length black hair and the other a deep amber, almost the color of flames. Both are wearing vicious smirks.

"If it isn't the little Sidus," the male with black hair sneers.

"Caligo," I reply with a smirk.

"The guards have put a pretty little reward on your

head. Should an accident befall you, well, the reward doubles." They share a savage smirk. "I'm afraid this is where your little journey ends," he taunts.

I feel the endless limits to my Sidus power brushing just under my skin, and when the black-haired male lunges forward, his shadows whipping out ready to slash, I'm ready for him.

I spring to the side, using the wall to kick off and flip over him. Landing in front of the other male, I punch him straight in the face, knocking him out.

I turn to the male now baring his teeth at me like a wild animal.

"You'll pay for that," he grits out.

His shadows rise up around him, and I wait until they are encasing his body before using my own shadows to join them. His pitiful attempt at a vortex of shadows quickly doubles in size. He frowns at the sight around him, a bead of sweat dripping down his head as he tries to contain it.

But *he* is not the one in control of it.

With one push, I move the shadows closer to him, and his eyes widen in shock and fear as the shadows envelop him whole, taking the breath from him.

Walking closer to him, I pull my powers back just as his knees hit the ground.

"I'm afraid this is where your little journey ends," I say, echoing his little taunt before hitting the back of his head. He drops to the ground with a thump.

Quickly moving out of the dead end, I stay watchful

and make sure to listen for any sound before moving around the next path.

The guards must be getting desperate if they feel the need to pay off some of the competitors to finish their task, finding it so difficult themselves.

I smile to myself at the thought.

Moving quickly through the maze, I come out to another long pathway, grateful it is not a dead end, when I hear a swish. Instinct has me ducking just as a blade shoots overhead before slamming into the wall beside me.

I take a step forward, attempting to move away from it, but I must have stepped on a hidden trap, as dozens of blades begin to shoot back and forth from the walls, not letting up for even a moment and completely blocking my way through.

I hear movement from behind me and know I must be quick. If I were a Caligo, I would use my shadows to form weapons and fight my way through, and if I had a weapon, I would use it to defend against them. But as I can't be seen using either, I bring my light to the surface and let it guide me. The urge to look up brings a smile to my face when a way out comes to mind.

Weaving a net with my Sidus light, I use it to climb up the wall to the top of the maze. With my new vantage point, I quickly spot the exit and head for it.

Once I'm at the end of the stone maze, I drop down onto an open path. Thinking I'm finally clear of the maze, I grimace when I spot the maze of steps and stairways as the next obstacle. It's covered in a green substance in the form of large rectangular structures in and around the steps.

But whereas the maze was on one level, this has multiple, the stairs and passages overlapping each other with small thin wooden bridges as underpasses.

I move closer to inspect the green substance and touch some of it with my fingertips, finding it slimy.

A plan to climb over it like the maze won't be an option, but a vantage point would give me an idea of where I should go. And this is an abilities test, after all.

Glancing around, I listen and look out for anyone before drawing up the cool, dark tendrils inside me and using my shadows to form small steps just big enough to get a foothold on. Jumping on one, I create another quickly and keep moving. The shadows are not as stable as my Sidus net and won't hold for long, so I need to move fast.

Moving quickly, I make it across the nearest bridge and overpass and move to climb up and over to a large open area above.

I land and find Oryn standing right in front of me, his eyes wide in shock as he watches my shadows disappear.

Damn it. How did I not see him?

"Is there anyone else around?" I ask, glancing around for anyone who may be hiding or concealed among the structures. But he doesn't answer me, his mouth still open with shock.

"Oryn?" I hiss, snapping him out of it.

"No." He shakes his head. "There's no one. How is this possible, Seren? You're a Sidus. I've seen your powers."

Guilt seeps into my chest at the look on his face. I knew I was eventually going to tell him. But so many things have happened since then that it became something I would do later.

I guess later is now.

"I didn't know if I could trust you," I tell him. I wince when I hear myself say it out loud, especially when he has trusted me this long with his. "But the truth is, I have both Sidus and Caligo powers. Just like you."

He snaps his mouth closed as he nods his head quickly. "Yes, I mean... I just—"

"Never met anyone else like you?" I finish.

"Yes..." Oryn gives me a strange look.

"I understand. I never thought there was anyone else like me, either. But I'm glad I have. It's nice not to feel so alone." I give him a soft smile, one he slowly shares with me.

"Let's keep moving," I tell him and turn to inspect the rest of this obstacle.

With the vantage point, I am able to spot the end of it easily. We move through the rest of the green stairway maze without much resistance.

Once we're clear of it, we come to a long tunnel with a roof overhead and sides that encase it. There is a slim stone path through the center of it. But the path doesn't reach across to the sides, and it is only held up by its connections to the end of the tunnel and the start of it where Oryn and I stand. There doesn't seem to be any other way around it, and should either of us fall, we most definitely will be falling to our death.

Oryn steps up beside me, swallowing hard when he sees it. "We should be able to just walk across it. The path isn't that thin. It's wide enough for one person to walk on at a time."

But it's not the path that I am worried about. The guards would never have something as simple or easy, and I have already sensed them.

Oryn moves to step forward when I reach out to stop him.

He begins to explain. "I'll go first to check—"

"No. Look." I tip my head toward the shadowed sides.

He turns to scan the area. "I don't see—" The shadows move slightly. "What are they?"

"Guards," I reply.

Oryn's head whips to me. "How are you so sure? They could be beasts or rebels."

A shadow slashes out at us before retreating, and I raise a brow at Oryn. "Rebels don't have Caligo abilities."

Oryn frowns as he looks to them. "Why are they doing this?"

"They don't want me to continue on in the competition," I tell him truthfully.

"I think they're doing it for *all* contestants, not just you." He gives me a sympathetic look meant to alleviate the worries he thinks I have. But he has no idea what the guards are truly like, nor how far they are willing to go to see me fail.

"Go first then," I tell him, ready to prove my point.

He pauses. "What?"

"Go first." I dip my head toward the thin path. "Use your Caligo abilities to keep you atop the path. Be quick about it, and you should have no problem."

"I'll prove it to you." He moves onto the path, his shadows coiling out of him to act like a rope to tether him to the path. They move along with him as he walks forward.

The guards' shadows don't move an inch, not until he's near the end, and then they make a feeble attempt to slash out at him.

Oryn turns to me at the end of the path, a wide smile on his face. He thinks he has just proven his little theory, but he hasn't seen mine come to pass yet.

The minute my foot hits the path, shadows from both sides whip out to slash and attack. Oryn looks on in horror, but I am ready for this.

I bring my Sidus light to the surface of my skin, letting it build and build. The world around me grows brighter and brighter until there is nothing but light around me.

Releasing some of the wildfire inside me, I let go and blind the guards with my Sidus light. Their shadows retreat and I quickly move across the path to Oryn.

I release my light as soon as I reach him, and he blinks it away before looking at me, a sad expression on his face.

"I'm sorry. I thought... I was aware the guards treated you differently, but I didn't realize..." He releases a harsh breath.

I shrug. "I've never known anything else. But coming here has helped me."

He frowns. "How so?"

"I'm no longer so close-minded as to judge all Caligo based on the guards' actions. A few of the Caligo I have met are some of the kindest people, with generous hearts."

A wide smile spills across his face. "I'm glad you don't think we're all bad."

"You're a little different," I remind him as we make our way to the next obstacle. Walking down the rocky path, we come to a long cliff. Glancing around, I find no other way around it.

"We have to climb over it," Oryn says, and I nod, agreeing before heading straight for it and starting my climb upward.

"Is there anything you can't do?" he shouts up as he follows close behind me.

"My mother told me there is no such thing. That the only limits we have are those we set for ourselves."

He grows quiet for a moment. “She sounds like an amazing woman.”

“She is.” One I miss terribly, even though I just saw her.

I grab the next piece of rock and then the next, making sure my grip is tight, my foothold firm as I ascend the cliff. Minutes pass as we both stay silent moving upward, our heavy breaths the only sound around us.

Reaching the top, I’m just about to pull myself over when I hear a resounding click from somewhere below. I glance down to find Oryn looking up at me, his eyes wide with fear.

“I think I’ve triggered some type of trap,” he says. And then he plummets.

Without thought, I push my Sidus light toward him and weave a net around him, catching him just before he slams into the ground.

Holding the net in place, I direct it toward the bottom of the cliff and keep it still as he gets a foothold and slowly starts to ascend once more.

It takes him longer than before to climb it. His face is pale and he’s out of breath, but he finally makes it up to the top. I grab ahold of his hand as he nears the edge and help him over.

“We’re not supposed to help one another,” he reminds me while trying to catch his breath, his face completely drained of color.

"I'd rather not watch you die," I tell him, and it brings a small smile to his lips.

"Thank you."

"Why didn't you use your own Sidus net?" I was glad to help him, but if it comes down to trying not to be caught by anyone or dying, the option should be obvious.

He glances back over the cliff, swallowing hard. "The trap caught me off guard. And I so rarely use them that I can't imagine ever being able to create a net like you can."

It hits me that he grew up in the Caligo city. A place where there are no Sidus. Which means he's never had anyone he could go to ask for help with his powers.

I was lucky. I had my mother. She found out everything she could about Caligo's powers and taught me it, making sure I was more proficient than any other Caligo.

"I can teach you, if you'd like?"

He turns to look at me, giving me a small unsure smile. "Maybe after everything is over."

I nod and let it go for now. But I will make sure he at least knows how to weave a basic Sidus net. Especially after today.

I turn and glance around at our next obstacle, my eyes widening when I see what it is.

"What is that?" Oryn asks, the horror etched in his voice.

"A pit," I tell him on autopilot as my mind tries to fully comprehend what I am seeing.

"Yes, but *what* are those?" He points straight at the familiar group of creatures inside it, clawing at the edges, trying to reach us.

My senses sharpen and the ice in my veins cool.

The guards don't just know about the dark creatures; they capture them to train against.

CHAPTER 21

Rage boils up inside me, threatening to unleash and seek out each and every Caligo guard.

Sidus have *died*. They have mourned their fathers, mothers, brothers, and sisters. And all while the Caligo play games with the dark creatures up in their mountains.

They could have told us about them. Helped us trap them like they have done so easily. We could have learned about them and better defended ourselves.

But they chose to hide this. To keep whatever they have learned to themselves. And for what? For the hate and distrust they have for the Sidus?

It doesn't make sense why they hate us so much and why they go to these extremes. Apart from existing, we have never done anything to make them this way.

There is no rhyme or reason to it. No logic that makes sense.

“What are those things?” Oryn asks.

“Dark creatures,” I tell Oryn as I move forward with purpose, needing an outlet for this blazing rage.

“Wait—”

“Aim for the head,” I tell him before I jump into the pit and strike, punching the nearest dark creature and spinning around to block and kick the next.

I spot a discarded sword on the ground and pick it up, slashing, slicing, and stabbing into every creature that gets near me.

I’m so lost to the rage and fury inside me that I let the need for violence seek out each and every dark creature as I imagine them all as the guards who put them here.

The guards who hide the creatures’ existence before capturing them and bringing them here to toy with.

With that thought, my attack grows more vicious and ruthless, and I decapitate and eviscerate each and every last one of them until there is nothing but dissipating black smoke around me.

Breathing heavily, I turn, ready to attack movement from behind, but freeze when Oryn jumps a step back and raises his hands in surrender.

“I’m not going to pretend to know what this is about. But from the look on your face, I can tell it is personal. Tell me what it is you need help with, and I will.”

The kindness and offer to help me without question

after seeing what I just did slowly quiets the rage inside me, bringing it to a soft hum in the back of my mind.

I throw the sword onto the ground, not wanting the Caligo to see me with it and find an excuse to kick me out of the trial, and glance around the pit.

It's empty; not a drop of blood or shard of evidence is left from my attack or that the dark creatures were ever here. No other competitor behind us will ever know they existed either.

"Let's just continue on ahead." I move to the other side of the pit and up and out of it as I try to gather myself and my thoughts.

I'm so lost in my mind that I jolt and whip around to Oryn when he speaks.

"I think we're starting to loop back around." Oryn is scanning our surroundings, and I follow his lead, glancing back and around us.

He's right. It looks like the landscape and layout is turning to move in the opposite direction we've been going in.

The mountain area opens up, leading to a brick archway and path. There is no ceiling covering us overhead as we move through what is left of a large crumbling building.

The sound of water hits my ears as we continue to stay silent and follow the only path available to us. Every other way seems to be blocked by huge brick walls that encase the side of us.

"*I told him not to touch it*," a voice hisses out from somewhere ahead of us.

I pause and Oryn freezes beside me.

"Other competitors?" Oryn whispers, and I nod a reply, staying silent.

"What will we do?" he asks. "We can't go around them."

No, that's not an option. Not with how this building is constructed. It also sounds like there is more than one. Which means there are a few that could potentially finish this before us. But we need to come in the top three in order to meet with the royals.

"We continue on and try to pass them if we can. But if they want a fight, they'll get one." I quicken my pace and move toward the area the sound is coming from, walking into another large open room with no ceiling.

Each side has small waterfalls of gushing water filling into the larger area of water that covers most the room, and the only way to cross it is the small circular crumbling brick paths on each side. But they're too spread out from the entrance to get access to, and there are hundreds of small crystal balls with blazing flames sitting directly on top of them while some float across the water.

I doubt their purpose is to light our path. It is another type of trap; it has to be.

The path would be an easy option if not for the water itself. It is completely black. And if it is the same water that comes from the black sea, then even the smallest of touches will bring about death.

I glance around the rest of the area to find half a dozen competitors at the edge of the open room. Two are injured, while the rest look exhausted.

None of them greet us with glares or hostility, just a weary sigh full of regret.

The male nearest to us looks to be the oldest of the group, with light graying hair and eyes full of knowing only years of experience bring. He must also be the chosen leader, as the others seem to refer to him for direction and advice.

He steps closer to us, raising his hands in surrender. "My name is Enver. I am not here to fight you. None of us here wants or would accept the deal the guards offered. We hate to admit it, but we have been stuck here for a while and just want to figure a way past this."

"What deal?" Oryn asks. But I ignore him to take a step closer to our newest obstacle.

"The crystal balls explode when you get too close to one. Using our shadows near them sets them off too," Enver says to me before tilting his head toward the water. "Lucius already tried it. He..." Enver glances over to a corner of the room, where a long dark cloak covers the shape of a body. "One touch and he was gone to a madness I have never seen. Then moments later he was gone completely."

"I'm sorry for your friend," I tell him.

He nods, glancing away to clear his throat. I've heard

many stories of Sidus accidently touching the black sea and a death that swiftly follows. It is not something I would ever wish upon anyone.

"We've tried to come up with everything, but anything we have risks touching the water or setting off the crystal balls."

I glance back at the crystal balls and around the room, realizing the mistake the Caligo guards have made.

"Your powers set them off, but what about mine?" I turn back to look at Enver and Oryn. "This course is meant to test Caligo abilities, not Sidus."

Stepping back, the others follow my lead and stand behind me as I reach down into the warmth inside me. I barely have to reach far, with it still brimming near the surface like a wildfire ready to attack. A luminescent string of light floats out around me before moving toward the nearest crystal ball.

Only the sound of the waterfalls echoes around us while we wait and watch as it curls around a ball before moving to the next and next.

When no balls explode after a couple minutes of testing, I pull back my light and turn to the others as a plan forms.

"I think I have a way to pass," I tell them with certainty in my voice.

"We're all ears," Enver says, a look of relief on his face.

I glance back at the path and balls of flames. "I can

weave a net of my Sidus light on top of the black water, and we can use it as a bridge to cross."

I turn back to find the group of Caligo growing hesitant and doubtful.

"I can vouch for its sturdiness," Oryn says with an embarrassed smile and wince.

"That's good enough for me," Enver says before looking to me with a worried frown. "But can you hold it long enough for all of us to pass?" He glances around at the wary faces. "It will not drain you?"

I give him a small smile, grateful for his thoughtfulness. "I'll manage just fine."

"How can we trust her?" a male with suspicious brown eyes says. "She's a Sidus."

"I don't care if she's a bloody mythical creature," a female with short white hair says. "She's the only one of us able to get out of here." She turns to me. "How can we help?"

"Try to move as quickly as possible." I turn back to the water and push out my warmth once more. Luminescent strings float a foot above the black water and slowly weave together to form a long path straight across to the other side.

"Go," I tell them, but they're still hesitant and move slowly toward it. And the slower they are, the more I feel the exhaustion catch up to me.

I try to focus on keeping the weaved light in a solid state, but any adrenaline I had previously starts to fall away the longer I hold my powers like this, draining me faster.

"If you are not quicker, I will not be able to make sure you all pass," I warn them.

The white-haired female moves onto the net and walks across it quickly.

Once she passes without injury, the others are quick to follow.

I wince as the strain to hold my powers in this state starts to grow painful. The warmth of flames inside me grows sharp, wanting to unleash and destroy instead. Having to pull it back and contain it only drains me further.

"Seren?" Oryn moves closer to me with a frown marring his brow. "Can you hold it?"

Enver is the last of the group to cross, with just Oryn and me. I should be able to make it a little longer.

"Go. I can hold it," I tell him—with hope instead of certainty this time.

He nods, taking my word for it before moving twice as quickly as the others to cross the weaved path.

"Come on. Now you," Oryn shouts. The others wait behind him, not moving on, and the small gesture has my hope growing, making me push harder.

Grasping hold of the wavering light, I drag it to me and rush forward onto the weaved path. But the minute I touch it, it starts to shake and become unstable. I run forward as the path behind me slowly starts to disappear, becoming patches of path that dissipate.

Not ready to give up, I jump from one broken weaved path to another while trying to hold them as steady and formed as I can.

The sharp slash of pain grips me just as I near the end, growing into a blaze of flames that burn me from the inside out.

I know that if it releases, it will kill us all.

I shove it down and use the pain to push me forward when I spot the entire path disappearing completely.

Rushing forward, I push my body and mind and focus on the group in front of me before making one last run and jump toward them.

I misjudge the distance and realize it only too late, when my foot heads straight for the black water.

But just before I fall, a hand snaps out and reaches for me. I grasp on to it like a lifeline as it pulls me over the edge and away from the black waters.

Kneeling on the ground and breathing heavily as I shove down the raging wildfire inside me, I glance up to thank Oryn when my gaze meets a pair of soft deep green eyes.

"Thank you for helping us across," Enver says before gently releasing my hand.

I nod to him with my own thanks, and together we move out of the end of the crumbling brick building and into the edge of the maze.

"Nearly there. Thank the gods," the white-haired female says with a sigh of relief.

I nod, agreeing, but keep my eyes watchful. Hopefully, there won't be too many surprises, but with the guards, I would not be shocked to find them leaving the biggest one until last.

We quickly move into the maze, only making it a few feet in before a loud shriek sounds out ahead of us, stopping us in our tracks. A sound that is definitely not another Caligo in pain, but more like a beast that seeks out bloodshed and violence.

Oryn looks to me with fear in his eyes. "Is it those dark creatures?"

I shake my head as a chill runs down my back. "They don't make any sound."

"What dark creatures?" Enver asks, making me frown.

"I'm guessing you didn't have the pleasure of meeting them?" Oryn says to him.

Enver shakes his head, a small furrow forming between his brows.

"Then you were lucky," Oryn replies, sharing a look with me.

They were before us. They had to have met them. Unless... unless someone was following us, following *me* to ensure I met them alone.

"What are they?" the female asks.

"You don't want to know, trust me," Oryn tells her with complete certainty.

She nods her head. "Then let's get a move on before whatever else the guards have concocted comes to greet us."

With a silent unanimous acknowledgment, we spread out while keeping watch for anything amiss.

"How are you feeling?" Oryn whispers to me.

"Drained but still capable." I glance around as something sets my senses on alert.

"No one would dare question your competence after seeing you fight, let alone what you just did for everyone here."

I find no obvious threat and give Oryn a small smile as we move on through the maze.

A few silent minutes pass before I hear a crackle and roar similar to that of a fire. Only when we move a little farther in do I spot the huge flames blocking one of the larger paths ahead.

"I bet our only way out of this is through that fire," Oryn says. But if that's all it is, a Caligo's shadows would easily be able to snuff it out.

"We just have to move through it?" the white-haired female asks with a frown. "It seems too easy."

An observation I have to agree with. It is too easy. There must be something—

A pulse of energy blasts out around us, hitting us all at once and pushing us a step back.

I glance around to check the others, but no one is injured, and all are still standing in semi-states of confusion and shock.

"What was that?" Enver asks as he glances down at his hands, frowning as if feeling something amiss even though he doesn't see it.

I reach down inside me, my stomach dropping when I feel it.

The cool, dark tendrils inside me are missing as if consumed and snuffed out. It must have been that blast of energy.

A bolt of panic jolts through me when I realize I'm completely powerless. But the warmth flares to life inside me, a violent slash of flames that reminds me of the strength I hold within.

"I can't feel my shadows," the white-haired female says as she reaches both hands out in front of her and watches in shock and despair as nothing happens.

Just like the bracelets blocked my Sidus abilities, the blast of energy has made this entire area a barrier against using our Caligo abilities.

"The trial is to test our abilities. Why take them from us?" she asks as everyone else attempts to use their abilities with no luck.

"Maybe we have to get them back?" Oryn says as he glances around.

"How? That blast could have gone on for miles," Enver replies, and I glance down at the empty space on my wrists, drawn to them as a thought creeps into my mind.

The guards could have blocked our powers in the entire maze if they wanted to, but they chose only now and here to do it. They like to play games, that much is obvious, to get into our heads and make something seem more challenging than it really is. Just like the maze and the structure of green bridges and pathways. Everything so far has been a puzzle we need to deconstruct or an obstacle that makes us think outside the bounds and restrictions that are the norm.

But there is *always* a way out. Another way or source...

Source. Just like my bracelets.

"Find the source," I whisper to myself, but they all turn to look at me. "There must be a source somewhere close by. Something that created the blast of energy and the block on your powers. If we find it, we can destroy it."

Enver nods as a determined glint enters his eyes. He turns to the others. "Spread out but stay close. Look for anything out of the ordinary, or anything that doesn't look like it belongs."

"If that's the case, we should all be looking at Calen here," the white-haired female says with a mischievous smile. "His head *is* unusually large."

The others chuckle around him, breaking some of the building tension in the air.

A male with a thick head of glossy black hair gives her a smug expression. "That is because I have a large brain."

"Full of air." She cackles, and the others join in before breaking apart to start their search.

Oryn shares a smile with me, his own tension eased from the small moment before we head off in separate directions.

Moving to a path on the left side of the flames, I get two steps in before I hear Oryn.

"Dead end," he shouts over, and I take note of his path to avoid before moving ahead, soon finding path after path empty.

I'm about to turn around and head back when something hard hits me from the side, slamming me into the wall.

CHAPTER 22

Dropping to the ground, my head dazed from the jarring impact, I immediately try to stumble to my feet to face the threat head-on. But I barely get the chance to move before a hand grabs my throat and slams me back against the wall.

Darkness clouds my vision as I claw at the hand holding me. My Sidus power rises up to slash out against the threat when something cold and hard clamps down on my wrists. The warmth immediately dissipates inside me, and I instantly know what they are.

The bracelets. I force my gaze to focus enough to spot my attacker—and find Levon snarling at me.

"I could easily end this all," he growls as his hand tightens painfully around my neck. The sharp pain burns down my throat, stealing each raspy breath.

"But the Breaker was promised your death." He

smiles and the vicious promise in it creeps down my back like ice.

Chuckling to himself, he shoves me hard against the maze wall once more before dropping me to the ground. I crawl away from him, putting some distance between us just as Enver comes around the corner, his eyes widening when he spots me.

"Sir? What is the meaning of this?" Enver asks Levon as he rushes over to me.

Levon takes a step back with a smirk on his face. "Just making sure the last trial is fair for all Caligo. Seren can't have an advantage simply because she is a Sidus."

Enver glares at him, but Levon ignores it as he turns and heads off into another part of the maze, disappearing in seconds.

"What happened?" Enver asks as he helps me to my feet and winces when his gaze finds the marks on my neck.

"It doesn't matter," I rasp, trying to clear my throat. "Did you find the source?"

Enver shakes his head. "No. Not yet, but we're still looking."

We move out of the passageway and into another when a man with long, dark hair walks toward us, a dead look in his eyes and a long blade in his hands.

"Lucius?" Enver says as his eyes widen in shock and horror.

Lucius...

"Wasn't he...?" The man who was covered in the dark cloak.

"Dead." Enver nods. "Yes."

Then how...? Maybe they just assumed he was dead and instead went into a healing slumber?

"Where did you get the blade?" I ask him. Apart from the one in the pit, there has been no other available. Unless the guards handed it to him. Which wouldn't surprise me.

Lucius doesn't reply but continues forward, moving stiffly. My instincts scream at me, telling me something isn't right.

When he gets closer, I realize his eyes are completely black.

Just as he reaches me, he raises his blade above his head. "For the gods."

I duck out of his way and avoid his blade before twisting his arm, breaking it. His blade drops to the ground, but he doesn't make a sound. He should be shouting in pain or screaming at me for hurting him, but he just attempts to get back up on his broken wrist.

It looks awkward and clumsy, but he manages to drag himself closer to me and tries to grab at me again. A swift kick to the head knocks him out.

Enver comes up beside me and slams the blade into his head. My eyes whip to his, and I find his own drenched in sadness.

"He was dead the moment he touched the black water. He would not like to live on like this."

I nod, figuring he would know best what his friend would want.

"Let's head back to the others. Hopefully, someone has found a clue at least," he says as he retrieves the blade with a wince.

We move back through the maze and spot the flames from the fire like a beacon that watches on, taunting us.

"I wanted to—"

Screams sound out, followed by a loud shriek cutting off whatever Enver was about to say. I share a worried look with him before making a run toward it.

We make it through the maze to the sound and come around a passageway to complete chaos.

A towering beast of a creature slashes out at the others, quickly tiring them out as they attempt to evade its vicious attack.

A soft black leathery skin covers its entire body, and it has thick hooves and small pointed spikes that run along its limbs and head. Its large head displays two large horns and a long snout with deadly fangs and even sharper teeth.

Dark, otherworldly energy is in the air around it as it moves. Its eyes turn to me, and the flames within them flare to life as it rears up with a shriek before slamming its hooves into the ground and rushing straight forward.

Snapping out of my shock, I look for a weapon and realize Enver has one.

"The blade," I shout to him, and he throws it to me without question.

I wait until the creature is close enough, slowing down each breath and tightening my hold on the hilt of the blade.

The creature rises up, ready to slam into me, but I drop and slide under it, slashing the blade across the flank of its body as it moves over me. It shrieks and the sound claws at my ears.

Moving swiftly, I roll to the side and turn back to the creature. "Run," I shout back to the others behind me.

"What about you?" Enver yells over just as the creature gets up, rearing up once more, readying another attack.

"Go!" I shout, twisting the blade in my hand. I might be able to buy them some time to hide.

"She has her Sidus powers. We have nothing. Let's go," one of the others shouts.

"She—" Enver starts to reveal what Levon did, but if they don't all get out now, no one is getting out.

"GO!" I shout once more just as the creature rushes forward.

Tightening the hilt of the blade in my hand, I run and jump, using the wall as leverage to rise up and twist my body over the creature and out of its way.

With the force of its attempt to skewer me, it slams into the dead end, and the maze wall trembles with the impact.

Quickly shaking it off, the creature turns and heads straight for me once more, its large horns bent down and aimed right for me.

But I've already turned and started running, pushing my legs to move quicker and out of the passageway with hopes of finding somewhere I can avoid it.

All too soon, the creature catches up to me. I turn and jump once more, this time slamming the blade down onto its back and pushing it as far as I can into the creature.

Before I get the chance to remove the blade, the creature dips its head and uses its body to slam me into the wall beside it, trapping me.

I hear a crack and wince as a familiar sharp pain spreads across my chest. Pushing down the pain for now, I twist the blade, and the creature bellows out in pain, slightly pulling back from the wall and giving me enough room to free myself.

A sharp burn slices across my side as I begin to move, forcing me to pause. Glancing down, I spot one of its horns bent and angled right at my side. There's not enough room to pass it without touching it, as the other way is blocked by the curved position of the creature's huge body.

With no other way out, I grit through the pain and slowly move around the creature to the front of it.

Grabbing hold of my side, I try to put pressure on the wound as the creature continues to slam up against the wall, trying to free the blade from its back.

With it distracted for a moment, I take a step back, and when it doesn't seem to notice, I get moving as fast as I can toward the flames with hope that the rest of the group will be near them too.

I leave a trail of blood behind me and attempt to push myself to go in multiple directions to throw the creature off, should it catch up to me.

It takes longer than I hoped, moving slower around each passageway, but I eventually find the flames once more, with the injured group all huddled around it.

Relief fills me as I make a start toward them. I'm halfway there when the flames slide open like a curtain, revealing a small path through the passageway and hopefully farther away from the creature.

Fighting the creature must have been part of the last obstacle enabling us to move forward.

"Go. I'll follow you," I shout over to them. There is no point in them waiting for me. I will be with them soon enough.

Enver gives me a worried look but must see my determined, stubborn gaze and nods before moving them all through the path.

Oryn follows him last before turning to me with a hand reached out. But in the blink of an eye, the flames quickly grow, making him snap his hand back just as they close once more, blocking me out.

My stomach drops as a loud shriek sounds out from behind me once more, and I know I do not have long before the creature finds me once again.

My choices are limited. I can either go through the flames and burn or turn back and die by the creature.

I clench my fists, wanting to scream to the heavens. This cannot be it. This cannot be my end. Not after everything. Not with everything I have to do and all who count on me.

I reach down inside me for any of my powers, anything I can drag up to help aid me. But I find none. Not a sliver of warmth or tendril of cool darkness.

But I can't give up. I won't. I keep searching. Looking deeper and deeper, until...

There.

Something flickers to life inside me, a small ember of energy and a fragment of something that doesn't feel like it is mine but at the same time feels familiar.

I pull on it, dragging it upward. Up and up until I feel it at the surface. Opening my eyes, I reach out and push every shred of energy I have toward the fire.

I feel it as it rushes through me. But instead of dark shadows of smoke forming in front of me, a small vortex of wind picks up, growing bigger and bigger, creating a whirlwind that swirls and slams into the flames, snuffing them out before swallowing it whole.

Releasing a harsh breath, I drop my hand and, with it, the whirlwind slowly disappears.

Taking a moment to gather my strength, I drag my body forward, wincing at the pain in my side and stomach before moving.

I head through the path where the fire once was, glancing over my shoulder to make sure the creature has not made it to me and quicken my pace when I don't see it.

I keep going, even when my body wants to give up, when my injuries throb and cry out for a break. I push myself, holding on to that sliver of hope that I will somehow make it and my plan will go ahead. Even when I know Enver and his group have had plenty of time to beat me. I keep going, knowing hope is all I have now.

Limping, I make it around the last corner and come to a complete stop.

There, standing before the exit and entrance of the maze, is Enver and his group. It doesn't look like they have gone through, some of the group still sitting with their injuries while others rest.

Spotting me, Enver stands up from his seated position and moves closer to me. As soon as he moves, the rest follow suit, slowly making their way over.

I ready myself should they wish to go ahead with the guards' deal, but pause when Enver gives me a look full of relief and gratitude.

"You helped us all when you did not have to. You fought for us, protecting us without question. Your place among the guards is well earned." He moves to the left of me, and the others follow, each taking a side until there is a small line each side of me and an open path that allows direct access to the exit.

"After you," Enver says, a gleam in his eyes and a knowing look on his face.

I swallow hard as my eyes begin to blur and burn.

They chose to wait. To let me pass ahead of them. They could have all easily moved through the exit, and one or more of them would have possibly won the trial. But they chose to stay and wait for me.

I glance at each of them, and they all give me warm smiles full of gratitude. There is not one glare or shred of hostility. Some of them are badly injured, and yet they waited. Waited for me to pass first.

"Thank you," I whisper. They will never know how much this means to me. To all the Sidus fighting daily who suffer. They will never know, but I will never forget this nor any one of their faces.

Struck silent with shock and gratitude for their gesture, it takes me a minute to realize that Oryn isn't among them.

"Oryn?" I question Enver, my stomach dropping when he gives me a strange look.

"He already made it through. He said you would understand." He frowns, but I nod, understanding completely.

His sister's life is on the line. I could not fault him for moving ahead. I just hope we both make it in time.

Taking a step forward, I move through the path they have created for me. They follow a step behind as I walk out of the maze and meet Alderic's and Amaro's gazes. Once they realize it is me, their eyes fill with nothing but wild rage.

I ignore them to search for Oryn and quickly find him standing beside another male, with wild bright red hair. I glance around, but there is no one else here, and that is when it hits me.

I've made it.

Relief and happiness seep into every muscle in my body, making my injuries feel twice as painful. But I don't care. All that matters is that I've made it. My plan will go ahead. And in the end, I have the Caligo to thank for it.

Amaro and Alderic storm back toward the palace. I spot Oryn as he makes his way toward me, a look of guilt slashed across his face, but I give him a small smile and it lessens.

Just before Oryn makes it to me, one of the males from Enver's group steps in front of me. His dark brown eyes are hesitant as he rubs a hand up the back of his neck to his wavy brown strands of hair.

When he doesn't say anything after a moment, I go to move around him, but he steps to the side, blocking me as he glances over at the guards.

"Please just give me a moment of your time," he says as he swallows hard. "My name is Sloane. I saw something the other night that I need to tell someone about, but the guards..." He glances back at them, a fearful look creeping into his eyes. "I know it's against the rules, but I snuck out the other night to meet my girl."

I don't really care about him breaking the rules, but I don't think he wanted to talk with me just to confess.

"What happened?" I ask, keeping my voice low so as not to draw attention to us.

He moves closer and lowers his voice. "I heard a noise, so I got my girl to go home and followed it. It was near the bridge, the biggest one, just at the end of it, near the gates. The shadow-jumping block only reaches so far, so anyone can reach it if they have the power. But when I arrived, no one was there." He glances back over at the guards before shaking his head to himself.

"I couldn't... I'm not strong like you. I won't survive it if I go against them."

"Who do you think you heard?" I ask, needing to confirm who I also suspect.

"The guards," he whispers, and my stomach churns at what this could mean.

I glance at Oryn, and he frowns at whatever he sees on my face.

"What did you hear?" I ask Sloane as my gaze stays fixed on Oryn while my mind tries to figure out a way to tell him.

"Someone cried out for help. That they were being kidnapped."

CHAPTER 23

After seeing a healer and taking a bath, I am placed in a room and told to stay there until someone comes for me. Oryn and Xavier, the other competitor to make it to the top three, were brought into a separate room. But all I can think about is what Sloane told me and how I can try to get to the end of the bridge without the guards noticing me. And if it sits just outside where the block on Caligo shadow jumping starts, it can't be a coincidence.

It makes me wonder how far the block goes. I've never been in the Caligo town, but it might cover the entire side of the mountaintop with all the Caligo homes.

It would explain why the guards, or whoever is taking these women, need to get to the end of the bridge before moving them.

I also need to go down and check on the dark creature in the cavern before my visit with the royals. Hopefully, this will all not have been for nothing and they are unaware of how corrupt and vile their Caligo guards are.

Though if they are truly unaware, it still leaves me with more uncertainty and doesn't give me any confidence in their ability as royals.

They should know what is going on in their kingdom. They should be vigilant and able to safeguard their people.

It is a fine line between knowing and not knowing. I just hope to come out of it with some form of help from them. The Sidus town will not last much longer should we keep up the way we are going.

The door is thrown open with a flourish, pulling me from my thoughts.

Visha walks in with Isolde by her side. Both are wearing wide smiles, and each has an armful of colorful gowns and jewelry.

"First, congratulations are in order. Although you are not the first woman to make it to this stage, or become a guard for that matter, you are our favorite and, as an added blessing, a Sidus."

I grow completely still at her words, my mind still trying to comprehend what she means.

"You think me being a Sidus is a blessing?" I ask.

"It is a *gift*. One you should cherish," Visha says with an intensity I do not fully understand.

I'm stunned silent by her words, but it doesn't seem

to deter either of them as they set about organizing the items they brought with them.

"I've never seen anything more beautiful than the light of a Sidus. It is magical," Isolde says as she lays out the gowns, matching up jewelry with them, and then starts to choose footwear.

"I don't understand..." I tell them. I know not all the Caligo hate the Sidus. And after spending my time in the palace, I know for certain that the prejudice stemmed more from the guards than anything else. But I never thought they would think of the Sidus and our powers as something beautiful.

Visha turns and gives me a sad look. "The guards fear what they do not understand. Your power, your light, draws people to it. It has a..." She frowns, wearing a contemplative expression. "Warmth that is pleasant. It can make those who come near it complacent."

My back straightens. "I didn't realize many others felt it, the warmth."

"The minute you entered the palace, I felt it. But it disappeared, only to be felt once more again yesterday." Visha glances down at my bracelets.

"The guards?" she asks, the question needing no further explanation.

I nod my head. "It seems they do not like that warmth."

"No. It seems they do not. But it is their loss." She turns and picks up a bloodred dress. "Now let's find you the perfect dress to wear."

"Dress?" I glance around at the array of colors and sparkles, the fabric luxurious and not something I ever thought I'd see, let alone wear.

"I don't usually wear dresses, and these shoes are not something I'd ever choose, as the heel is too high. Though they make a good weapon should I need it."

Visha takes the shoes off me and places them aside. "No fighting tonight."

I share a knowing smile with Isolde.

"Here, try this one." Visha hands me a blue floor-length tulle dress. I hide a wince at the huge layers threatening to engulf me. "Come now, I'll help you try it on."

"I—"

Visha drags me behind a changing screen and starts pulling at my clothing, attempting to strip me.

I pull back from her, covering myself. "I think I can manage by myself."

She places her hands on her hips with a sigh. "So be it, but be quick. We have many others to try on before tonight." She moves around the screen and mumbles something to Isolde. It's too low to hear, but I'm more focused on her words I *did* hear.

Many… I wince. It's going to be a long day.

The blue tulle dress is beautiful, but I can't move in it. And if I can't move in it, I definitely can't fight in it.

I don't tell either woman my reason for not choosing it, but they don't question my decision and easily move on to the next.

A tight cream wrap dress that gives me far too much movement but even less coverage is the next one I try on. It looks more like a cloth of soft bandages than a dress. The slit goes right up past my thigh, and the top wrap barely covers my modest cleavage.

"It is beautiful," Isolde says, standing back to admire it.

"Yes, but where is the rest of it?" I ask, wide-eyed and in shock that anyone would wear something like this. There is no place to hide any weapons; everywhere is on reveal.

Visha chuckles at my expression before telling Isolde to pass me the next one.

This one isn't too bad. The color is a dusty pink, and the simple fitted bodice has built-in underwire but is extremely comfortable. The skirt has enough volume without it being too big, and the slit and length reveal my leg without being too provocative.

I turn, ready to tell them this one is fine, when I find Visha standing in front of me, a dress in hand.

"I can see that you may be set on that one, but for an old woman, I beg you to try this last one." Visha hands me the dress and chuckles quietly at the expression I give her. She must know now that I can't deny her my trying it on. Not when she's been so kind to help me and let me borrow one for the meeting with the royals.

But the minute I slip the dress on, I know that it is the one. A glittering white fabric with strings of black lines woven into a tight bodice that drips down the skirt like black rain. A juxtaposition of my Sidus light and Caligo shadows.

The bodice conforms to my body shape, giving my cleavage some support while also not being too revealing. The skirt is floaty and light enough that I can fight in it should I need to. Though with how beautiful it is, I would hate for anything to ruin it.

The slit climbs up my leg, stopping mid-thigh, and gives me room to hide a small dagger.

"This. This is the one," Isolde says as she claps her hands, and I have to agree with her. It's stunning.

"It's perfect," I tell them both.

"The black could be the Caligo shadows and the white glittering fabric, your Sidus. It will help let the Caligo know that you accept their side as well as your own," Isolde says.

"Yes." Visha nods. "It is good to show them you are willing to bend to some of their rules. But remember never to bend so much that your shape, your being, molds into something different from what you are, because what you are is perfect. And anyone that tells you otherwise is wrong." Visha steps forward and cups my cheek as I try to get my foolish emotions under control.

Clearing my throat, I glance down at the dress to see what Isolde sees. The black lines and shimmering white, each a representation of the Sidus and Caligo but also, what I am.

I am both Sidus and Caligo. Both light and dark.

That is what this dress represents to me. My secret. And even though I will never truly fit in on either side, tonight it will be on display for all to see.

"Now sit down and I'll do your hair," Isolde says with a warm smile.

The minute I sit down, Isolde gets to work, detangling my knots and leaving it silky soft with whatever creams she uses. She then curls my hair, leaving it down and sweeping the right side up, pinning it with a hairpiece that matches the dress.

She moves on to my face next, using other creams to make it look like it's glowing, dark dyes to define my brows and lashes, and a brush of brown powder on my eyelids to make my sea green eyes stand out. And lastly, a shimmering pink lip cream to finish off the look, only making my lips seem fuller than they are.

"Are you a witch?" I ask her, only half in jest. Surely some of her creams are actual potions crafted through spells and witchery.

Isolde chuckles at me. "I doubt any of the Caligo will be thinking about what you are after seeing you tonight. Neither male nor female will be able to resist you like this."

"And the finishing touch." Visha sets down a pair of shoes in front of me. They are completely see-through, as if made from glass. Drops of rare white gems sit neatly all over the front, back, and outside of them, with even smaller gems crawling up the sides.

They are the most beautiful pair of shoes I have ever

seen, but my eyes immediately fall on the heel and how high it is. High enough to break my ankle should I fall, but sharp enough to use should I be without a weapon.

I look to Visha, not knowing whether to thank her or ask her if I've insulted her somehow that she now wants me injured.

She gives me a wicked smile, as if already knowing where my thoughts have gone, and pats my shoulder.

"Your feet will regret it by the end of the night, but you will manage."

"I wasn't planning on dancing," I tell her. One small mercy, I suppose.

But both women freeze on hearing my words and turn to me with wide eyes.

"You have to dance," Isolde says, and Visha nods.

"I don't know how. I've never learned." I wince. Sidus don't have many celebrations, and those we do have are usually full of drunken Sidus men who need constant reminders of where their hands should be.

"I've never needed to," I tell them.

"Well, we can't have that now, can we? What if one of the royals wants a dance?" Visha says.

"I doubt—"

Visha moves over to me and quickly helps me into the shoes before pulling me to a standing position and taking my hand. I stumble a little but quickly steady myself, getting used to the new height.

I'm not a complete stranger to heels. Jarek somehow found a pair and made me wear them to ensure I didn't miss out on the experience, saying all women needed to try it at least once.

So of course I made him wear them with me, and we never had so much fun or laughter as we did that night.

Visha places my hand on her shoulder, and her matching hand takes my waist. She then takes my free hand in hers and looks at me with nothing but warmth in her eyes. With the heels on, I am a half a head taller than she is, and with her leading the dance, it makes it a little awkward, but we manage.

"It's very easy," she says as she begins to sway, at first side to side before attempting to twirl me around.

I duck and bend, laughing as I bow under her arm. We practice a bit more, and I find the dance steps to be simple enough.

"Let your dance partner lead you, and he will be too busy being lost in those eyes of yours to wonder about your dancing skills."

I shake my head at her, but she gives me a secret smile before attempting another twirl.

We dance for a bit longer, and I get used to the heels once more while we laugh at each other, and a lightness fills up the room with happiness and joy. By the time Visha and Isolde have to leave, I start to wish I could spend the rest of the day here with these two beautiful, funny women rather than meet with some hidden royals and their guards.

I make note to try to figure a way to come visit Visha

and Isolde after everything is over, knowing I have made a lasting friendship with them both.

Once they are gone, I take off my shoes and leave them in the room while I sneak down to my cell to the hidden tunnel to check on the dark creature.

I pull my dress tight against me, careful not to let it touch the dirty walls should I ruin it and all the work Visha and Isolde have put into making me look and feel beautiful.

Moving through the passageways, I find the one I used to hide the dark creature in and head toward it. But when I come around the corner, my heart plummets, my stomach twisting when I find it empty.

Glancing around, I check that I am in the correct spot before moving to the next passage and the next, checking every path and room. Continuing my search, I find more rooms, passageways and caverns that open up to more paths than I realized was here.

It should be an impossible feat for the dark creature to escape those iron chains. But if it has, maybe it got lost among the underground maze of passageways and rooms down here.

But what am I going to do now? My entire plan is based on bringing the royals proof. The Caligo guards could easily deny the dark creatures' existence, but with proof, they will not be able to.

Damn it. It is too late to go hunt another dark creature now, but this is my only chance to meet with the royals.

I glance around the passageway I am in, not really seeing anything but my mind and despairing thoughts. I can't stay down here for much longer; the guards will eventually find me missing, and the celebration will start soon.

The only thing I can do now is go ahead with what I was planning to do. Meet with the royals but without the dark creature. Maybe I can suggest catching another and bringing it here as proof. It might be enough.

With a heavy sigh, I head back through the passageways and rooms, through the cavern, and up the tunnel. Resealing the hidden door, I listen for sound before moving through the cell room and back up into the palace.

I'm halfway down the hall from the room I was placed in after the trial when a heart-wrenching scream bellows out around me.

Without thought, I rush toward it, running through the hallways and down the corridors. Another scream sounds out, and my stomach drops when I realize it is directing me toward the servers' rooms and kitchens.

I push my legs twice as fast, and as soon as I'm close enough, I feel it.

The dark creature.

All my fears rush up inside me, threatening to choke me as I move into the kitchen and straight for it.

Grabbing a large knife from the counter, I lunge for it, kicking the dark creature off whomever it has cornered, and slam the knife into the back of its head. It drops to the side of the floor, disappearing into smoke before it hits the ground.

I turn to help whomever it attacked when I spot who it is, and my heart plummets, my eyes widening as I rush forward.

"No. No. No. No." I drop to the floor beside her, trying to stop the bleeding. But it doesn't stop. It spills out onto the floor around me, seeping into the ends of the white dress.

The dress *she* chose for me.

I push against the large open wound, but I know it is too late. I know it and yet I still try to stop the bleeding. It covers my trembling hands and arms, and the shock of what has happened finally hits me when I see them.

Visha is dead. She is dead and gone from this world. And it is my fault.

The guards come in a moment later, surrounding me with their swords. But I don't care. I don't see anything but Visha and her still body, her ghostly white face, and her open eyes as they stare upward in shock and horror.

Numbness seeps into my mind and body, an icy coldness following soon after it, clawing at the corners of my mind.

I don't feel it when the guards yank me up and shove me forward, moving me down hall after hall, stair after stair. I don't feel it when they shove me forward into a cell and lock it behind them, leaving me to the heavy silence that slams on top of me, mind, body and spirit, shoving me down.

The cold creeps further into my bones, and I curl up into a ball, trying to find some warmth inside me, quickly finding none.

Time moves in waves that drag before speeding up to crash against my chest as it grows tighter and tighter.

I have seen many people die and had to watch on as others lost their loved ones in front of them. I have seen it, but I have never truly *felt* it. My mother and those I love are all still with me.

My chest grows heavy as my eyes catch on something red. I lift it up and realize it's my hand. Her blood is on my hands. It's on my hands because it is *my* fault. My fault she's dead.

My eyes burn and cloud with tears, and a deep sob is ripped from my chest.

I brought that dark creature here. I brought it here, but I didn't think it through. *I didn't think.* And now she is dead. Gone.

She was a kind soul who did no harm to anyone and helped me when she didn't have to. She helped me and, in return, I killed her.

Her death is my fault, and I will forever—

"Hello?" someone calls out, ripping me from the self-loathing and guilt attempting to swallow me whole.

"*Ren*?"

CHAPTER 24

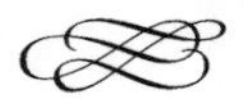

"How do you know that name?" Only one person calls me that, and by the sound of this male's voice, it isn't Jarek, someone I desperately wish was here right now.

"I'm Wylan. Jarek told me about you."

Jarek...

"Are you... okay?" he asks with hesitance in his voice.

"How do you know him?" I ask, ignoring his question.

"We are..." He sighs, pausing for a moment before answering. "I am his and he is mine."

His soft statement brings a small smile to my face. It feels strange and stiff and quickly drops when I realize I have no right to feel any happiness right now. Not after...

Swallowing hard against the lump in my throat, I focus on Wylan.

"You're the one he was talking about? The one he met not long ago?"

"Yes... Well..." He chuckles. "I've been wanting to meet you for a while."

A while...

I get lost in my thoughts. The ones of Jarek and the smile he wore when he told me about someone he'd met. And the ones now that seem to overshadow everything else.

The dark creature. The kitchen. Blood. Visha...

A sob is wrenched from me.

"Seren? Are you okay?"

"What does it matter?" I whisper, thinking he won't hear me, too lost in my pitiful grief. But he hears me.

"It matters because Jarek is... He means a lot to me. And you mean a lot to him. He is mine, but you are also his, and that makes you mine too. My family."

"It's my fault," I tell him. And everyone. And no one. "It's my fault." My chest grows tight, and a heaviness settles in my stomach.

"What is?"

Cold. Why is it so cold? I glance around the cell as an icy chill works its way into my bones.

"Can you tell me what happened?" he asks.

I hear movement to my right as if he has moved closer to the wall between us.

"I let it in," I whisper as the scene flashes through my mind over and over again.

"Let what in?" he asks, but my mind is still replaying the scene again in agonizing detail.

"Talk to me," he pleads.

"It won't change anything." I can't bring her back. I couldn't save her.

"No, but it might help to talk about it," he says gently.

"I killed her..." Admitting the truth out loud sends a painful jolt throughout me. "She's dead because of me... because of..." Because of my foolish choices. Maybe if I had checked on the creature earlier or placed it somewhere else...

I frown, realizing that the only thing holding it was the iron chains. It should not have been able to escape them. But maybe I should have used more.

"How did she die?" he asks.

She would be alive without my mistake. Alive and happy, with her kindness and warmth. But...

"The dark creature," I whisper more to myself than him.

"You brought a dark creature into the palace?" There is no judgment in his question, just a gentleness that wants to understand. And the softness in his voice eases something inside me.

So, I tell him. I don't know why I do. But I tell him everything. About my plan to capture a dark creature and finding the hidden tunnel to keep it chained up in.

"Somebody released it," he says, making me pause.

"The dark creatures are smart, yes, but they cannot

unchain themselves from something made from iron. We've tested it. Someone must have set you up."

He's right. I knew it. I knew it the minute I saw the empty chamber. But I had hoped it was not the case.

That means someone must have followed me and found it. Or maybe they were aware of the tunnels and stumbled upon it. But someone had to have unchained it and released it.

"But it doesn't matter," I tell him.

"How can you say that?"

"That woman's death is still my fault. I brought that creature here."

"You didn't set it on people. You trapped it. It wasn't your fault."

I grow silent, knowing that is not true. I am not blameless.

"Do you deserve to die for it?" he asks, so softly I nearly miss it, too lost in my chaotic thoughts.

I pause and start to think on his words.

"*No*, you don't," he snaps, as if angry with me now. "You have a great deal to accomplish before that. A great deal. Some will not get that chance. But *you* deserve to live a full life of happy moments." He pauses with a heavy sigh, and something about his words makes me pause.

"Wylan?"

"Yes, Ren. Can I call you Ren?"

I hear the smile in his voice, reminding me so much of Jarek and his playfulness.

"No," I answer immediately, and he chuckles.

"Why are you here in a cell?" Or in the palace at all.

His chuckles quickly dry up as he releases a harsh breath. "Someone betrayed me. And because of it, I am to die."

My already cold body turns to ice.

"In two days." He chuckles again, but this time, there is no amusement in it. "I have two days before I am sentenced to death."

My mind tries to scramble together some form of a plan to get him out. He can't die. Not him too. Jarek will be… I have to get him out. It's the only thing I can focus on that makes sense right now.

"I would have liked to have seen him again. One more time," Wylan says almost wistfully, but I'm already up and moving, searching my cell. It doesn't look like my old one, the layout and bars similar to the one Veles was in.

My eyes slide to my right and narrow as an impossible thought drops into my head. Pushing it to the back of my mind for the moment, I find a basin of water at the side of the cell and shove my blood-red hands into the ice-cold water to wash them.

Turning my head away from them, I try to wash the blood off my hands and arms while focusing on something else.

"Why are they sending you to your death?" I ask, hoping it will pull me away from the small spiral I'm about to lose myself to once more.

"I wanted to help the Sidus. I've seen them suffer time and time again. All I wanted to do was help."

I freeze. "You're not a Sidus?"

He pauses as if realizing his little slip. "No."

Ah. Now I realize why Jarek was too nervous for me to meet him. He thought I would judge him. And he would have every right to think so. I did judge the rebels too harshly without ever really knowing them. And I did the same to the Caligo.

My impossible thought comes to the forefront of my mind, and I reach down, only to instantly feel my Caligo powers. And if I have access to them, surely he does too. Unless... "You're not Caligo either, are you?"

Wylan pauses again. "No."

Getting back to cleaning the dried blood off me, I focus on my small plan now that I have confirmation it may work. The bracelets are still on me, with no way to remove them, so I won't be able to use my Sidus light. But the guards don't know about my Caligo side. And hopefully this new cell doesn't hinder them either.

As I pull my clean hands out of the basin, my eyes fall on the now reddened water. Visha's blood.

Wylan. Wylan. Wylan.

I squeeze my eyes tight, reminding myself what I need to do. Again and again, before I can think of anything other than the blood and what it means.

Wylan. Wylan. Wylan.

Taking a deep breath, I reach down and feel for my shadows. They immediately roar to life inside me.

Opening my eyes, I watch them coil around my hands and move upward to brush against my cheek as if trying to soothe me.

It helps. I don't know why or how, but it does, centering me and allowing me to move ahead with what I must do.

"Do you know how to get out of here?" I ask him while forming more and more shadows around me.

"I wish I could. I wish I could get you out—"

"No. I mean, do you know how to get out of the palace? Do you know your way out?" The palace is a colossal maze that many could get lost in.

"Yes, I know my way out. But it doesn't matter. The bars on this cell alone make sure I can't use my abilities or leave. That is without the many guards guarding the only exit I know."

I ignore the part about the guards, having a plan for that, but my stomach drops when I realize what he means about the bars.

"The cell has a blood spell on it?"

The cell next to me goes completely silent. "How do you know what a blood spell is?" he asks.

I hear him rise to his feet, and I glance to the wall he's behind, narrowing my eyes on it when my shadows move toward it as if reading my mind.

"Did they place it on the entire cell or just the bars?" I ask.

"Just the bars, but it doesn't matter because it also

stops me from using my abilities. Now that I have answered your questions, I'd like to know how you know about any of this."

"Stand back," I order as my shadows continue to build around me.

"What—"

"Move away from the wall between us. Now!"

I hear the quick movement of feet just as I let go, and my shadows slam into the wall, destroying it and leaving nothing but crumbling, destroyed brick.

The dust starts to clear as a man around my age with shoulder-length dark brown hair and dark brown eyes steps over the debris. But as he attempts to move closer, I turn, pulling my shadows back before pushing them out toward my cell door, ripping it from its hinges and throwing it to the side.

Wylan stumbles into my cell, his eyes wide. "How?" He glances around at the destruction and then back at my shadows as I pull them back into me.

"I thought... you're a Sidus, Seren." Glancing at my face, he searches it for something but only frowns.

"I know you have questions, and maybe one day I'll get to answer them, but for now, I need you to trust me. You have no reason to—"

"I do," he says with absolute certainty.

I pause and search his eyes, seeing it there too before nodding.

"You said we are family?" I ask.

"We are," he says without question.

"Then keep my secret. For it will only get us both killed."

He searches my face once more, but this time, he finds whatever he's looking for. He nods his head. "You have my word."

We turn and head up into the palace. I have to figure a way to get all the guards to follow me. If I draw them to the palace garden, it will be in the opposite direction Wylan is—

"Come with me," he demands, just as we reach the main corridor.

"I can't," I tell him, meaning it. If I escape, what I'm accused of will fall on my mother and Ryuu. They will be implicated for it and pay for my foolish mistake.

"I can't leave without you," he snaps. "Not only because I know what they will do to you, and I don't want to ever see that happen, but because Jarek will kill me if I allow anything to happen to you."

I shake my head at him while keeping an eye out for any guards. "I need to follow through with this. I will draw the guards to me. Find someplace to hide until they come for me. You should be able to make a quick exit with them distracted."

"And if they try to kill you?" he hisses.

I narrow my eyes on him. "I am not that easy to kill."

"Seren—"

"Go." I push him, turning him, hoping he'll find a

good hiding spot while I distract the guards. "And tell Jarek I give my approval."

He stops and turns, giving me a boyish smile. "You do?"

"But break his heart, and I'll rip out yours," I warn him with just a hint of a smile, letting him know I'm only *mostly* serious.

He pauses and squints his eyes. "I don't know who I should be more afraid of, the lieutenant or you."

"Me. *Definitely* me," I warn him. But instead of taking my warning seriously, he smiles and shakes his head, a determined glint in his eyes.

"I'll come back for you and get you out of here. I promise."

"I can look after myself. Take care of Jarek for me."

"I will. And I'll see you soon," he promises once more before turning and disappearing into the night.

I turn and head for the guards' watch and soon come upon one of the guards who take me to and from my cell.

"You." His eyes widen in recognition. I take his blade before he notices and give him a smug smirk before turning and running, slow at first so he has a chance to catch up with me.

"Stop! The Sidus has escaped," he shouts out, running after me and making a scene just as I had hoped. It garners more attention, and more and more guards join him.

I make my way through the palace and out to the

wide-open gardens. They're on the opposite side of where I hope Wylan has gone.

I stop halfway and turn to them as they surround me.

"How did this Sidus killer get out of her cell?" the guard with the scar on the side of his neck snarls.

Killer... I tighten my hand on the blade. He's right, I *am* a killer. And was one long before I got Visha killed.

Instead of turning the pain inward, I let it out. I push it into the blade in my hand and strike, attacking the nearest guard.

More and more guards show up, but I don't stop; I keep fighting when all I want to do is lie down and cry. For Visha. For my foolish mistake. For the gut-wrenching pain that now fills my spirit and soul.

I keep fighting because it's all I know. And I don't know how to fill this black hole that has somehow opened up inside me.

I want to cry and scream and shout. But I can't. I can't because I don't deserve to.

It was my fault, no matter what Wylan said. If there was no dark creature here, then whoever released it would not have been able to do so. She would still be alive and I... I wouldn't feel this rock crushing against my chest.

My body moves, stabbing, ducking, and fending off as it comes second nature to me.

With ease, I spin sideways, eluding another guard's attack before advancing and slicing the guard in front of me.

More grunts, snarls, and hisses sound out as I make my way through them with ease.

The guards quickly change tactics and try to overpower me with a distraction while more sneak up from behind. But I sense them immediately and evade their attempt to catch me.

I carve a path through them and fend off another attack, but more and more guards show up, replacing those that have fallen.

They soon overwhelm me, and it gets harder to defend against them all. One falls but another quickly replaces him.

A blade slices against my shoulder, another across my side. But I feel nothing. No pain bar the ache inside me slowly crawling its way throughout my body.

More and more slices cut me, the guards eyes lighting up as they watch me grow slower and more drained.

I can see it in their eyes; they're toying with me. They don't use their shadow powers, because they know I will pay with every cut, every drop of blood shed, every bruise and broken bone.

They know it and I do too. And instead of fearing it, I welcome it. I welcome the thought, knowing I deserve much worse.

"You are all ordered to stop." A shout bellows out from somewhere behind me, but none of the guards stop, and neither do I, continuing our fight.

The guard with the scar tries to outsmart me, but I

drive my blade into his shoulder, eliciting a curse before twisting around to my next attacker, when my sword clashes with another. But instead of another one of the guards, my gaze meets with steely-gray eyes full of thunder.

Kestral.

CHAPTER 25

He sees something in my eyes that makes his own widen with pity. And I can't bear it. I can't because I don't deserve his pity. Or anyone else's. I deserve nothing but the sharp edge of my own blade.

So I don't stop fighting him, and he doesn't ask me to. I continue to purge the pain from my heart, using my blade to funnel it out of me. He becomes my conduit, my channel and inner resolution.

"Leave," he shouts. And even though his eyes haven't left mine, his blade is still as quick, his moves swift. I know he's talking to those around me.

I hear their grunts and curses but don't see them leave. But I feel them. I feel it and know that it is only Kestral and me here now.

Kestral, me, and my inner demons all fighting as one.

He doesn't ease up when I grow tired, and it only makes me angrier; in turn, giving me the energy I need to continue my fight with myself.

"Where did the creature come from?" he asks, but it only reminds me of what happened, and the claws that were slowly falling away ensnare me once more.

"What was your plan?" he continues, but I tell him nothing, instead striking each question harder, moving quicker to try and relieve some of the suffocating tightness trying to envelop me whole.

"Did you capture it?" he continues, even when I say nothing.

Even when I push harder and harder. Even when I beg him with my eyes to stop.

But he doesn't, and then I see it all again.

The blood. My hands. It's everywhere. And Visha as she gazes up in horror, her ashen face completely lost of any warmth or light. Warmth and light she will never see or feel again because of me.

"From where?" he asks again, but all I see is Visha.

Visha. Visha. Visha.

The claws slice into my mind and heart, ripping it, tearing it apart. And I can do nothing but let it. Let it pull me under once more.

Kestral sees something on my face, his own softening with a sadness I do not deserve.

"It is not your fault. Her death," he says, his voice soft. But it only scrapes against my ears, making me want to silence it.

He met me but once. He does not know what type of person I am or how horrible and foolish my decisions have been lately.

He does not get to declare a verdict for me when I know my mistake is unforgivable. He does not get to hold that power, nor will I let him.

Something bursts up from inside me, and I let it out. I attack without thought, without the bounds or confines I normally give myself.

I let it out because, somehow, I know he can take it. And he does, with ease. Each hard clash of my blade, each swift turn and attack. He moves with me as if he knows how and where I'll move and follows.

I stop thinking. I stop letting fear and pain shove me down, and I just move. I let my body do what it was born to do.

Attack. Defend. Block. Counter. Strike.

The clash of steel becomes a music that soothes, the swift spins and stride my dance. I get lost to the dance, to the elegant entwine of our swords, the retreat and rise of each step.

I let go this time and allow myself to feel nothing. To let everything around me fade away.

The slash of my sword becomes more precise, my movements more swift.

"I knew you were holding back," Kestral says, looking more intrigued than angry. But my moment of sweet oblivion is quickly ripped from me with the sound of his soft voice. It jolts through me, and everything rushes back.

The pain. The self-loathing. The endless tightness that suffocates.

It's enough to distract me to make another foolish mistake. And before I realize it, he has his blade blocking mine and forcing me backward, my steps losing their footing as he shoves me up against a wall.

The cold brick slides against my back as he leans into me, the swords still crossed between us.

The sound of our heavy breathing mingles as he pushes even closer to me, forcing me to look up at him and into his eyes.

But what I find there nearly breaks me entirely.

A newfound admiration that's slightly masked by a sliver of frustration. A strange longing that I don't quite understand. A disbelief but one that I feel is more for himself than anything else. A stunned bewilderment. Sympathy. Compassion.

But *not* pity. Or judgment. Or anger or suspicion.

Or any of the other things I've been placing upon myself.

He's given me a glimpse into his own soul, and in this quiet moment between us, I allow myself to feel vulnerable, powerless. To feel the regret and remorse for my actions without letting them swallow me whole.

"It. Is. *Not.* Your fault," he says, each word a definitive statement on its own.

"*I* brought it here. It is *my* fault. The blame is solely

on me. If the blame is not mine, then whose is it?" I glance away from him and those eyes that want me to reveal every secret I behold.

He steps back from me, and my sword falls with a clank to the ground. Exhaustion finally makes its presence known, hitting me with the force of a steel ton.

I glance away, hoping the guards will come soon to take me back to my cell. Whichever one they choose.

"The one who set it free," Kestral replies, making me pause.

I look back at him with a question in my eyes, and his own brighten when he sees it.

"You were followed and betrayed. Your *friend* released it."

The word *friend* sounds like a twisted thorn on his tongue. But what he means finally hits me, making me freeze.

I don't have many friends here at the palace. For him to assume I am this person's friend means he would have to have seen me with them.

Which means I must know the person who released the dark creature.

Rage spears through me, ripping the numbness and heavy exhaustion from my mind and body.

"You know this for certain?" I ask.

Kestral nods his head, a look of complete certainty on his face. "He has confessed to it."

He... I glance down at my sword on the ground and

the drop of blood clinging to the edge of the blade and shake my head.

"I still brought it here. I am still at fault." No matter who betrayed me. I am still to blame for the outcome.

"Tell me what your goal was," he says again, without judgment or anger.

I glance up at him and see it in his eyes; he only wants to understand, nothing more.

"I wanted to make them listen. *Only* listen." I frown. "I did not wish for any more death."

"Them?" he asks.

"The royals," I explain, and his eyes widen a fraction before a frown mars his brow.

"Why not the guards?" he asks.

I shake my head again as a quiet chuckle slips past my lips, though there is not an ounce of amusement in it.

"They know. They *know* and do not care. I had hoped... I had hoped the royals would be unaware and want to help us." It would seem I had hoped many things that would now never come to pass. And now my mother and Ryuu will end up paying for it.

They trusted me. Had trust in me. And now—

"Where did you get that creature from?"

Kestral's question quickly pulls me from my turbulent thoughts. I try to remember what he's asked, and when I do, I give him an irritated look.

He is a Caligo lord, if the power he wields so easily over the guards is anything to go by. He obviously knows the lieutenant and holds some power over him too. So, it does not matter what I say anymore. My one chance has gone with my hopes to meet the royals, while he will continue to come to his own opinion based on what suits him and his people.

"You wouldn't believe me if I told you," I tell him.

"Try me," he insists.

But why bother? I am just a Sidus here, and a Sidus holds no power in a world full of Caligo.

"Just like anyone listened to me before I was placed in a cell?"

"One you so easily escaped." He takes a step closer to me, his own frustration flickering to life in his eyes.

"Ah, I see the celebrations have started without us," a familiar voice shouts from somewhere behind Kestral.

Kestral quickly moves aside, revealing a wide-smiling Veles as he makes his way over to us. Beside him is another familiar face. Asra, the Caligo I stole the wine from. And beside him is another man, though his face is unfamiliar.

His dark hair is pulled back from his face, and his bronze skin tone is a similar shade to Ryuu's. But it is his eyes that make a sliver of ice crawl down my spine.

The color of the sun pierces from within them, and there is a hidden knowing beneath them that comes only from years of experience. Years he does not look to have lived. He looks just as young as Kestral and Asra, if not slightly younger, which only leaves me more confused than anything.

He drags a moving bag behind him, and once they get close enough, I realize there is someone inside it.

"We all were coming to free you, but it seems you've freed yourself," Veles says with a proud smile.

"All?" I give Kestral a questioning look.

He nods his head. "Veles told us everything. We didn't realize so many of the guards were corrupt."

Veles moves beside Kestral, a smile of familiarity on his face.

"You two know each other?" I glance between them both.

"Unfortunately," Kestral mutters, and Veles's smile only grows.

I feel Kestral stiffen as Asra steps forward and pulls me into a hug.

"It has been too long. Have you missed me?" he asks with a small mischievous smile that reminds me of Jarek and his tricks.

"Not even a little," I reply, making the new male laugh.

Asra exaggerates a sigh. "There is no need to fight this thing between us. We are meant to be."

I give him a deadpan look. "I'm glad to see delusions are highly acceptable in your world."

"I like her," the new male says, drawing me to him and his smile.

He dips his head to me. "I am Cyra. It is nice to finally meet you, Seren. I have heard a great many things about you."

"I don't understand." I glance between them all, wondering what this is.

Cyra's smile vanishes as he shares a solemn look with Kestral. "Veles has explained to us your situation."

My situation? I look to Veles for some answers and what he means.

"I told you I would help you. Vowed it, in fact," he says.

"And you all trust his word so easily?" I question, glancing between them.

Asra crosses his arms, an intense look on his face. "Veles does not trust anyone. For him to have made a blood-bond vow—"

"Don't remind me," Veles mutters, making Asra smile before he continues.

"For him to have made something so binding means we all trust you as much as we do him now."

"Just like that?" I ask, glancing around them all to see them wear the same intense look.

Asra nods. "Just like that."

"I'm a good judge of character," Veles says as he looks me in the eyes, holding my gaze. "Know now that I would *never* choose to complete a blood vow with someone who I know I can't completely trust nor feel is not honest or true." He says it with complete conviction in his voice, leaving no room for doubt.

But he barely knows me.

"I know," he whispers so only us both can hear. It sends a chill down my back as he says it, and the expression he gives me tells me he knows far more than what he says.

I nod my head, trusting him for now until I can understand more.

"Now that your innocence is cleared up..." Asra says before turning and yanking the bag open and shoving Nevan to the ground in front of me.

"Your betrayer."

CHAPTER 26

N*evan*... It was Nevan who betrayed me.

He glances up at me with pain in his eyes. A similar pain I have felt since the dark creature was released.

Pain *he* helped cause.

"Why?" I ask, needing an explanation of some kind. "What could you possibly have gained from releasing that dark creature?"

Nevan swallows hard. "A distraction and time. I just needed time to continue my search and the guards' attention otherwise occupied. I didn't think... I didn't realize..." He shakes his head, not saying another word.

And all I can think is how he could have come to me.

"If you had asked, I would have helped you," I tell him. "But you followed me in secret. You went behind my back, and then you..." I shake my head. "A woman is dead." Visha is...

"I know. I *know*." He slams his hands into his chest. "It is my fault, and I will have to live with that."

His eyes grow vacant as he glances away. And I see the guilt and regret and remorse. I see it and I don't know if it is because I hate myself for what happened or because he also shares part of that and reminds me too much of it, but every time I look at him, all I see is Visha's face now. And it may be a selfish need, but I don't want to be reminded of it every time I see him. I will remind myself of it enough on my own.

"I played a part in this too. I also accept that responsibility. But I would advise you to stay far away from me," I warn him before moving back and stepping closer to Kestral, hoping a measure of his self-control and calmness brings some comfort to the thrum of torment rushing through me.

I feel his eyes on me but ignore them to watch Veles step forward. He whips out his blade with a smirk on his face and moves toward Nevan.

Cyra blocks him with a narrowed look. "We cannot kill him, you know that. He is one of the three that holds potential."

I frown. *One of the...*

"You ruin all my fun." Veles sighs, placing his blade back at his side.

Cyra gives him a pointed look. "I keep you alive."

Veles rolls his eyes at him. "Don't bring rational thought into this. You know it's hard to kill a thief."

A thief?

Kestral glares at them both. "Let's move this along. We need to—"

"What are you doing here?" Veles asks, cutting off whatever Kestral was about to say.

I glance in Veles's direction to find Oryn rushing toward us, a sword in hand as if ready to fight.

His eyes widen on Veles. "You."

"Me." Veles smiles but it's not a nice smile meant to reassure; rather, it's one meant to frighten. "*Again*, I will ask. What are you doing here, and with a sword in your hand?"

"What am *I* doing here?" Oryn asks, looking exasperated. "I came to help, Seren." He points his sword toward me. "I overheard the guards talking and came as soon as I could. But... what are *you* doing here?" His question is full of ire and accusation, but Veles gives him a bland look, crossing his arms.

"How convenient of you to show up when she no longer requires any help."

Oryn opens his mouth but glances down at Nevan and does a double take. "I—*Nevan*?"

Nevan doesn't answer him at first, still lost to his thoughts. "I just wanted to find my wife. I did not mean for any of this to happen."

"Any of what to happen?" Oryn asks, but Nevan remains silent.

Veles takes it upon himself to explain. "Nevan is the reason you were rushing so gallantly to save Seren."

"What?" Oryn asks with a growing frown.

"He ruined her plan and managed to get someone killed," Veles says.

I wince at his bluntness, but he doesn't notice and continues on with his little tirade.

"And all for his own selfish needs."

Oryn opens his mouth and closes it a couple of times before glancing over at me.

"He didn't mean it, I'm sure." He looks to me for understanding, but I have none for him. "We were running out of time. He prob—"

"*We?* What do you mean *we*?" Veles snaps, taking a step toward him.

Oryn's shoulders drop as he rubs a hand down his face. "It is the entire reason we are here in the palace for the guard's competition. Our females have been going missing."

Kestral, Cyra, and Asra freeze.

"How long?" Asra asks, his tone like ice.

"A few weeks. My sister was taken not long ago, his wife before that, and there have been many more," Oryn rushes to explain.

"We have dark creatures entering this kingdom, missing women, and more. It seems the corruption goes beyond the guard," Cyra says, sharing a look with both Asra and Kestral.

It reminds me of one of the competitors. *Sloane.*

"One of the competitors approached me after the last trial," I say without thought.

They all turn to look at me.

"He mentioned overhearing something one of the nights. He said it sounded like someone was being taken," I tell them.

"Where?" Kestral asks.

"Why didn't you tell me?" Oryn says, but it sounds more like an accusation than inquiry.

I narrow my eyes on him. "I've been a little busy."

"This is important!" he shouts, his eyes filled with fury.

Veles whips out his blade and has it at Oryn's throat before he can blink. "Speak to her again like that, and I will slice off your tongue."

Taken aback by Veles's warning, it takes a moment for me to reply.

"My own blade works just fine," I tell Veles before glaring at Oryn.

"Of course." Veles merely smiles at me before pulling his blade back. But not before nicking Oryn's neck, making him wince.

Oryn steps back and tightens his hand on his blade. "I'm sorry. I'm sorry. I just... I want to find my sister. She's been gone too long as it is."

Kestral turns to me, ignoring him. "Did he tell you the location?"

"At the end of the bridge. The entrance from the Sidus side," I answer.

Once the words are out of my mouth, everyone is up and moving, heading through the corridors and halls within the palace and straight for the bridge. It's not until we're halfway there that I realize I haven't seen one guard.

"Why aren't there any guards here?" I ask, wondering if they've also noticed it.

Cyra gives me a look. "The royals needed to update them on something important."

"I guess it's lucky we have chosen to go now, then," I mumble more to myself at the strange luck we seem to have.

Veles chuckles but covers it with a cough, while Cyra gives me a patient nod and smile.

I narrow my eyes on them both but choose to ignore whatever they're hiding from me and stay focused on finding more information as we move across the bridge and down the steps to the location Sloane described.

But once we get there, we find nothing. No guards. No women. And after a few minutes of searching, we find no clue left behind either.

We turn, ready to head back, when shadows start to form and someone's shadow jumps right in front of us. His back is to us, so he doesn't notice us as he bends over to catch his breath before turning.

His eyes widen as Kestral grabs him before he can disappear and drags him up the steps, assuring he is within the confinements of the shadow-jumping barrier.

"What were you doing out here?" Kestral asks him with a hint of violence in his tone. The man's eyes are as wide as his fists, and his entire body trembles in fear.

"I'm just a palace guard. I was checking the area. I thought I saw something."

"Lie," Veles shouts.

Kestral yanks him harder. "Lie to me again, and you will pay for it dearly," he growls.

"I would listen to him if I were you," Asra warns.

"Tell us what you know about the missing women," Kestral demands.

The guard's eyes widen even more as he glances between them. He must see the promise of violence in their eyes, as a glint of true fear flickers across his own.

"I don't know where they take them, just that I have to be in a certain spot for collection."

"You kidnap the women?" Asra asks before he pulls him from Kestral's grasp and grabs him by the throat.

"I was told to, or they would kill me," he splutters.

"Another lie," Veles says, narrowing his eyes on him. "Kill him."

"*Don't* kill him. We need him," Kestral says, giving Veles a sharp look.

"He deserves to die," Oryn agrees, making Veles narrow his eyes on him.

"I agree," Kestral tells him calmly. "But we will never find the other women if he dies."

"We need a plan," Cyra says.

"What do you want me to do?" the guard asks with complete and utter terror in his eyes. "I take females to them, and none of you are..." He glances over and finally spots me.

I guess we have a plan after all.

* * *

"The Caligo don't disappear like the Sidus do when we leave this world," Veles says as we make our way back to the palace. The others have already left with the guard. But after they got what they needed out of him, Veles pulled me aside and asked me to go with him.

I follow him to the gardens and out past it to a little spot full of wildflowers. Every color imaginable. And with the darkness of night and the stars watching over, they seem to sparkle back at us.

It is a small haven I would like to visit again, should I get the chance.

"We bury them." Veles dips his head to the ground, where a small piece of land has been overturned, and my stomach drops.

"Your friend Visha," he says softly, and I glance over at him. "I thought you might like to say goodbye." He dips his head again and moves over to a tree nearby, giving me the space to say my piece alone but close enough should I need him.

And I don't care if it is the blood bond or the beginning of a true friendship; I'm just grateful for his presence right now.

I glance back down at the dirt, and it hits me that she is beneath it. And I don't know why it gives me a small measure of peace, but it does. To know that she is here whenever I need to see her. To plead and beg for her forgiveness.

The Sidus don't leave behind anything. They disappear and rise up. Some say they join the stars and watch over us from above.

I don't know what will happen to me when I die, but I hope wherever I go, I get to meet her again one day.

"I don't have enough words to tell you how sorry I am. You were kind to me when no one else was and found me when I wanted to give up. You renewed my hope for the Caligo and, along with Isolde, made sure I felt it. You brought me happiness in the dark and taught me that I could be who I am and that it is enough. I will be forever grateful for you, for the time I got to spend with you." I glance out around at the world she will no longer get to see, and my eyes blur and burn.

"I do not deserve your forgiveness," I tell her and then stop when a wretched sob pulls from somewhere deep within me and right into the center of my chest.

It pulls and pulls until I have nothing left and my tears have run dry.

As I'm staring out at the world and nothing at all, a hand rests on my shoulder, and I turn to find Veles there.

"Visha was a special woman."

"You knew her?" I ask.

He gives me a sad sort of smile, one that speaks of familiarity. "I have been on the far end of her wooden spoon many times for trying to"—he glances over at me with a wince—"*borrow* some of her cooking."

I roll my eyes at him, but he smiles with a soft look in his eyes and continues, growing serious.

"The first death is the hardest. But you cannot let it pull you down."

"It is not my first death," I tell him. Nor is it likely to be my last.

"It is the first one you've loved," he says softly, and it makes me pause.

He's right. Visha felt like home to me. Like my mother and Ryuu and Jarek. She felt warm and full of light. And now it feels like it was ripped away from me.

"Does it get any easier?" I ask.

"No," he says with a sadness that makes me turn to look at him. "It's a hole that forever stays with you. And sometimes it hits you out of nowhere and feels like it is the very same day." The grief in his eyes makes me want to reach out and protect him from the pain he must be feeling. And then his eyes brighten, and a shadow of a smile forms as if he can hear me. It grows into a real one, with a sliver of joy in it.

"But then time passes, and you find other things to fill up that hole with. So many things that bring you laughter and joy that, when it hits you again, it doesn't feel as hard. And you get through it."

"You get through it?" I ask him, and no one but he answers.

"Yes. Especially when you have new friends like me

who will make sure your days are spent with laughter and games."

"We're friends now?" I ask with a small grin.

"We have a blood bond. technically we're *more* than friends." He gives me a mischievous smile, and I narrow my eyes on it.

"What does that mean—" I hear movement from behind me and turn around to find Nevan walking over this way.

Veles turns and glares at him and reaches for his blade as he grows closer, but I place my hand on his, stopping him. We don't get to choose who visits her. That is not our decision to make.

I may not want to see him, but he has his own piece to say.

Ignoring us completely, he drops to his knees beside her and bends his head. His shoulders start to shake as I say one last silent goodbye to her before turning around and heading back to the palace.

I still know that I am to blame for what happened to Visha and that I will carry her death with me for a long time to come—maybe always. But for now, at least, I can focus on doing something helpful and make sure another person does not lose their life.

CHAPTER 27

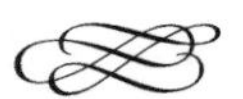

Gold gleams all around me. It is speckled in the white marble floors, adorned as intricate carvings on the ceiling and bedpost. It is woven into the hem along the opulent gold velvet drapery that hangs along the spacious white bed. A bed large enough to fit a small Sidus family. The pile of white pillows, silken sheets, and thick, filled comforters are enough to keep them warm all through the harsh winters.

There is handcrafted furniture placed thoughtfully around the room, a small alcove with a desk and matching white wooden chairs that look too delicate to sit on, and small white flowers that are spread throughout the room, leaving a subtle floral smell that soothes something inside me.

The entire space speaks of grandeur, extravagance, and elegance. A room fit for a royal, and not someone like me. It only makes me wonder who my new friends really are.

I was too lost in my thoughts after the bridge and visit with Visha. The long day caught up with me, and my mind became blissfully blank.

A healer had come and gone after Kestral's relentless claim that my small cuts and bruises needed healing, and then sleep finally dragged me under.

But now that I am alone and fully rested, I get a good look at the room they have placed me in. A room that is somehow still filled with a natural light and warmth.

I thought I would be taken back to my cell. Or any cell. The guards hate me; the lieutenant even more so. It doesn't make sense for Kestral, Cyra, and Asra to hold this much influence over them, even if they are Caligo lords.

A knock on the door pulls me from my thoughts as it opens, and a handful of the servants come in with a large tub. They place it on the other side of the room and pull a dressing screen across it as they finish preparing it.

From the corner of my eye, I see a servant move toward me. It takes me a minute to realize it is Isolde.

She rushes over to me and pulls me into a hug. I'm so shocked by her actions that I don't immediately wrap my arms around her.

"I'm sorry. I know I'm not supposed to..." Isolde starts to pull away, but I finally snap out of my shock and pull her closer.

"I know you tried to save her," she whispers, making me freeze.

My shoulders drop when I finally speak. "I was too late," I tell her.

"It is not your fault," she says with vehemence in her voice.

"You don't know that. I..." I pull back to look at her, swallowing hard at the complete sadness in her eyes, knowing that I am the one who put it there.

"I am the one who brought it here," I tell her, dipping my head in shame and guilt as I wait for her wrath and rage. But all I am met with is silence. And after a moment, I glance up to find no anger, hate, or resentment, just sad eyes that hold nothing but compassion and understanding.

"I was there," she says, taking my hand in hers. "I was there when you killed it. In the room."

"Then you know," I whisper.

"I know." She gives me a look. "I *know* it was not your fault."

"But Isolde—" I start, but she stops me with a shake of her head.

"Many think the servants do not know what goes on around them. We are told to be quiet, to make ourselves invisible. They taught us to be unseen and unheard. But they became complacent and forgot about us completely. They forget when we're in the rooms and along the halls. And we hear things. Things about how the Sidus suffer and starve in a town full of darkness. Of creatures that seep in through the shield and kill."

Tears start to run down her face as she grasps my hand tighter. "Things about a Sidus competitor that was placed in a cell and beaten by the guards for their amusement."

I shake my head, but I don't know what to say to her. I do not want to lie to her anymore. But I also don't wish to cause her any more pain either. So I glance down at our clasped hands and wait for her to tell me what she needs from me.

"I do not blame you for her death," she says, and my head whips up to meet her eyes. "It is not the first time we have seen one of those dark creatures, and I fear it will not be the last."

"Isolde? What do you mean?"

She shakes her head. "There is an evil in this palace, and it is not the dark creatures but the guards and their leaders."

"Isolde?"

She shakes her head once more, not telling me any more. "I heard you are putting yourself in danger to try to save those missing women." She gives me a look that would rival Visha's meanest glower.

"I just want to help. I don't want any more people to lose a loved one," I tell her, and she gives me an expression full of sympathy and gratitude before shaking her head and clearing the tears from her face.

With a determined glint now in her eyes, she gets up

and swipes a hand down her wrinkled clothes. "I will make sure your bath is warm and lay out some clothing for you."

"You don't have to—"

She turns and gives me a sharp look. "Just say 'Thank you, Isolde,' and let me take care of you."

Warmth fills me at her words.

"Thank you, Isolde," I whisper.

She nods her head and begins to turn but pauses. "Visha... Visha would not want you to be sad for her. She would want you to live."

I swallow hard against the burn in the back of my throat. "I'll try," I tell her.

"And you will succeed," she commands with a look that makes me smile.

She turns and walks to the tub and starts moving about as normal, and as she does, something loosens in my chest, making me feel slightly lighter.

Once the tub is warmed, Isolde leaves me to enjoy it, demanding I take my time and try to relax.

I scrub every inch of my body and then lie back to let the warmth and soft floral scent seep into me.

Closing my eyes, I try to focus on the plan we came up with when I hear the door open as Isolde comes back in. She moves closer to the dressing screen, but once she's there, she starts pacing back and forth as if distressed. I open my mouth to ask her what is wrong.

"You don't have to do this," a familiar male voice insists.

I freeze. It's not Isolde, but Kestral.

My face grows hot as I glance down at myself, dragging my body farther under the water as he continues to pace beyond the screen.

"You don't have to put yourself in danger to prove anything," he insists.

I narrow my eyes at his words. That is not why I am doing this. I don't need to prove myself to anyone. Least of all him.

"I can take care of myself," I tell him, hoping he will leave soon so I can enjoy the bath while the water is still warm.

"It's too dangerous," he declares with the hint of a command beneath it.

"I wasn't asking your permission," I hiss. "Now get out so I can enjoy the rest of my bath in peace."

I hear and feel Kestral freeze, and it brings a wicked smirk to my lips.

"You..." He clears his throat. "You are—"

I raise a brow. "Taking a bath? Yes." I splash a little bit of water to make my point.

"I..." He clears his throat again, making my smirk grow. He stays where he is until something snaps him out of his frozen state, and I hear him quickly move toward the door. But before he leaves, he pauses.

"The royals have agreed to help with the dark creatures and shield."

My body stiffens as my head whips in his direction. "They have?"

"Yes. You have their word." I hear the smile in his voice and find one spreading across my lips. The Sidus will not suffer by the dark creatures' hands. The royals will help. They will *help*.

My time here was not for nothing after all.

"Be careful," Kestral says.

I hear something clink onto a table before he leaves.

Quickly drying myself off, I throw on a robe that Isolde left me and check to see what it is.

There sitting on the small table is a gold dagger with rose carvings down the center of the blade. Most of the handle is white, apart from the gold trim. I pick it up with a smile teasing my lips.

The door opens and Isolde sees the dagger in my hand.

"I see you had a visitor. He is quite handsome, is he not?" She gives me a secret smile. "Come, I have a dress that will suit your needs."

Isolde helps me dress just like last time, curling my hair and leaving it down to fall around my shoulders.

Demanding I keep myself safe, she hugs me one last time before leaving me alone in the room.

Oryn arrives not too long after, freezing the moment he sees me.

"I... You look... I mean to say..." He stumbles over each word, his eyes dragging up and down my body.

"Oryn?" I snap and he looks to my face. "Spit it out."

He nods his head and takes a step closer. "I'm sorry, I just... I don't know if you should go ahead with this anymore. What if something happens to you? What if something goes wrong?"

"Then I will think on my feet and stay alive long enough for the big, strong men to come along and save me." I give him a deadpan look just as Asra and Veles arrive, walking into the room chuckling.

I give them both a smile before glancing back at Oryn. "I will figure a way out myself, fight if I have to, and kill if I must."

"Why don't you forget about everything else and come elope with me?" Asra says with a wicked smirk on his lips.

"And deny the line of women a chance at your fine breeding and modest nature? I wouldn't dare," I tease, raising a brow at him.

He shakes his head at me, his smirk firmly in place.

"Ignore the brute. Focus on what you need to do. You are more than capable. Just remember, stab first, ask questions later," Veles says, and it reminds me instead of my new little gift.

Taking my new dagger, I lift my leg and slide it into the strap on my thigh. A door opens and closes as I'm adjusting it.

"Enjoying the show, Your Highness?" Veles asks with a smirk.

I glance up to find Kestral standing frozen on the spot, but I ignore his expression to focus on Veles's last word.

"Highness?" I ask him.

Kestral quickly snaps out of his stunned expression and gives Veles a sharp look.

Veles smiles to himself but stays silent as he gives Kestral an expression full of amusement.

Kestral's eyes narrow on him but then light up as if he recalls something. "Did Veles tell you that he is now bound to help you until his death—the blood bond ensures it—and that he also cannot lie to you?"

I freeze and straighten up before turning to Veles. "Is this true?"

He nods with an exaggerated sigh. "I have a life of servitude, and all you had to do was steal a bottle of wine."

He sulks, making me roll my eyes as I find the shoes Isolde left me. I find a flat pair and silently thank her for her thoughtfulness.

"I had to scale the side of the palace with broken ribs and a bruised and battered body to get that bottle of wine. I have earned your help." I slide on the shoes and stand up, only to find everyone in the room silent and stiff as a stone.

"*Why* were your ribs broken and body battered and bruised?" Kestral grits out, the fury and anger in his voice ready to boil over.

"It doesn't matter," I tell him, cursing my stupidity for even mentioning it.

"Tell me—"

"I heard whispers from the servants..." Veles starts, his face full of rage. "That I thought were not true. When

I met you, you were..." He sighs, shaking his head. "They said a Sidus was placed in a cell and met with the guards regularly."

A torrent of violence spears through the room, promising bloodshed and chaos.

"You were in a cell? This entire time? Why didn't you tell me?" Oryn steps forward, wearing a distressed expression.

"It's not important. Can we focus on the missing women?" I ask, hoping to move away from this topic swiftly.

"They also mentioned gold bracelets that were placed upon the prisoner to cut off their Sidus powers," Veles continues, and four pairs of eyes draw straight to my wrists.

I've gotten away with it for so long, most people assuming they were an accessory, but I guess that time is now up.

"I need to... I forgot I need to do something," Oryn mumbles before leaving the room without a backward glance.

The others don't seem to notice his absence as they share a ruthless, vicious look between them.

"Let's hunt them down. One by one," Asra says to the others before looking to me. "I'll bring you each head as a souvenir."

Kestral steps in front of me and takes my wrists in his hands. I attempt to pull them away when he stops me with a sharp look.

I stare into his eyes and find nothing but clouds of swirling gray. I'm so lost in them that I jolt when the bracelets unlock and drop to the ground with a clank.

"You should have told me," he hisses.

I rub my wrists, feeling my Sidus powers return, but unlike last time, the warmth settles inside me instead of flowing out of me in rage.

"How was I to know you were able to remove them?" I reply, and he tenses up as if just realizing that too.

"You're not a Caligo, are you?" I ask him before glancing around at the others.

"No," Kestral answers, watching me warily.

"You're both like Veles?" I ask, and Kestral and Asra turn to Veles, giving him a narrowed look, one he ignores.

"Yes," Kestral says as he looks back to me, his body growing more and more tense.

But I need an answer to the question that has been on my mind since I woke up in this room.

"Are you the royals?" I ask them. I have had my suspicions. The way they can easily command the guards and lieutenant at will, the way they can move about the palace without question, and the luxurious rooms they are in.

They couldn't just be Caligo lords; they have to be more.

My question is met by silence, with no one willing to answer it. So I look to Veles, knowing that he will have no other choice, thanks to Kestral's little reveal.

"Veles? Are they the royals?" I ask.

He sighs at the glares from both Asra and Kestral. "You both know I cannot lie to her." His gaze then zeroes in on Kestral. "*You* are the one who made sure she knew that little fact," he says before looking back at me.

"Yes, they are," he tells me.

Before I get the chance to call them out on it, Cyra steps into the room, dragging the guard from the bridge beside him.

"He has been told what he must do," he tells us. "We must leave now if we want this plan to move ahead."

"We will talk about this later," I tell them all before making a move toward the door. But Kestral beats me to it.

"I will meet you there. I have something I must do first," he grits out.

Cyra frowns at the thick tension in the room. "What has happened?"

"Let's get this over with," I tell him with a weary sigh.

Once the guard is thoroughly aware of what will happen to him should he attempt to betray us, he covers my eyes and brings me to the new location he was told.

I pretend to sleep as my body is carried and moved from one place to another.

Time drags on and just as I think we have finally reached our destination, a sharp sting slices against the side of my neck, and a moment later, darkness pulls me under.

CHAPTER 28

I wake with a gasp, my gaze falling on the dark, dirty cell around me. This one is far worse than any other I have been in, with thick grime around the bars and floor and a foul stench that only adds to my already churning stomach. It is lucky I haven't eaten anything, or it would already be on the ground in front of me.

With no sign of the guard, I can assume he decided to take his chances with whomever he is working for instead. A foolish mistake he will learn to regret.

Pushing up on my arms, I sway a little before the dizziness finally stops.

"It's the sleep-inducing mixture they have given you."

I glance over at the voice to find a girl around my age looking back at me. Her skin is pallid, her brown hair unkempt, and her clothes as dirty as the cell we are in.

"It makes you sleep and feel nauseous when you

wake," she says with a wince. "It will pass. Just try not to breathe through your nose."

"Too late," I tell her, and she gives me the ghost of a smile, as if she is no longer used to it.

"I don't remember consuming anything," I tell her and check over my body. My hand falls on the dagger on my thigh, and I breathe a sigh of relief.

"It's from a small knife they have dipped into a mixture. They only need to nick you for it to work."

My hand reaches up to my neck and the slightly raised skin there.

"How do you know all of this?"

She sighs and it's full of weary despair. "I've been here a while."

My stomach sinks at the dejected expression on her face. "You were taken?" I ask, and she nods a reply.

"Are there many others here?"

She scans my face, searching for something before dipping her head toward the cell bars.

On shaky legs, I move toward them and peek out, my entire body freezing when I see it.

Half a dozen cells around this one, each with at least two or three women in them.

"They'll kill half of them by the end of the week," she says with a whisper.

I whip around to her. "And the rest?"

"To be sold. It's the only reason I have lasted so long."

I turn and move over to her but stop when she stiffens. "I'm Seren."

"Leora."

"Are you all Caligo?" I ask.

She shakes her head. "Some of both, though they kill the Sidus quicker," she says, and I clench my fists at my side at the thought.

"Why have you not tried to escape?" I can feel both of my Sidus and Caligo abilities, so I know they must not have any shield or block that restricts them.

"If we attempt to use our abilities, we are killed." Leora swallows hard, her eyes misting over as she drops her head to look at her hands. "I'm not a fighter. None of us are. I think they know that. They pick the ones who won't try to fight back. Those who are weak and vulnerable."

My hand tightens around my blade. "Do you know how many guards there are?"

She glances up at me with a frown. "On this corridor?"

My stomach drops. "*This* corridor? There are more?"

She nods. "Two that I know of, but there could be more."

"How do you know if it's night or day?" I glance around, seeing no windows, so I can't tell how long I have been out for.

"There are more guards at night," she tells me.

Moving back to the bars, I glance out and see no guards about, so it must not be that late yet.

"What are you doing? The guards will be here soon," Leora says before getting to her feet.

"We're getting out of here," I tell her.

"How?"

I pull the dagger from my thigh and show her. "Through them, if we must."

Leora's face pales.

Using my shadows, I conceal them with my body and unlock the cell door, sliding it open as softly as I can.

"They will kill us," Leora says, her voice panicked and her face drenched in fear.

"We cannot stay in a cage, no matter how scared we are." I take a step out of the cell, but she rushes over and takes my arm, stopping me from moving any farther.

"Please, Seren. They killed another for using her powers and another for trying to escape. They made us all watch." She drops my arm to wrap hers around herself in comfort.

"I know you are scared because of what you saw. But you cannot stay here. You are to be sold or killed; those are your choices if you stay." I reach a hand out to her. "Come with me."

She shakes her head, stepping back into the cell. "I can't."

Moving out of the cell, I glance around at the other women, all huddled in the back of their cells.

"Are you all going to stay here? Lie down and die for them?" I ask them.

"Look behind you," someone says.

I turn to the end of the cells to find the bodies of two women.

"*That* is what happens when we try to fight back. Death. And none of us wants to die," she hisses, but her eyes are wide with fear, not anger.

"But they will kill you either way," I tell her and them as I glance around at each frightened face. "Or sell you off to the highest bidder."

"We're not fighters," another girl says, so softly I nearly miss it.

"But you can be," I tell her. "It does not have to be just one. All of you can join together and fight your way out."

The girl with the soft voice glances up at me. "But they're stronger than us."

I glance around at them and their already defeated faces and realize that it is not the bars keeping them here. Any one of them could have used their powers to unlock their cells. It's their fear. *That* is what's stopping them.

"The world can be an unforgiving place. It can be cruel and full of hardships no one wants to face. It can break you down until there is barely anything left of you, but it can also build you anew. It is also filled with laughter and love and the people who care about you." I glance around at them all, pleading with them to fight. "Don't you want to see your families again? Don't you want to feel the light?"

Some of the girls move closer to the bars, giving me hope.

"Your freedom does not belong to them. It belongs to

you. And *only* you can take it back," I tell them, but they stay behind their bars, and I start to wonder if I'll ever get them out.

Until one girl steps forward.

"I don't want to be a prisoner here," she says, looking at me with wide, fearful eyes. But there's also a glint there—a glint of hope.

"I don't want to die or be sold off." A small shadow coils around her hand as she unlocks her cell and steps out. "I choose freedom and whatever may come from it."

The other girls hesitate, but I can see it in their eyes now. That hope. It's a small flicker that I want to watch grow into a flame that burns.

"If you won't fight for yourselves, fight for one another. Fight for a cause bigger than yourself."

They glance around, and then one after one, they unlock their cells and step out.

I glance back at Leora as she stays further back in the cell.

"Your freedom is yours to choose, but it can only be found through courage. Don't give them this power. Don't let them win."

"Come on, Leora. Oryn will miss you," another girl says from beside me.

Oryn? My eyes widen. "You're Oryn's sister?" I ask her.

She nods, moving closer to the cell bars. "You know him?"

"He's been searching for you this entire time. He's in

the palace right now," I tell her, hoping it will get her out of the cell.

Leora glances around for a moment before hesitantly taking a step outside her cage.

"I would like to see my brother again," she tells me. And it's enough for now. Enough until she can fight for herself.

I gather the girls together and put the strongest at the back as I take the lead.

We move past more bodies, and a girl beside me with short black hair and brown eyes gives me a sad look.

"They don't like the ones that talk back either," she says, and my hand tightens on my blade.

Two guards come into the corridor, their eyes widening when they spot us. But before they get the chance to call for backup, I move swiftly and slam my fist into one before spinning the blade in my hand and striking the hilt of it into the back of his head. Both fall to the ground with a thump.

"I am feeling a little better about my choice now," one of the girls says with a smile.

"Let's keep moving," I tell them.

With slightly more determination than a moment ago, we move forward. I quickly silence three more guards before moving to the end of the passageway and around the corner. Only to come face-to-face with Levon and at least a dozen guards behind him.

CHAPTER 29

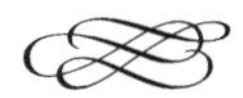

"Take those you wish to sell. Kill the rest." Levon points to me. "But leave *her* to me."

So it seems Levon is a part of this. He steps forward, meeting my eyes with a smirk before whipping forward. Our blades meet in a resounding clash, his sword to my dagger.

"What a pitiful blade," he sneers.

"This *pitiful* blade is going to gut you in a minute," I tell him with a smirk.

I push forward and he leans back to gain his balance, but before he does, I slash my blade across his arm, leaving a nice, long gash.

"A taste of what is to come," I tell him.

Instead of hissing in pain, he looks me in the eyes and laughs. A deep chuckle that crawls down my back like ice.

I shoot forward and he blocks my next attempt to gut

him, but he leaves his side unguarded, so I twist and slash my blade across the top of his thigh before spinning out of his range.

Again, he doesn't cry out in pain or check the wound. Instead, he looks at me with eyes filled with venom.

"Go back to your cages and we won't hurt you."

I quickly glance over at the girls to see them huddled together and frightened as the guards surround them. The guards smirk at the indecision in their eyes.

"You are not powerless," I remind them as Levon lunges forward to attack. I block him and slash my blade across his other arm. "Protect one another. Do not let them win."

This time when I circle Levon, there's more than just loathing in his eyes; he's livid. It seems I have provoked him enough to take this personally.

Good. Now he realizes that this won't be as easy as he assumed.

I hear a scream and glance over to see the guards reach the girls. The guards have them surrounded and are trying to break them apart.

I let my Sidus power build within me, dragging it up and up from the depths of me before reaching out and releasing it, aiming at each guard. My strings of light snap out, coiling around each of their necks and tightening, cutting off their air supply.

I block another attack from Levon as I hold my Sidus light and shout over to the girls.

"Do not let them take your power. Take it back. Take it back and *unleash* it upon them."

I catch something flash in one of the girls' eyes, the one who was the first to leave her cell, and she steps out as her shadows begin to build around her.

Just like last time, it takes just one. Just one person to light the flame. I release my hold on my Sidus light as one grows to two and then three and four, until the entire group of them are joining their shadows to the first, growing and expanding it to become a shield of shadows and smoke, pushing the guards back and blocking their path to them.

The guards try to use their own shadows to slash at the shield, but it doesn't budge.

I turn my full attention back to Levon and attack with unfaltering strikes, my movements swift and the slash of my blade precise. I manage to cut him another two times before he is foolish enough to open his mouth.

"Chaos and death will come for you all," he says in an ominous tone.

"*Chaos* is already here," I remind him as I raise my blade. "And your death is near." I strike again, this time managing to get close enough to his face. The red line slashed down his left cheek is a nice addition to the rage now pulsing throughout his eyes.

His hateful eyes pierce me as he grows completely still, wiping a drip of blood from his chin.

I move and he follows. I attack, and he does the same, his movements a mirror of my own. I attempt another attack, but he does the same, mimicking my movements once more.

I spring forward but spot my mistake too late as his eyes narrow and he dips to avoid it, catching my wrist to slide his blade along my arm, drawing a hiss from my lips before he moves back with a chuckle.

"An eye for an eye. Isn't that what your kind says?"

My kind. He says it as if he is not the same. As if what we are is beneath him.

I think back to when I've seen him use his shadows and realize I never have. He is strong, yes, and a fighter, but he has never wielded any shadows around me. And his immediate disgust for the Sidus and our powers assures me he has no light.

"You're Fae," I say, and his smile widens. I should have expected it after Veles said his blood had trapped him in the cell.

"You are *all* going to die here," he says before surging forward with a thrust of his blade.

But I quickly catch it and get the upper hand, twisting around to swipe his legs from under him. He slams to the ground with a grunt as I step back to put some distance between us.

A small black ball rolls toward me, hitting my shoe before turning white.

I glance over at Levon, wondering if this is one of his tricks, when I catch his eyes widen on the ball.

"Orbis," he whispers before looking at me with eyes full of interest.

A loud bang rumbles throughout the passageways, and the ground shakes beneath me, throwing me sideways and distracting me from Levon's strange expression.

But instead of panicking, something inside me loosens, and I know somehow that my new friends have arrived. I just need to hold off Levon and the rest of the guards long enough until they make it here.

After gaining my feet, I glance back at Levon, only to find him gone. But I don't have much time to think about where he went, as more guards spill in from every position and surround me.

They eye me up with a smug grin before attacking. They use their swords and shadows to strike, but I evade their shadows and fend off any attack.

Time quickly disappears as I fight without mercy and block any of them from getting past me to the girls. I can't see them anymore, the dust and crumbling brick blocking my view. But I can hear them fighting back with their shadows, so I know they must be close.

I continue to hold my own against the onslaught of attacks from all angles, but it won't be much longer before they overwhelm me.

Another blast bellows out around us before tapering off to a deep rumble. But it's enough to throw the guards a few feet away from me, allowing me to get my footing once more before they continue their attack.

I spot Asra and Veles first. They make their way over to me and gain ground with the guards farther away from me before cleaving a path through them. They're beside me within minutes, guarding me as if I'm the one who needs protecting. Though I am grateful for their help.

"The girls?" I ask.

"With Kestral and Cyra," Veles answers before stabbing the nearest guard in the neck and pulling it out with a pointed look. "Stab first, ask questions later, *remember*?" He nods without waiting for a reply and continues to stab, maim, and carve a bloody trail wherever he goes.

It's brutal and chaotic, but even I can admire the efficiency with which he works through each guard.

A female voice shouts out in rage, and it reminds me of the other women. Those Leora mentioned in the other corridors we had yet to find.

My eyes widen, and as if they sense my inner panic, Asra and Veles both turn to look at me.

"There are more women in the other corridors. Go, now. Find them and free them. I can take care of the rest." I nod my head to the half a dozen guards stumbling around us.

"Are you sure?" Asra asks.

I give him a narrowed look that makes him smirk before he grabs Veles by the collar and pulls him away in the opposite direction.

Turning back to the guards, I move through them quickly, avoiding their slash of shadows and sloppy attacks before turning to find the others.

There is dust and debris everywhere, but I scan my

surroundings and spot Veles and Asra leading a group of women away from here, and the tightness in my chest slowly unravels.

My gaze lands on Oryn, and his eyes widen when they meet mine.

"Seren," he shouts as he makes his way toward me.

I open my mouth to let him know his sister is here and hopefully safe with Cyra and Kestral, but just before he reaches me, a sorrowful bellow rings out around us.

I glance over to find Nevan holding one of the women's bodies we passed earlier, and my stomach drops.

His wife...

He clutches her tightly to his chest, his face drenched in agonizing pain and heartbreak.

Oryn stares at him in horror, his face ashen as he moves to search the bodies around him.

I rush to him and stop him. "She's alive," I tell him. "Leora is alive."

Once he hears her name, he stops his search and whips his head to me.

"You've seen her?" he asks, and I nod. "Where is she?"

"Kestral and Cyra led them away from here. She was with the group when I last saw her."

He nods to me, a determined glint in his eyes now as he gets up to go search for her. But just as he takes a step forward, a light blares to life beside us. A *Sidus* light.

I turn to look at it and find Nevan's hand weaving

light to encase his wife. More and more surrounds her before encasing her entire body and absorbing it whole.

Just like when a Sidus passes, nothing is left behind. Nevan stares blankly at his hands as I glance up at Oryn in shock.

"I'm sorry I didn't tell you," he says and winces at me. "Nevan is also like me."

My eyes widen. "He has both Sidus and Caligo powers?" I ask, and he nods, confirming it.

I'm so lost to my shock that I don't realize Asra and Cyra have stepped up beside us until it is too late.

"What happened?" Asra asks.

I share a worried look with Oryn, hoping they didn't hear us. But before either of us gets time to worry about it, another blast roars out around us, flinging us all apart from one another.

My head smacks against something hard, and the world around me dips and spins, my vision clouding with dark spots.

Squeezing my eyes tight, I try to right myself and shake the loud ringing from my ears before stumbling to my feet.

When my gaze finally clears, it lands on Levon and the smirk on his face as he holds Leora in his grasp, a sword to her neck.

My heart drops, my chest tightening as he drags her backward and out of sight.

I follow without thought, quickly catching up to them as his hold tightens on her, and she gasps.

"Let her go," I demand.

"Is your Sidus power quicker than my sword?" he taunts and slides it closer to her neck while his cruel smirk grows.

I pause and he chuckles. He knows I cannot use my powers. Even the ones he isn't aware of. Neither of them would be able to pull her away before he slashes the blade across her neck, instantly killing her.

"I'm going to kill this spineless stain of a being, and you will be able to do nothing but watch," he sneers before continuing to drag her away as she whimpers.

He brings us to another long corridor and through a passageway before I hear it. A loud bellowing blast. And another and another.

The rumbling roar ripples out behind and beneath me, and I whip around to find my way back quickly closed off.

Steeling myself for what I must do, I turn back around and carry on, following Levon's callous laugh while sending a silent prayer to the gods, hoping that everyone else behind me is safe and alive.

I'm not so naive to believe this isn't a trap. I know he has lured me here. But it is for that reason that I blindly follow him, because I know it is me he wants, not Leora.

With my sliver of hope, I move ahead and follow them, hoping I will have a chance to buy Leora a moment to escape.

We quickly move upward and along the inside of the

palace, to a long, open hall with huge pillars on each side.

I glance around for anything to use as a weapon, having lost mine in the blast, but find nothing.

Levon brings Leora to the edge of the hall before he looks to me with a smirk and slams the hilt of the blade into the back of her head. Her eyes roll backward before closing as she drops to the ground.

I lunge forward to catch her when shadows whip around my arms and legs, encasing my entire body, only leaving my head free.

A man steps out between me and Levon before he turns to me. My eyes widen as a slash of fear shoots through me.

"I was hoping we'd meet again," the Breaker says.

CHAPTER 30

Once the initial shock and fear releases me from its icy grip, I take stock of my body as they drag me out to a large open area.

I can't move, the shadows too tight, constricting. I try to use my powers, but it is like dragging up a brick wall from the bottom of the ocean, the attempt alone already weakening me.

It is as if the shadows coiling around me are draining me, pulling every sliver of energy from me and ensuring I can't use my powers or do anything else for that matter.

We stop moving and I find myself glancing up at a dark night sky covered in stars. We're so high up that if I weren't tied up, I would think I could reach out and touch them.

Huge white columns lie in a circle around us, rooted directly in the mountain itself.

The shadows move me to the center of the area just as a familiar face comes into view.

Amaro.

"She has the orb?" he asks.

Levon steps up beside him, coming into view. "She does. But it is *inside* her."

Amaro's smile only grows. "Kill her if you must. But get the orb."

"With pleasure. But let us be certain."

A beaming light is placed in front of me, blinding me. I blink away the light from my eyes, only to find the Breaker there with an eager smile on his face.

"I knew I sensed something inside you," he says before stepping back.

His shadows spiral around me, expanding slightly before constricting once more, leaving me completely drained before pulling away.

I drop to the ground with a thud and a groan.

Sliding my hand under me, I try to push up, but my arm trembles and shakes so hard I have to stop and drop it back to the ground.

Drawing on my abilities, I try to pull up even a sliver of power, but nothing comes to my aid. I try again, not ready to give up yet, when a whip of pain slashes down the center of my body, burning me from the inside out.

I cry out as the pain builds and builds, expanding and shrinking inside me as it twists and turns and moves about before centering around my chest. As if someone has physically placed their hand directly into it and is trying to pull out something from the inside.

"There," I hear the Breaker say from somewhere far away just as agony like nothing I've ever felt before surges through me, rippling outward and striking again and again as it tries to cleave me in two.

A crack rings out as something fractures inside me. Something more vital than bone or body.

A light glimmers, a luminous shine from within me, and I scream out as the pain becomes too much to bear.

The illuminated light expands, sending small pulses that create a growing sphere, but as it grows, it slashes and slices across my body.

Lost beneath the layers of pain, defenseless and without power, my mind fills with despair and my heart grows defeated.

But something small begins to grow inside me. An ember of power that reaches out and curls around me, giving me hope. I focus on it, and it expands, just like the sphere of light around me.

The familiar thread of power slides through me, helping me gain control over my body, slowly strengthening it and easing the pain within.

A storm builds and builds inside me, and on instinct, I reach a hand out and push it outward and straight at the Breaker, Amaro, and Levon. A small twister of wind quickly grows into a whirlwind of power, growing and gathering more and more strength before rushing through them all and unleashing the hold the Breaker has on me. The whirlwind continues to rush forward and slams into Levon and Amaro, knocking them off their feet before disappearing completely.

My moment of reprieve quickly disappears as the sphere of light continues to spread inside and around me, expanding and growing until it bursts out of me in one giant blast.

"*Seren*!" a familiar voice shouts out as I drop to my knees and can only watch as the light passes through everything until it hits the shield.

Once it touches it, the shield ripples and cracks open, revealing something that should not be possible.

A gurgle of pain sounds out from somewhere beside me, but I can't look away from the sight in front of me.

Another kingdom sits farther across the black sea, its outline and magnificent palace close enough to see, and straight across from it is another.

"They've escaped," Veles says to someone as he moves beside me, but my eyes don't leave the sight before me.

Two kingdoms. Each on other islands far enough that one would have to sail a boat to reach them but close enough to be able to see. And yet when the shield is up, nothing but the sky and sea exists.

Kestral moves in front of me, checking me over, his face growing more furious the longer he looks, but I can't look away.

And then the shield ripples. Once. Twice. Before

pulsing around the kingdom and closing off my view of another world.

Asra and Cyra arrive just as the two kingdoms disappear completely.

"What. Was. That?" I breathe, my voice hoarse from screaming so much.

They share a look between them, and I see it in their eyes. The worry, the guilt, the fear. They know. They *know* what it is and what it means.

And it is about time I also find out.

CHAPTER 31

"Levon and Amaro have escaped," Veles says to Asra and Cyra, though his worried gaze keeps veering to me.

"We'll deal with them later," Kestral says.

"The girls?" I ask, and they jump to answer my question, probably hoping that I will forget what I just saw. But there is no hope for that.

"Most are accounted for," Cyra says.

"Most?" My stomach drops as I look up at him from where I sit on the ground, my body completely drained of energy and spent after the Breaker's cruel search for the orb.

Cyra gives me a somber look and nods.

The last few hours were nothing but chaos and mayhem. No one could have predicted the outcome. But the guilt now seeping into my chest, making it hard to feel the air hit my lungs, does not want to listen.

I asked them to trust me to lead them out of the dark and help them find their light and strength, only to turn around and abandon them not a moment later.

A spear of dread shoots through me when I remember the reason I am here and not with them.

"Leora?" I ask, my body growing more and more stiff the longer they don't reply.

"Leora?" Kestral asks with a confused frown.

"Oryn's sister. She was here with me before, in the hall. Levon used her to lure me out."

Kestral's eyes grow cold and hard. "You knew he was luring you, and yet you still followed?"

"I had no choice. He was going to kill her." I stay calm. Too calm. Too quiet. Too empty. Too *broken*.

"We haven't found her, but I'm sure she is safe with the others," Asra says, giving Kestral a look, but he will not yield on this, his rage already starting to boil over.

"You—" Kestral starts, but I cut him off, already looking to Veles for the distraction I desperately seek. To think of anything other than my failed attempts to help those women and Leora. I can only hope that she and the others are safe and unharmed.

"Veles?" I know none of the other three males around me will tell me the truth of what I saw. They will try to cover it up somehow. The look they shared when I first asked about the shield told me just that.

But Veles cannot lie to me and feels the need to answer my questions because of our blood-bond vow. He will *have* to tell me. Whether he wants to or not.

"What happened when the shield cracked? I saw it. Tell me everything you know."

Veles sighs as he looks to the others. But I stay focused on his face as he slowly gives in to my request and nods.

"Let us move you someplace more comfortable first and away from here." He glances to the right of him, and I follow his line of sight to find the Breaker's body completely broken. It is as if someone has literally ripped him apart.

My eyes find Kestral's steely gaze.

"She needs a healer," he grits out.

"I will make sure she is looked after," Veles tells him with a wary expression.

Kestral clenches his fists but nods once. "We will not be far."

He heads back toward the palace, and Cyra follows him, but Asra stays for a moment, staring at me as if he wants to say something but is stopping himself, thinking better of it, before giving me a sad look and leaving.

I turn to Veles. "Veles—"

He stops me with a look. "I will tell you everything. You have my word, and you know I will only tell you the truth. Let's see to your injuries first and take it from there."

Veles helps me up, practically carrying me inside to the palace, where a healer is already waiting. Once I'm healed, I move to the long hallway I first met Kestral in and gaze out at the view of the sunrise.

"It has something to do with the Fae, doesn't it?" I ask as Veles walks toward me and climbs onto the small wall between the columns, using one to lean against.

I climb up to the same wall and sit opposite him, and he gives me a small smile when I do.

"I'm hoping you won't hate me too much, because I'm only half. Whereas..." He pauses and glances out at the rising sun.

"Veles?"

He releases a harsh breath before looking at me, his face full of apprehension and concern, and it makes none of my already turbulent thoughts nor my churning stomach ease.

"In order for me to explain everything, I need to start at the beginning," he says before giving me a look.

"Were you ever told or taught anything about the gods?" he asks.

My mind flashes to the statues in the cavern beneath the palace.

"I have a little knowledge about them," I tell him. "I know that there were many gods long ago. They were revered and loved by all."

Veles winces. "What I must tell you is a lot of information to absorb, but also try to keep in mind that I cannot lie to you."

"I understand. Please, just tell me what you know," I plead.

He scans my face for something before nodding to himself and starting.

"Many millennia ago, eight gods were said to have been created by the goddess Danu to help the world grow and evolve. All were beloved and worshiped by many." He gives me that wince again before continuing.

"But over time, they grew in power. So much that it caused an imbalance and started to affect everything around them. An era of despair and misery began with sickness, war, death, and destruction following. But even then, some of the gods grew vengeful and hungered for more power. A restlessness came about, and they fought amongst one another. It was then decided that each god would take a piece of the world and rule it alone, staying apart from the others so as not to cause any more conflict. But the imbalance had already started. And their relentless need for power slowly became a taint that spread, corrupting everything they touched."

I already have so many questions and so many things I don't understand, but I fear he will stop if I interrupt him, so I push them to the back of my mind for now to listen.

"One night, a powerful prophecy arose. One that foretold the ending of all living things. A darkest night without moon and star and a world that would fall to chaos and destruction." He gazes out at the mountain with a heavy sigh.

"The gods were told that they must leave this world in order to stop this and take their taint and imbalance with them. But they did not listen. Seven gods stayed, and now their tainted essence has spread into every corner of the world and corrupted it."

But his words bring me no clarity, only further confusing me.

"And the world outside the shield?" I ask. Is that why they kept us in here? Because of this taint.

"It's not what you think or how I assume you are imagining it. The world is still habitable. There are cities, towns and many people, animals and beasts." He gives me a look full of unease.

"But there is also darkness because of this taint, corruption from its spreading, manipulation that creeps into everything it brushes up against, and cruelty and malice."

I frown at his words. "Isn't that in every world? How can you blame the gods for something us mortals do so easily?" I ask.

Veles glances out around him, and whatever he's thinking ages him in a moment. "The black sea was not always this dark mass of death. It was the gods and their presence in this world that did that. That is a small piece of their taint, along with the dark creatures." He turns to me with a pointed look, and I freeze.

Shock seeps into my body, making it cold. "The dark creatures were created by the gods?"

"Not on purpose. It's the imbalance, the corruption. They form from their essence and spread the taint farther."

"But they reached this kingdom through the black sea?" I ask, needing to know their origin.

He rubs a hand down his face. "They should not have been able to, but it seems they are drawn to the Sidus light, the very essence of the Sidus, because they are without it. You all are like a beacon to them."

"The Sidus are drawing the dark creatures to the kingdom?" I ask in a shaky, disbelieving voice.

"Yes, but it is the gods and their taint that are the cause of it. Those creatures seek you out only because of their darkness and lack of light. But know that the shield would have always protected you from them had Amaro and Levon not attempted to bring it down."

"Amaro and Levon. They're both Fae?" I ask, and he nods.

"No one knew they were corrupt and possibly siding with the gods. The shield does more than just cast an illusion; it stops the Fae from using most, if not all, of their abilities." He gives me a wary look. "Had you met Amaro or Levon outside the shield when they were at their full strength, you would not be alive right now."

"The Fae are that powerful?" I ask as ice trickles into my veins.

Veles nods and chooses his words carefully. "And dangerous. We investigated a little after the dark creature was released by Nevan." He gives me a worried look as if he is afraid I'm about to come apart at the seams and break once more. But my heart is too tired to think of my mistakes, my mind too full of questions that I need the answers to. I have later to fall apart and crumble.

With a small nod, I encourage him to continue.

"Amaro and Levon have been trying to take the shield down for as long as they have been here. They must have people on the outside helping them." He frowns. "They have been telling the Caligo guards that the Sidus are the ones who are tainted. And with the dark creatures being drawn to you all, it acted as proof to them that the gods must have chosen the creatures to rid you all from this world."

"So that is why they hate us? They think the Sidus are evil because of what Amaro and Levon told them?" I don't know whether to laugh or scream at the idea.

"The dark creatures aren't as drawn to the Caligo and their shadows, so this only plays into their story, making them believe that they are favored by the gods."

A small chuckle falls from my lips, but there is no amusement in it. The Caligo guards think the Sidus are the evil ones, and yet they have no objection to making us suffer, torturing us, or killing us.

It makes no sense how they can justify their actions to commit the evil they call us.

"I saw two other islands when the shield cracked open. Who is on them, and do they know about us?"

Veles gives me a look as if he was hoping I would forget about it. But knowing now that it is the gods who created the dark creatures and that there is a whole other world out beyond us just makes me want to know as much as possible.

"There are two other kingdoms of Caligo and Sidus. They are kept apart from each other and shielded just like this one."

"Why keep us hidden from one another? Why hide us at all?" It makes no sense. The entire world is unhidden, and yet the Caligo and Sidus are hidden from everyone and everything. Even each other, it seems. But *why*?

"They thought it best," he says, too vague for me to understand.

"*They*?" I look at him and quickly surmise who *they* are. The Fae.

"Why didn't they ask us what *we* wanted?" Maybe we didn't want to be hidden and caged off from the rest of the world.

"They wanted to protect you," he says with a sad sort of smile that makes my anger retreat for a moment.

"And what is it that they are protecting us from?"

"The gods," he says, and my eyes widen in shock as my stomach drops. "They want you all dead. They don't know where the Sidus and Caligo are. The Fae have kept this location a secret and protected it along with the other two kingdoms. The only way on and off any of the islands is through a portal and the land of the Fae. All of which are heavily guarded."

"Why do the gods want us dead?" Surely if the Fae

are as strong as he says, they would see them as more of a threat than any of us.

"Your existence alone is a threat to them."

"How could any of us possibly be a threat against a god?" I doubt even the Fae would stand a chance.

"The gods must fall before all can rise," he whispers to himself before looking at me. "The prophecy spoke of their taint and corruption, yes, but it also foretold their ending. They thought killing the one who foretold the prophecy would end it completely. But a loophole is always created when fate is defied. The Sidus and Caligo are descendants of the original prophet and the one who foretold the prophecy. Which means you all are that loophole and the only thing standing in the way of the gods and their foretold ending."

CHAPTER 32

Leaning against the pillar and lost in thought, still trying to wrap my head around everything Veles told me, I glance out at the sky, or the illusion, and the sun now raised high above the clouds.

There are so many questions I have unanswered and so many things I don't fully understand, but the heaviness sitting atop my brain now makes any further questions left aside for another day.

"I regret not being able to make it to you in time," Veles says with a frown, pulling me from my jaded thoughts.

"Kestral killed him, of course, but I would have liked to torture that vile male after what he did to you."

My body turns to stone. "You saw?"

Veles nods at me, a blood-fueled rage that quickly tapers off to a look of intrigue.

"I caught the ending. But not before I saw you free yourself by creating a whirlwind. Something no Sidus or Caligo has the power to do." He looks at me with a question in his eyes. One I feel drawn to answer.

He told me everything I asked, and even though it was most likely because of the blood vow, I still feel that the small friendship forming between us requires my own truth. Or at least a part of it.

"I used it one other time, when my powers were blocked. I don't know how I have come to have it or understand why, only that I am grateful for it." I would have died by the Breaker's hands if I didn't have it.

"It doesn't belong to you," he says softly, and my gaze snaps to his.

"And it will not always come to your aid. You need to be close enough for it to work. At least until the bond fully forms."

"How do you know any of this? Close enough to *what*?" I sit up as my mind races with his words, searching for an answer I do not have.

"Not what, *who*," he says, a deep frown marring his brow. "You borrowed it from another."

That is not possible. "How can anyone *borrow* a power that belongs to another?"

He cocks his head to the side and hesitates as he observes me for a moment.

"It is not unusual for... *mates* to share powers between each other." His voice is strained, tense.

Everything inside me freezes. "Mates? Caligo and Sidus do not have mates."

"But Fae do," he says slowly, and a heaviness settles on top of my chest. "A Fae's mate can be any being, and the bond between two fated is created by the goddess Danu herself."

He leans back as if to give me more space to think or breathe. "You borrowed your mate's power," he says with unwavering eye contact and complete certainty in his voice.

"My *Fae* mate," I reply, but it sounds more like a question.

He nods and I spot something in his eyes, a glint of knowing that makes me suspicious.

"You know who it is," I accuse.

He releases a drawn-out exhale before continuing. "There is only one able to control all elements and one who is known to wield the whirlwind you created."

"Tell me, Veles. Whose power did I borrow?"

"Mine," Kestral says as he moves from the shadows and steps into the hall beside us.

It takes a moment for the shock to leak away from my mind and body as I slip down off the wall to stand in front of him.

Mine. Mine. Mine.

Veles quickly slips out, avoiding Kestral's cutting look.

Once he's gone, Kestral focuses back on me, his face now devoid of emotion. But I can see the truth in his eyes. He doesn't want to have this conversation, the sharp look he gave Veles a moment ago proof of that. He didn't want to reveal this to me. Maybe he never would have. And for some reason, that makes me incredibly frustrated.

"Has the healer checked you over? The orb might cause some—"

"Have you ever been to the Sidus town?" I ask him, wanting to know more about him and hoping my offhanded question might remove that hollow mask of his.

The first flicker of emotion seeps into his face and he frowns at me.

"The town?" he asks.

"The *Sidus* town, down the mountain and into near complete darkness."

His frown only grows. "No."

I nod, expecting as much. He isn't a real royal, only masquerading as one. It was just a task to him. An obligation that spanned out centuries.

"Veles told me that you all did this to protect us. To keep us safe. But there has been nothing *safe* about living here. In fact, there has been no living or joy. There has only been suffering and death. And had we not been confined to this *cage*, we might have stood a chance to survive."

Something flickers in his eyes before he shoves it down.

"It will not happen again. The shield will be fixed

soon. And Amaro and Levon *will* be found and punished." He clenches his fists at his side.

But what about the Sidus who lost their lives because of the dark creatures? It may not be the Fae's fault that they exist. But keeping us hidden and locked away only kept us ignorant of the truth. We could have been more prepared for them. We could have found a way to escape.

His power. It was *his power*.

"You kept us caged up," I tell him as the slow-building rage burns through me.

"It is to protect you all," he says.

"You expect me to keep this secret?" The confusion must show on my face.

"You cannot tell anyone." His eyes harden with determination.

"You expect me to lie to everyone I know?"

"Yes," he hisses.

"No." I shake my head. "I will not lie to them."

"You have no idea how long we have…" He shakes his head, trying to gain his vacant look once more.

"I do not care what you have done. We are not something you can control, cage, and hide away when you feel like it. You do not get to play God," I grit out.

"You need to be protected," he roars, finally losing the rein on his emotions. "You need to be protected because you all are our last hope. We have nothing without you. *Nothing*. No future. No world. Millions will die. Do you understand that? Millions. Every living thing in this world will be gone. Wiped out. And I will not allow that to happen." He moves a step closer, forcing me a step back.

"So, if I need to bound, cage, and conceal each and every last one of you, I will," he sneers.

Rage unfurls inside the tightness of my chest, creeping outward.

"Do you want me to hate you? Is that it?" I snap.

"I don't want a mate," he whispers, but his eyes tell me something different.

"You knew?" I ask.

"From the moment I met you."

No hesitation. No denial. No true emotion.

"I don't want a mate. I never have," he tells me again.

Never. Never. Never.

Pain lances through my chest before I push it down and away, ignoring it completely.

"Do you expect me to cry about it? To beg you to change your mind? I don't care if you want me or not, or if we are mates and whatever that may mean. It does not change anything between us. Nor the fact that you lied. That you would have continued to lie to me and everyone here had I not seen the shield fall."

"I do not want one," he whispers fiercely as his eyes darken.

"I do not care," I snap.

"Say it," he demands, stepping forward as I become aware of every movement and breath. "Tell me how you really feel." His smile turns cold and cruel, and something about it makes me snap inside.

"I *hate* you," I hiss.

"Good," he says and then slams his lips to mine, awakening something I thought would be long left to slumber.

Desire. Hunger. Passion.

It ignites inside me, spreading like wildfire throughout my entire body before pooling low in my stomach.

He pulls my body flush against his, and I gasp and feel every hard inch of him. The caress of his tongue slides across my lips again and again, roaming my mouth, tasting, teasing as his grip tightens on me, demanding more.

A building frenzy and need spirals through me, and I bite his lip. His throaty groan ripples through me, tormenting me further before he bites me harder and pushes me away.

"I hate you more," he breathes. His eyes draw to my lips and then eyes before turning and leaving me there without a backward glance.

The delicious burn of his lips and taste of him still linger on my own.

"Damn him," I pant, attempting to get my breathing and the growing tightness in my chest under control.

My thundering heart soon slows down, but the tightness in my chest only grows, spreading out to my arms and legs. A small ache quickly becomes an agony that burns, leaving me breathless.

Darkness clouds my vision as the world around me becomes a deafening roar. The hall tilts and spins, and my knees hit the floor. My head follows next, hitting the ground with a crack. And the world shutters to a stop as the darkness snares me whole.

CHAPTER 33

KESTRAL

The haze of pleasure enthralls my mind, body, and soul, holding me captive. It entices my senses, consuming me whole.

She ensnares me. Her eyes bewitching, her beauty an allure and temptation I cannot resist. Her endless strength and wicked tongue soothe the beast inside me while also bringing him to life.

If I hadn't ripped myself away from her, I would have shoved her up against that wall, slid down her body, and...

A vicious hunger rips through me as a series of images flash before my mind; her beneath me, spread out as I explore, tease, and taste every enticing curve and dip. Molding her body to mine as I savor every inch of her. Absorbing the feel of her as she moves above me, tormenting me, trapping me with the thread that slowly binds us as one.

Her. Her. Her.

Damn it.

Blood thunders in my veins, making me lightheaded.

I cannot claim her. I cannot *have* her. Clenching my fists, I grit against the sharp pain the thought alone causes.

She will be my ruin, and I, her damnation. We cannot be. She is a beautiful cruelty the fates have condemned me with. A hypnotic flame that will only burn me to ashes.

I try to erase the feel of her. Of her enticing scent and soft hands and lips. But the ache, the hunger, and savage need only snare me more.

I need to push her away and put more distance between us, farther away from the powerful desire building and growing.

I move to the large balcony outside the royal suites with hope that the fresh morning air will extinguish a sliver of this heat.

A moment later, a palace servant stiffly walks up to me, his face growing paler the closer he gets. He stares at me but says nothing, flinching when I raise a brow in question. When he continues to stare at me in fear, I decide to use this opportunity to make sure Seren is at least checked over once more, to play it safe.

We do not know the extent of potential damage the

orb may cause farther down the line. She may need to be watched closely.

"Send a healer to check on the Sidus competitor. I feel the orb may have left some unstable energy from its aftermath."

"Sir. The Sidus you speak of. She is..." He glances around as if searching for a quick escape, his hands trembling in front of him.

Every sense in my body is set alight and on alert. This particular servant knows what and who I am. He has worked for me for years and does not normally fear me. But he is also aware of what happened to Seren and the orb, and my instinct is telling me something is amiss.

"Another servant. They said they saw her being captured. She's gone."

Gone... My body turns to stone. A bitter ice that spreads through every nerve in my body before constricting and flaring to life as flames, igniting a fire that blazes throughout me.

Rage. Violence. Bloodshed.

It slashes across my mind in waves and thunderstorms, heightening each one of my senses.

Gone...

The servant slips away as Asha, Cyra, and Veles arrive, coming up behind me, but I do not move. I do not speak or turn around to them, the vicious impulse to slaughter anything that comes near me too great. To ruthlessly rip apart, destroy, and decimate everything until nothing but carnage and chaos are left behind.

Asra slowly steps up beside me but keeps his distance. "We will find her, Kestral. We will get her back. You have my word."

Gone... The flames claw and burn across my chest, piercing through my thundering heart.

A storm begins to build inside me and spill out, causing the light around us to be shuttered by dark gray clouds sweeping across the sky, completely obscuring the sun. They unfurl across the three kingdoms, swelling into a powerful windstorm, a tempest that upheaves the turbulent waters below.

Asra's eyes widen. "He is not supposed to be able to use his powers within the shield."

My power expands, charging outward with a rumble of thunder that reverberates across the sky.

The turbulent waves crash against the side of the mountain as the wind picks up. Twisting, spiraling, growing, before unleashing an onslaught of twisters that slam into the black sea.

"He is a direct descendant of those who created the shield, and his mate was just taken. I doubt that little restriction is going to stop him now," Veles says, my heightened senses picking up the strain in his voice.

The storm surges and swells, forming a powerful whirlwind that roars around us in fury. In rage and vengeance. In pain and torment.

Until everything stops and grows calm. A still silence that is a deceptive lull and ominous warning.

Energy fills the air, cracking around us, stalking outward.

Gone... The lightning hits, a booming strike that seeks out a ruthless revenge.

* * *

SEREN

The ground beneath me shudders and shakes, making my stomach roll. I try to move my arm and any other limb, but no part of my body obeys my command.

Flashes of light flicker across my lids, and my eyes blink open a sliver, too spent, too painful to fully open.

I can't move my head, but I can see the wooden edges of the open carriage I must be in. There are bodies beside and above me, their warmth bleeding into me, keeping me warm as we travel through the bitter winds outside.

I know I have to try to get out of this, to awaken my body from this strange unmoving slumber, but no matter how hard I try, nothing moves.

I try to pull up my Sidus light and then attempt to release my shadows, but nothing happens. I reach down inside myself and search for that familiar thread of power, but it is as if it has been carved out of me with only a hollow space left behind.

The carriage jolts, turning my head to the left, and my eyes slightly widen when I spot a familiar face.

Leora is by my side, her eyes closed, her body still. Too still. Focusing on her, I catch the rise and fall of her chest, and the tightness in mine slowly eases.

I can't tell where we are, the edges of the carriage high enough to block me from seeing directly out but low enough to see the sky above.

It can't be my town, as it's not dark enough to block out the sun above like it does in the Sidus town, and the ground is too smooth and straight to be up in the mountains.

It can only mean that whoever has taken us is taking us someplace *outside* the kingdom. Which should not be possible. The shield and wall alone should have stopped them, and that is without the dark creatures preventing them a way past.

Veles's words cross my mind about the mention of a portal, just as energy slides over my skin, an icy rush that fills me before dissipating.

Panic assaults my mind and silent body as dread fills me, and I realize my fears have come true.

The carriage stops and two males come into view, their side profiles now revealing one with a slight point to his ears.

It seems the shield does more than just hide the other kingdoms; it glamours the Fae's appearance too.

The Fae looks slightly older and taller, but the other male is familiar. It takes me a moment to realize who it is as my eyes attempt to close, my body wanting to rest. I force them to stay open and watch on as the Caligo guard we caught at the bridge stands in front of me. The one who betrayed us.

"I hate that bloody shield," the Fae says to the guard. "I hate not having my full abilities and how it makes me feel as fragile as a weak human," he sneers.

The guard glances backward before looking at the Fae, a thoughtful glint in his eyes. "We have no new orders to go back..."

A smug grin crosses the Fae's face. "What will—" A rumbling thunder ripples across the sky, making the two males jolt and quickly lose their smiles.

A dark storm of thundering gray clouds and twisting whirlwinds expands out toward us as if it is trying to follow us.

"What in the blasted heavens is that? I've never seen anything like it," the guard says, the fear in his voice evident.

"That is not natural. Let us get out of here. *Now*." The older Fae moves out of view, but the guard pauses and frowns.

"What should we do with them?" He tilts his head toward the carriage.

"They will be sold," the Fae replies.

The guard turns to me with a smirk, a small knife in his hand as he reaches out and nicks my neck.

Lightning strikes from somewhere far away, the force of it a violent vengeance that reaches out to pursue just as darkness drags me under once more.

ACKNOWLEDGEMENTS

To Mum, words cannot express how much I appreciate you. I could not have done this without your endless support and encouragement. I am forever grateful for you. Thank you for everything and more.

To my daughter, thank you for always making every journey enjoyable and fun. For being the bright light that always brings a smile to my face. I love you endlessly and always will.

To my sisters, thank you for always being my biggest cheerleaders. For being with me through each stage and lending me your strength when I need it.

To you, the reader. I hope you enjoyed the start of Seren's story and I can't wait for you to see what I have planned for the next book. Thank you for giving this new fantasy author a chance. I am forever grateful for each and every one of you.

Soraya x

ABOUT THE AUTHOR

Soraya Cole is a fantasy romance author. All Gods Must Die is her debut fantasy series and is inspired by Irish Mythology. When she isn't creating fantasy worlds with strong female leads and swoon-worthy heroes, she is spending time with her family in Ireland or trying to chip away at her never-ending TBR.

Soraya can be found on TikTok and Instagram @sorayacoleauthor

Made in United States
Orlando, FL
08 December 2024